DARK DANTE

DARK DANTE

Maggie Rose

Matador
9 Priory Business Park,
Wistow Road, Kibworth Beauchamp,
Leicestershire. LE8 0RX
Tel: 0116 279 2299
Email: books@troubador.co.uk
Web: www.troubador.co.uk/matador
Twitter: @matadorbooks

ISBN 978 1800463 639

British Library Cataloguing in Publication Data.
A catalogue record for this book is available from the British Library.

Printed and bound in Great Britain by 4edge Limited
Typeset in 11pt Baskerville by Troubador Publishing Ltd, Leicester, UK

Matador is an imprint of Troubador Publishing Ltd

Many thanks to Sal Cabras, Riccardo Cassarino, Elisabetta Ceccariglia, Rino Garro, Marjory Peckham, Robert Peckham and Jan Sewell.

To Alice and Charlie Rose.

Maggie Rose lives in Milan. She is a playwright and teacher, whose work has been performed in Italy and Scotland. For most of her life she has travelled between Britain and Italy, sometimes building cultural bridges between the two countries. *Dark Dante* is her first novel.

1

It was midnight in the spring of 2000, and a dilapidated Alfa Romeo Giulia drew up outside an elegant nineteenth-century town house in a wealthy area of Florence. A woman of around sixty got out of the car, walked around to the passenger side and helped her elderly companion out and onto the pavement. They exchanged a few words and a kiss on the cheek, after which he lurched towards the house, seriously drunk. Fumbling in his pocket for his keys, he turned to blow a second kiss at the departing car, before unlocking the main door and going inside.

In the dark hall his hand pressed the light switch. When it failed to respond, he let fly a string of Italian swear words, cursing the Madonna, Baby Jesus and all the miserable swine in Christendom in quick succession. He was groping his way towards the lift when two strong hands gripped his neck. As the fingers tightened, he lost consciousness.

A torch flashed on, revealing a man called Kim, which isn't his real name for reasons I prefer not to disclose. Picking up the victim's keys from the floor, he dragged the heavy, flaccid body towards the lift, opened the door and pulled it inside. On the third floor, Robin, his accomplice, was smoking outside the victim's flat. His hand was shaking as he put the cigarette to his lips and inhaled the smoke. The minute he saw Kim emerging from the lift, he knew the moment had come. Kim grabbed the fag from Robin's mouth, throwing it angrily down and intimating that he needed a hand to get the body out of the lift.

Robin felt sick as he obeyed the orders. This was the first time in his life that he had touched a dead body. He and Kim took hold of the corpse and hauled it out of the lift. There were three locks on the flat door and a dozen or so keys on the bunch taken from the victim, so it took Kim a minute or so to fathom out which keys would work. Once the door was open, he pocketed the keys and the two men carried the body into the flat. Quietly pulling the door shut behind them, Kim breathed a sigh of relief. They were safely inside, so no passing neighbour could see them.

In the bathroom they undressed the body, lathering it with spicy gel, rinsing and then drying it on a couple of luxury towels. As a final touch, Kim chose some perfume from about ten bottles neatly arranged on a dainty blue table by the window and proceeded to spray the body. Now for a heavyweight polythene bag that he had bought specially for the occasion. The two men opened it and carefully put the corpse inside, fastening the top with some string. They then carried the bundle through to a room beside the kitchen, which housed three chest freezers. Opening the middle one, Kim began transferring most of the food to the freezer nearest the door. Reading their labels – 'Lamb', 'Singh's ragout', 'Chicken curry' – he thought grimly that the body had found a suitable resting place in the meat section. The pair lowered the corpse into the freezer and arranged it amidst the remaining frozen food.

By now Robin was about to throw up and made a move towards the door, but Kim was having none of it. He swiftly grabbed his accomplice's arm and propelled him into the victim's bedroom, where he opened a wardrobe. Kim's eyes roamed over a collection of about fifty ties hanging neatly on two racks. After a moment's indecision, *he chose the first tie on the nearest rack — narrow, navy-blue striped, with a crest — for Robin; while for himself, he chose the last one on the second rack, made of yellow silk. The two men stood side by side, eyeing each other up in the wardrobe mirror. Kim smiled, satisfied that everything was going according to plan, while Robin's eyes looked haunted. A voice in his head kept repeating that he was now an accomplice to a murder.*

With the job almost finished, they wrapped the ties around their necks and adjusted the knots. Now for the bathroom, where they meticulously cleaned all the surfaces and scrubbed their hands and faces, Kim tidying his hair with the victim's comb. Looking for all the world like two office employees off to their place of work in central Florence, the pair left the flat. It didn't matter that it was two in the morning and not a soul was stirring.

2

"For crying out loud! At this time in the morning?"

I run to answer the ringing phone, rapidly fastening the top button on my pyjama jacket and pulling the collar straight, half-imagining that whoever is on the line can see me. Grabbing the handset, I stand poised, waiting for someone to speak.

"Hello, is that Signora Maria Farrell?" The voice sounds foreign.

"How do you know my name? Who are you?"

"I am Dottor Giuseppe—" the voice responds, irritated.

"For Christ's sake, Dottor Whoever-You… It's eight o'clock. And Easter Sunday!"

"It is nine here; very sorry. I am Dottor Manetti," the man says apologetically.

I decide it might well be some actor friend trying to set me up, so I attempt to catch him out. "You sound Spanish, or is that an Italian accent? Perhaps from near Rome? A *dottor* of what exactly?" Picking up a pile of paperwork from the divan and plonking it onto the carpet, I sit down and wait for his answer.

"*Sì, sì, sono Dottor Giuseppe Manetti. Calma, Signora, calma.* Yes, yes, I'm Dr Giuseppe Manetti; don't get angry. May I have a word with you?"

Even more convinced that it must be a scam, I hang up, but two seconds later the phone's ringing again. It's the same voice, only more insistent. I decide to try blasting him with a barrage of words. "Whoever you are, I am up to my eyes in paperwork. I'm a theatre-producer-cum-director-cum-coffee-maker-cum-usherette-cum-toilet-cleaner – actually, whatever is needed, depending on the emergency. And this morning, while most people in England are snoring their heads off, I have an Arts Council application to get in. The deadline: Tuesday at twelve noon... Are you still there?"

The phone's gone dead, and I breathe a sigh of relief.

Then it's him again. "Signora, Signora, please listen; my secretary has been trying to contact you for several days."

"And of course she didn't catch me; I'm generally out early and back late. A hectic schedule, not for the faint-hearted."

"So I thought, perhaps on a Sunday morning I'd manage to—"

This time I snap. "It'll have to be quick, though; I've got far more urgent things on my plate."

There's no reply, and for a moment I think he's hung up. I suddenly have a dreadful feeling. What... what if this call isn't a joke? It might be something really important. I'll try coaxing him. "Well, come on, get to the point; I don't bite, Monsieur, or Signor, at least not over the phone. I'm busy, remember, working my socks off."

"Socks off?! What? No socks?"

"Figuratively speaking, *Dottor*."

"I'm the *notaio* dealing with—"

"I don't get you. Didn't you say you were a doctor, *Dottor*?"

"Dottor Giuseppe Manetti, *notaio*, Signora Farrell. That's Italian for a notary or a solicitor. I'm specialised in deeds and wills, that sort of thing, and I'm phoning from Florence—"

"Florence?"

"Yes, Florence, Italy."

My eyes flash to a black-and-white photo on the desk near the window. Rigged out in his grammar-school uniform, my Uncle Peter stares back at me, reminding me that he lives in Florence.

"Signora Farrell, I'm very sorry, it's something very serious. It's your uncle, Professor Peter Farrell – my client. The police have informed me that…"

"What? He's dead, isn't he? My dad always said Peter was a sickly child." I take Peter's school photo off the desk, clasping it close to my chest.

"I'm very sorry but your uncle has died, but not of natural causes, according to the police report. They've opened a murder inquiry."

"Oh my God!"

"Let me reassure you." His voice softens. "I am presuming you weren't in Florence when it happened, so you aren't a suspect. There's a will, you see. Signora? Are you still there?"

"A will? It must be my Italian uncle. Well, no, he's not Italian. It's a long story. I really don't know."

"What do you mean, 'really don't know'? Aren't you sure? Is he or isn't he your uncle?"

"It's complicated. I never met him, but I feel strangely very close to him. It's probably to do with the fact he was my dad's identical twin. All I've seen are photos from when he was young. I'm actually looking at one right now. He must be about twelve in this one. Mm… He's looking rather fey… What? You don't understand? I can assure you, 'fey' describes him beautifully. And I think… You see, Dad would have been seventy-three this year. He died ten years ago, so that makes Peter, his twin brother, seventy-three. Even I can work that out, and I only managed to scrape through my O Level maths exam on my second try."

A faint chuckle is immediately overshadowed by the gravity of Dr Manetti's tone. I scrutinise the photo again, letting my eyes run over every item of Peter's school uniform: the navy-blue cap and striped tie, the blazer with the owl crest on the pocket. Were those his first long trousers? Sturdy lace-up shoes and a bulky leather satchel complete the picture. The news of the murder has knocked me for six, and suddenly the handset weighs a ton.

I can hear Dr Manetti again. "The murder was committed at Professor Farrell's home, in the early hours of the morning two weeks ago."

"Two weeks? Jesus! Why wasn't I informed sooner? Am I in time for the funeral?"

"I am sorry, it took us some time to trace you. The funeral was two days ago. There were lengthy forensic procedures to be dealt with."

"Would you mind telling me, was he buried or cremated?"

"In his will he asked to be buried in the English Cemetery, Ms Farrell."

"An English cemetery in Florence? Really?"

"I'll tell you about it once you are here. It's a very special place."

My hand reaches out towards the television for a packet of cigarettes. There isn't one. Although I gave up smoking six months ago, I still make an automatic gesture in that direction any time I'm feeling fazed. I breathe deeply, listening to the silence around me, pretending to inhale the smoke I am craving. There's something else I just have to ask. "How was Peter killed?"

"I'm sorry, I can't tell you. But about the will – you're one of three beneficiaries: Professor Gabriele Foschi, Countess Caterina Guiccioli, and you."

"A professor and a countess. Can that be right? I mean, a countess?"

"They were his closest friends."

"Can you at least tell me what I've inherited?" I mutter, still refusing to quite believe what has happened.

"I've already told you, I'm afraid I can't disclose anything further. I've made tentative arrangements for the official reading of the will on Tuesday. It'll be at 3pm at my office here in Florence. Is that all right?"

"You mean the day after tomorrow?"

"If that's okay, I'll notify the others."

"I suppose it'll have to be. I'll book a flight to Florence."

"Not Florence. The easiest airport is Pisa, and then a train to Florence, Ms Farrell. My office is a ten-minute drive from the railway station."

I can feel my stomach tighten. I think of the many commitments I have in Manchester, and the ordeal facing me in Florence. It strikes me that, if this is a sample of what the new millennium has in store, I am in for a rough ride. My mum passed away at the beginning of the year, and at about the same time Derek, my long-term partner, legged it. A new woman, a new life. And now Peter has been murdered. Is there some sort of cosmic cataclysm pointing straight at me?

As Dr Manetti rings off, his voice sounds warmer. "*Arrivederci*, Ms Farrell. I look forward to meeting you very soon. *Buon viaggio!* Have a good trip!"

Clutching Peter's photo, I stretch out on the divan. Holding it close to my eyes, I imagine the face and body of this adorable twelve-year-old mauled and disfigured. I beg him to tell me what exactly happened to him, and my mind drifts to the dozen or so snaps Dad kept of his twin. I drag myself off the couch, lift the bureau lid and rummage around until I find the bundle. According to Dad, he and Peter fell out before they went to college and never saw each other again. When I was growing up there were scraps of news from their cousin, Edith, who'd kept in touch with him. But then she died, leaving a vacuum behind her. I never understood what caused the rift between the twins and probably never will, now they're both dead.

I flick through the black-and-white photos, and the people captured therein spring back to life, firing my imagination and prompting me to speak aloud even if there is nobody here to listen. "In this one Peter must be about five; longish, wavy blond hair; a girlish, winning smile. In this one he's in his early teens; his hair darker and shorter. He looks nervy; the spontaneity of childhood has disappeared. In this one, he and Dad are on the beach at Scarborough with my nan. They look about ten, their arms wrapped round each other's shoulders, heads touching, as if they're joined there. They are the spitting image of one another. And in this photo, the war must be on; they are poking their heads out of the Anderson shelter in Nan's garden. They're holding gas masks up to the camera, and Peter's blowing a raspberry. He's jeering, seemingly oblivious to the tragedy unfolding around them. For some reason my dad never wanted to tell me why he and Peter never met up again. No more love, no more friendship between two people who were once so close. The silly sods. That just about sums them up."

I let the photos fall onto the carpet and get back to writing my application. I force myself to concentrate on the topic: a drama workshop aimed at empowering second-generation women migrants.

3

It's 9am on Easter Monday and I am cycling to the theatre to let my assistant know I am leaving. As I walk into our little office in Deansgate, Joanne is printing out her part of the Arts Council application, moaning that she's had no holiday. In the same breath she complains that the toner is very low and there are still twenty pages to print. We need to buy a new one, and the shop round the corner is closed.

"I'm leaving for Florence tomorrow," I call, ignoring her.

Her face falls a mile. "And who's going to finish this lot?" she asks, pointing at the pages. Then a far more terrible thought strikes her, and her face crumples. "And what about *Hamlet*? Who the heck is going to get the show on? You can't just walk out on us. You'd never do that, Maria. Are you sure you're feeling okay?"

"My uncle has just been murdered."

"Christ almighty! I am so sorry! Why didn't you say so? I didn't even know you had an uncle. You kept that a secret."

"It's a long story. I never met him, you see. But now I've just got to get to Florence. Peter's solicitor's been on the phone and I need to deal with my inheritance."

"Wow! That sounds grand!" Joanne looks like I've drenched her with a bucketful of icy water.

"Come on, Joanne, pull yourself together. Remember Prince Hamlet's line: 'The readiness is all.'"

"Thank you very much, Your Majesty."

"That's enough of your sarcasm! Look on the bright side. You've just turned twenty-five and I am offering you the chance of a lifetime to direct Shakespeare's greatest play. Go for it."

As I am telling her this, Joanne doesn't budge from near the printer, where she is rhythmically patting the pages she's holding as if trying to get a grip on the situation.

"I realise you've got to go, but you're our captain, sort of. I'm quite happy being your second in command, Maria." Her voice is shaking. "And I wasn't being sarky before. The moment they know you're not here, the actors will go to pieces."

I push the button and the printer sets in motion. "Don't be silly. I'm going, Joanne, but I'm not, if you see what I mean. That could be another line from Hamlet!" I quip, then turn serious on seeing her worried face. "What I mean is, I'll be on the phone every day to find out how things are going with the rehearsals. We've already done three weeks' hard slog, and most of the cast are on their way to finding their characters. I'm confident you'll manage to get them through the final weeks."

In reality, I am not at all confident she will pull it off, and feel sick at the thought of leaving her to manage, but I have no alternative. I've just got to go to Florence.

A touch of colour has returned to Joanne's cheeks, and she flashes me a glimmer of a smile. "I'm flattered you believe in me. I'll give it my all. If we talk every day that will be a big help. And—"

I cut her short, a long list of things-still-to-do racing through my mind. I've got to book my ticket to Italy. I need to pack, and talk to my cleaner and my neighbour. They are in for a surprise; they'll have to do some cat-sitting.

It's nearly midday and I give Joanne her instructions for finishing the application. I sign the final page so that tomorrow she can take it to the post office and send it off by recorded delivery. That done, I take myself off to the airport; the only place I feel pretty sure of finding a ticket on Easter Monday. As I drive, I go over what I am going to tell Jean, my daily help, whom I've arranged to meet later this afternoon.

A persistent purring welcomes me home. Richard and Henry, my two furry black friends, advance rapidly down the corridor, heading straight towards me. Still with her coat on, Jean hovers near the door, looking fraught. My human dynamo, as I call her, can't stand anything that spoils her usual routine. Being summoned to my place on Easter Monday has set the tic under her eye going a frightening nineteen to the dozen. Once again, I have no choice. I've just got to tell her I'm off to Italy.

"How long will you be away, Maria?"

Jean's question leaves me nonplussed, and I hesitate. "I've bought a single ticket, so I'm not tied to a particular return date." The truth is, in my mad rush to head off to Florence, I've given no thought to when exactly I'll be back.

"I said, how long will you be away?"

I pause again. "A couple of weeks, I suppose; a month at the longest. You see, Jean, I don't know what exactly is waiting for me over there." Then I drop the bombshell. "My uncle's been murdered."

By the look on Jean's face I could be telling her that World War III has just broken out.

I try and comfort her. "So I'm sure you can see why I've got to keep an open mind and take things one step at a time. But listen, I want you to keep to your usual days, but instead of cleaning and washing, you can mollycoddle the cats – feed them, stroke them, talk to them. And don't worry, there'll be no change in your wages. The cats know you, so if you come over as usual, they should be fine. My next-door neighbour will pop in on the days you're not here."

A jumble of thoughts races through my mind as I'm packing. After some dithering, I go for my largest case, putting in clothes for all weathers, from Siberian cold to African heat. They are mostly jeans and pants, T-shirts, a fleece, a couple of sweaters, a well-worn anorak, a heavy coat and a raincoat. As a final thought, I put in a little black dress I keep for first nights. There might be some formal occasions and it could come in handy. I throw in my copy of *Hamlet*, and search my bookshelves for the next two plays in our season: Shakespeare's *The Tempest* and Joanne's new play, a thinly veiled autobiographical account of the anorexia she suffered in adolescence. Now for emergency medicines. I stuff in an assortment, mostly of the 'anti' sort: anti-mosquito, anti-runs, anti-hangover. At just turned eleven I press the case shut and feed the cats, wondering how long it will be until I see them again.

I roll into bed knackered, but can't get to sleep. I've got a nagging feeling that my present circumstances are in some respects like Hamlet's. As in the Danish royal family, in my family there has been a feud between two brothers, with one of them getting murdered. But I tell myself not to get cocky. Lots of things are different; not least the murder. Somebody poured poison into the old king's ear while he was asleep in his orchard. I don't imagine that this happened to Peter. What's more, while Hamlet was still in mourning for his father, like lightning his Uncle Claudius ascended the throne and married Gertrude, his sister-in-law and Hamlet's mother. In contrast, I have just lost an uncle who never married, as far as I know, and had no connections with royalty.

With Peter's young face firmly impressed in my mind's eye, and a voice telling me to forget *Hamlet*, I doze off.

4

The next day, I'm slowly pulling my suitcase along the platform at the train station in Florence. It is the Tuesday after Easter Monday, and the flight from Manchester to Pisa, followed by a train ride, has taken five hours. I head for the exit, weaving around the crowds of people, some rushing to catch a train, others waiting for one, or perhaps to meet somebody. My ears attune to the different languages being spoken all around me, and I wonder for a second if I really am in Italy.

Outside the station, I notice a McDonald's on the other side of the dusty road skirting the building, flanked by sleazy bars, cafés and a couple of takeaways. The view strikes me as a far cry from the Renaissance city I read about in my guidebook on the flight over. The Uffizi Gallery, the Palazzo Pitti and the magnificent Boboli Gardens are nowhere in sight. Still, I tell myself, I've not come to Florence to visit the wonders of the historic city, or to go roaming around the Tuscan villas and farmhouses belonging to British celebrities who have second homes here. I've got more serious business to attend to.

I feel a buzz of excitement at the thought of the money I could be about to come into, then stifle it. I might be in for a shock. Peter may have been penniless, having squandered his money on gambling or drink. I glance at my watch –half past one – then look at a clock in front of me, which says half past two. I forgot that Italian time is an hour ahead of the UK, and I need to grab a taxi, fast; the reading of the will is in just half an hour.

The crowds have grown denser and the noise is deafening. People are milling in every square inch, reminding me that I have just landed in one of the busiest tourist cities in the world. Shoved to the left, right, and right again, I perch on my case, sweating and taking deep breaths. I have to keep calm. Still, a second later I jump to my feet, scanning round for a taxi rank. Standing beside me, a dark-haired young woman is engaged in what sounds like one hell of a row with the man cowering next to her. Thinking she sounds like a local, I decide to imitate her and shout, even louder, "Taxi? Taxi? *Per favore, per favore!*"

"Over there, Signora," the woman replies quietly, looking at me as if I'm mad, while pointing round the corner to a straggly queue.

Feeling anxious that I'll never make it to Manetti's on time, I have no alternative except to plonk myself and my case at the end of the queue. At last, at ten to three, my turn comes, and an elderly driver emerges slowly from his cab. Without a word, he takes the handle of my case, wheels it round to the back of his car and opens the boot. Picking the case up, he does his best to lift it inside. Then the fun begins. In a flash the case bangs back onto the pavement, and a bizarre concoction of English and Italian swear words fills the air; something like "Madonna fuck *maremma maiala* sod of *porca miseria.*" Then, looking daggers at the case, he makes a second attempt to heave it into the boot, resulting in an even louder thud and more swearing. As the seconds tick by, I imagine Giuseppe Manetti reading the will without me. I take the bull by the horns (or, if you'd rather, the case by the bottom end) and manage to help the by-now-exhausted cabbie to push it into the boot.

Once installed in the back of the taxi, my twenty words of Italian are getting me nowhere when the driver suddenly starts to speak in a cross between Italian and Liverpudlian. "I'm Francesco, or Frankie to my mates in England. You see, Signora, I lived and worked in Liverpool for more than thirty years. Just tell me in plain English where you want to go and we'll be off."

I fumble in my bag for my diary, where I've written the solicitor's address. Smiling to myself, I think that Frankie-Francesco is in for a disappointment. Not in a month of Sundays will I manage to pronounce this Italian address in plain English. As the taxi sets off, the crowds grow thicker and we are moving at a snail's pace. Some pedestrians are in the middle of the road because the pavements are chock-full. With no traffic lights or zebra crossings in sight, others are trying to dodge the moving vehicles in an attempt to get across. I am astonished that this part of Florence is just as seedy as the area immediately outside the station. I wind the window down, letting the smells of Chinese food, cheese-and-onion crisps, and exhaust fumes drift into the car. Sign after sign says, 'Hotel', accompanied by a bizarre assortment of proper names like Galileo, Dante, Derby, Roma and Leonardo, interrupted at one point by a plaque on an anonymous building announcing, 'Percy Bysshe Shelley wrote his *Ode to the West Wind* here between 1819 and 1820.' *Not with this din*, I think; *pull the other one*. Recalling Shelley's delicate, elfin face in one of his best-known portraits, I imagine him scribbling a very different poem amid the chaos unfolding here. He would have hated the fumes, dirt and noise just as much as I do.

"That's the main entrance of Florence Cathedral," Frankie murmurs, breaking into my thoughts. "Santa Maria del Fiore. Are you on holiday, Signora?"

I make no reply but let out a "Wow!" as I see the cathedral's majestic facade in mottled grey-green-pink marble. The taxi is going even slower, and as we skirt a side wall, I realise the sheer size of the building.

A few minutes later, after negotiating a couple more narrow streets flanked by anonymous, dark buildings, Frankie draws up in front of a nondescript grey-stone condominium and points at the front door. Holding out the palm of his hand to me, he murmurs, "*Ventimila lire.* Twenty thousand, Signora."

This sounds like an exorbitant amount for such a short journey, but I've no time to quibble, and I count the notes into Frankie's hand. Still, he glowers, muttering something about his aching back and my hugely overweight suitcase being a big problem. He's evidently expecting a tip, but I mumble apologetically, "Sorry, Frankie, I've no change; I mean, no coins. Not one! You see, I've just arrived in Florence."

5

The main door of Manetti's building is open and I find myself in an entrance hall with dark wooden panelling and a splendid black-and-white marble floor. There are six doors, each with a brass nameplate, and I look around, searching for the solicitor's office. There it is: '*Studio Associato Notarile: Dott. Giuseppe Manetti*', inscribed in fancy lettering on the right-hand door.

The minute I ring the bell, a furious barking flares up inside. Then the door swings open and a bright-faced, stylishly dressed young woman greets me, waving me into a waiting room. "I am Dottor Manetti's secretary," she says hesitantly in broken English, asking me for some identification. Pointing at the clock, she intimates that I am ten minutes late. However, the moment I start to explain, she brushes my apologies aside and opens a door just behind her.

The barking peaks and I brace myself, ready to face an angry pit bull. I needn't have worried. The culprit is a little Scottie dog, prancing frantically on the end of a lead. Tied to the leg of a table, it is doing its utmost to break free. As I walk into the room, I catch sight of two people sitting at a table. One has his back to me, while the second leaps to his feet the moment he sees me, introducing himself as Dr Manetti. His mop of curly blond hair, his fair skin and his greyish-blue eyes come as a surprise. Since his phone call I've been imagining a middle-aged, dark-haired and dark-eyed Italian, with olive skin.

Although he can't be much older than thirty-five, Manetti is poised and confident and manages the introductions with the aplomb of a master of ceremonies. "May I introduce you to Professor Gabriele Foschi, Ms Farrell?"

The professor approaches, shakes my hand and tells me that his dog, Phoebe, is actually a lamb in disguise once she gets to know you. In the next breath he reveals that he was a close friend of Peter's, and that my uncle has mentioned me so often it feels like we are old friends. With a faint chuckle, he asks if he can call me Maria. Seeing as I never met Peter, I am astonished that he should have talked about me. And on top of that, here is a complete stranger wanting to treat me like an old friend. Just the same, I nod to indicate that first names will be fine.

I take in Gabriele's tanned face and intelligent eyes. They look spent and weary, making me wonder how close he actually was to Peter. A pale blue cotton shirt and slim-fitting linen trousers show off his lean, agile body. The gold and steel of what looks like a Rolex watch, a heavy gold neck chain and a ring speak of money. Still, there is something just too perfect and polished about him. As he smiles, I notice his immaculate teeth and have to stifle a laugh. I can just see him in one of those television ads for upmarket Italian cars, behind the wheel of a state-of-the-art Ferrari – red, of course. He is tearing past the Colosseum in Rome, a gorgeous young woman in the passenger seat, her arm draped seductively round his shoulders. The image is nauseatingly romantic, but probably an excellent marketing strategy.

In a flash Gabriele cuts into my thoughts as he pushes a handkerchief into my hand and gestures that I should dry the sweat off my forehead and arms. His face shows what looks like genuine concern, and he tells me I should be careful not to go down with a fever. After all, a sharp change in climate can play havoc with the immune system. Manchester this morning, now Florence this afternoon to deal with a truly unpleasant situation. Gabriele's concern for my welfare makes me feel guilty; I've been having a laugh at his expense and he probably doesn't deserve it.

Unannounced, a woman enters the room and, after shaking her hand, Manetti introduces her as Countess Caterina Guiccioli.

"Good afternoon, Ms Farrell; I do hope you had a good journey," she says in almost perfect upper-class English. At nearly six foot, she towers four inches above me, her head held high, almost regal. She is Sandro Botticelli's Venus from his *Birth of Venus* painting, forty years on; not naked, but attired in a stunning blue silk dress over a shapely figure. Though she possesses Venus's exquisite features – her high forehead, sharply defined chin, delicate eyebrows, narrow mouth and full lips – the goddess's pale, translucent skin has turned wrinkled and dry; her flowing strawberry-blonde hair slightly faded and pulled back in a bun. She comes close, her spicy perfume overpowering me, and grabs my hand, whispering how deeply sorry she is about what happened to Peter.

The moment I've been waiting for has arrived, and Manetti takes out some pages from a large envelope. His gaze runs from one of us to the other, a radiant smile attempting to deflate the tension bristling in the room. "Ladies and gentleman," he announces in a solemn voice, his eyes still trawling, "you'll be glad to hear that Peter Farrell left a detailed will. He bequeaths his flat and a part of its contents to his niece, Maria Farrell."

"I can't believe it! That's amazing," I murmur, breaking the silence lying heavy on either side of me.

Unruffled by my outburst, Manetti's eyes stay glued to the paper. "Yes, Signora Farrell, you inherit the deceased man's flat, his furniture, his clothes and most of his possessions; the exception being Professor Farrell's collection of paintings – Picasso, Warhol, Dalí and other less distinguished artists. Have a look at the list."

He hands me a sheet of paper listing eleven paintings, each one with a short description. Out of the corner of my eye I glimpse Gabriele looking visibly shocked. I hand him the list, making eye contact, while wondering what exactly is going through his mind.

"I honestly can't believe this is really happening to me. You see, to me my uncle was more like somebody out of a fairy tale; never very real. I had an idea he was a university tutor, so these valuable paintings come as a complete surprise. Dr Manetti, would you mind telling me who the recipients of the artworks are?"

The reply strikes me like a bolt from the blue. "Peter Farrell leaves the collection to you and Professor Foschi, with the exception of a single painting. Before the division begins, Countess Guiccioli will be given first choice. But first of all, my client stipulates that each artwork should be carefully appraised. Only when this is done will you and Professor Foschi be allowed to select the paintings of your choice. In turn, you'll each choose a painting until the entire collection is divided between you. Oh, I was forgetting – you are to draw lots to decide which of you goes first. Regarding the art specialist, my client asks the countess to appoint one she trusts. You have three months to arrange everything. Is that clear?"

"Peter always loved a little party game," the countess mutters sardonically.

"What do you mean?" I ask, thinking that if this is a party game, it is worth thousands, if not millions of lire.

The countess's face has turned mischievous. "Knowing Peter… But seriously, Ms Farrell, as soon as you are settled in, I'll take you to visit his grave and tell you more about him."

I turn to look at Gabriele, hoping he might be more forthcoming, but there's no joy there. He is hugging Phoebe to his chest, moving his hand erratically up and down her fur, his face pale and grim.

Manetti tells me that I am now free to go to my uncle's flat, where a Mr Singh is waiting for me. Seeing my quizzical expression, he adds, "Don't worry, Mr Singh is the caretaker of the flats where the professor lived. He's Indian, but he's been living and working in Florence for almost two decades. He speaks fluent English, too, which should be a help. The two detectives in charge of the case should also be waiting for you. They've a few questions for you, and after that they'll be handing over the keys. Shall I call a taxi?"

I nod, speechless, so overwhelmed that my tongue and lips refuse to move. Struggling to my feet, I start wheeling my case towards the exit, when the tapping of high heels resounds behind me.

A second later the countess has overtaken me and is blocking the exit. She grabs my sleeve. "Ms Farrell," her voice is thick with excitement, "I hope you realise you're a very lucky lady. The contents of the will come as an absolute surprise to us all. Still, that's Peter all over. He was always a dark horse. I called him my unpredictable Albion! And he's proven himself true to form, even from beyond the grave. I still can't believe that he made his will without saying a dicky bird to his closest friends."

At that moment Gabriele joins us, his expression betraying signs of despair. With Phoebe hanging over one arm, he silently tucks his other through the countess's. As I walk away, I can hear her voice chiming in the hall, and I wonder why they are still speaking in English.

"Gabriele, cheer up. Remember, Peter did leave you half the paintings. I only got one. How about going to Giocosa's for a drink? You look like a ghost out to haunt me, darling."

"Do I really look so pale? It'll have to be a quick one, though. I've got to meet somebody in half an hour."

6

Outside a taxi is waiting, but this time I carefully weigh up the driver before getting in. I certainly wouldn't relish a repeat performance of the Frankie cock-up. The man, in his early twenties, whips my case into the boot, making it look like it is full of feathers. Relieved, I clamber into the back seat, sinking into the well-worn upholstery and running over what Giuseppe Manetti has told me. I feel elated and ready to tackle whatever comes my way. In my broken Italian I give my instructions: "*Andare Via Alfonso la Marmora… Numero Sessantasei, per favore.*"

Once again, the taxi makes its way along the narrow streets, skirting the cathedral, where the crowds of tourists show no sign of dispersing. The cabbie seems to be making for the outskirts, and skilfully navigates a complicated web of roads, followed by a junction seething with traffic. As a teenager I imagined Peter like a character in an E. M. Forster novel, pedalling around Florence on a rickety old bike en route to the library. Predictably, perhaps, he sported a 1920s tweed jacket, flannel trousers and handmade leather brogues, while a tattered briefcase was tied to the pillion. As the driver vies with the relentless stream of hooting cars, buses and lorries, I realise that, for all these years, my imagination has conjured up a picture of Peter that is probably way off the mark.

A little later the cityscape changes abruptly. On the right are some botanical gardens, and the crowds have almost disappeared. We shoot past a stark grey-stone church, and I glimpse a well-heeled-looking woman walking a black poodle. Her pace is so leisurely it makes me think that walking her dog is probably all she does each day. We are driving through a residential area of elegant town houses when a street sign indicating Via Alfonso la Marmora catches my eye. I stiffen as the taxi slows down, a lump wedging itself in my throat, and prepare for the worst. Through the window I gaze at the building in front of me: Number Sixty-Six. After careful scrutiny, I decide it is just as splendid as the others in the street. It is three floors high, with huge windows and bevelled balconies decked with boxes of yellow primroses and multicoloured pansies.

I climb out of the car, breathing in the calm of the place. The air definitely feels fresher and more fragrant than around the station. Staring back at me from the middle of the front door is an old-fashioned brass knocker in the shape of a lion's head, a ring through its mouth. To the right a keypad for the entryphone instructs: '*Premere 1 per Portinaio*'. (Press 1 for Janitor). I tap in the number, wait for a moment, and the door clicks open.

Inside the high-beamed entrance hall, I stop short. The orange-and-black marble floor is so shiny it seems to be defying me to walk across it. But cross it I must, and I teeter towards what looks like a porter's lodge. Through the spotlessly clean window, I peer into a tiny room where a hulk of a man is sitting. Dark-skinned, around sixty, he is dressed in bottle-green trousers, a white shirt and a green tie. With one hand he beckons me inside, while with the other he grabs a pan lid from the table and quickly hides some half-eaten spaghetti.

"Welcome, Ms Farrell; sorry I can't help you with your case. My foot's plaguing me." He bends over, rubbing his swollen foot as if to prove the veracity of what he has just said. "You see, I'm in a real mess today. You *are* Ms Farrell, I presume? Dr Manetti called to let me know you were on your way over."

"That's right... Mr Singh? Sorry for barging in on your meal," I murmur, pointing at the dish of spaghetti.

"Not to worry, I can eat it later," he replies, without much conviction. "Yes, I'm Singh."

He points to a chair next to his, and I perch on the edge, ready to dash back into the hall. The lack of natural light and fresh air in the room is making me feel claustrophobic. On the table I clock the single plate, glass, knife and fork. There's a small bed-settee against a wall, and a door in the corner, presumably leading to a toilet. The place is full of telltale signs suggesting that Singh lives alone.

"Please call me Maria. In England, only my bank manager calls me Ms Farrell. Here in Italy you are so formal."

"Oh, I couldn't possibly. It wouldn't be..."

"I'm English and work in the theatre. In my field we don't stand on ceremony. No surnames, not usually."

I am beginning to think I'll never hear any Italian; almost everyone I've met so far has spoken English. Singh's accent is upper-class and posher than mine. I ask him where he learnt the language, and his voice swells with pride. After leaving India, he lived in Sussex, where he worked as a manservant to a wealthy family. His employer, the owner of a leading London publishing house, was a stickler for grammar, Singh adds gravely, which meant he soon learnt impeccable English.

As if wishing to change the subject, the caretaker's eyes dart to a black-and-white wedding photo on the wall above the fridge. "Then I met her. That's Anna Paola, my wife. She was a Florentine. That's me standing next to her." Noticing my look of surprise, he adds, "Of course, that was taken quite a few years ago, when I was much thinner! Anna Paola came to England to work as an au pair for the children in the family who employed me. There was an instant spark. I taught her English. She was a very special woman," he concludes wistfully.

"And then what happened? I mean, what brought you both to Italy?"

"Some years later, after we married, her father fell ill and we moved here. She wanted to nurse him. But, to cut a painful story short, ten years ago Anna died. She had cancer, and I finished up here." He is rubbing his foot even harder. It is as if his unhappiness has settled right there. "Working as a caretaker is a steady job," he concludes. "And besides, I have no qualifications to find anything better."

Prompted by the sight of a noticeboard on the wall in front of me, with bunches of keys, each with a number, I ask Singh if he can give me the keys to Peter's flat.

"The police, Ms Farrell." He points apologetically at an empty hook. "They still have them. They phoned an hour ago to say they'll be here soon and will bring them. But may I ask – does this mean the professor's left you his flat?"

As he pronounces the words 'left you his flat', a glint of envy crosses his face, visible in the way his features twist very slightly. Then he checks himself, pulling a handkerchief from his pocket and coughing into it. Tears well in his eyes. "You know, Signora Maria, I haven't been up to the professor's place since it happened."

"I'm sorry you're so upset. Tell me – what actually happened?"

"I can't; the police have sworn me to secrecy."

"Oh, come on. Please."

"I found the professor's…" He hesitates. "After they detained me at the station for hours and made me repeat over and over what I'd seen, what I'd done after I found the body—"

A bell rings and, once Singh has dragged himself to his feet, he goes to answer the entryphone. A second later three men come striding into the hall. Two take the lift upstairs, while the third heads in the direction of the lodge. A second later his face is pressing against the window, his dark eyes peering at us through the glass. His gaze is no longer sad and angry, but alive and inquisitive. It's Gabriele Foschi.

7

Coming through the lodge door, Gabriele greets Singh and me, before sitting on the edge of the table and lighting up. The tiny room is soon full of smoke, prompting Singh to grab a brush and scuttle off, declaring that he has to clean the stairs.

Once we are alone, Gabriele explains briskly that the detectives have gone up to the flat to check that everything is in order. The forensic team left yesterday and from this morning the police have lifted the sequestration order, so I can get to work on the clear-out as soon as I like.

"Well, it gives me the creeps. I mean, the idea of going through my uncle's possessions and private papers…" I blurt out, surprising even myself.

"Why's that?" Gabriele's voice is confrontational. He moves swiftly to the door and closes it, presumably not wanting Singh or anybody else to hear what he is about to say. "Peter evidently wanted you to have everything he possessed, or almost. Anyway, it's written in the will in black and white. You heard what Manetti said. Truth is, Peter, or Pietro as we sometimes called him, was very attached to England, and you were very special to him. He even said – I remember it like yesterday – that you and I could have been brother and sister."

"What did he mean by that?" The idea amazes me.

"He felt very close to both of us. Yes, even though he never met you. Then there's the age factor. You're just three years older than me."

"That makes you forty-two." I grin. "No more secrets."

"For many years he had regular news from a cousin in England. What was her name?" Gabriele pauses, thinking for a second and then lighting up again. "Edith from Liverpool, that was it! You should have seen Peter's face when he heard you'd managed your first job in that theatre in Leeds. He was over the moon. I bet you'll find a stack of Edith's Christmas, birthday and Easter cards stored away somewhere in his office."

"When I was growing up, Edith was our only link with Peter, but after her death there was total silence. It was very sad," I say.

"She'd always scribble some news about you and your family on the backs of her cards. Your uncle relished reading them."

"Even if he had become Italian, or almost. Pietro – wasn't that what you sometimes called him?"

Gabriele's voice turns playful. "What's in a name? A Farrell by any other name would smell as sweet."

I quickly continue with more of Juliet's lines, charged with so much emotion and common sense. "Oh, Romeo, Romeo, wherefore art thou, Romeo? Deny thy father and refuse thy name."

"But seriously, Maria – I mean, I don't know you well, but when all's said and done, you are his niece and his closest living relative, so this might be the explanation."

Gabriele's eyes are scrutinising my face, and his voice has grown confidential. "You've got some of his features. His blue eyes, and there's something about your chin, too..." Noticing my embarrassment, he changes tack mid-sentence. "Listen, in my opinion, you've only got one problem at the moment. You've got to decide which room in the flat to clear out first. From today the property is yours."

The jealousy I saw on Singh's face flits over Gabriele's too as he pronounces these last words. He's evidently still feeling staggered by the contents of the will and making a huge effort to be friendly. Was he, I wonder, thinking that Peter would leave him his flat, all his possessions and all the paintings? And, again I wonder, what was their relationship exactly?

A rattling of keys on the lodge window interrupts my thoughts, and Gabriele moves to open the door, gesturing amicably in my direction while talking to the newcomer. "Inspector, here is Signora Maria Farrell, in the flesh. She has just arrived from Manchester."

The man at the door looks to be in his early sixties. Everything about him is rather faded: his light grey linen suit and matching shirt; the few remaining hairs on his otherwise bald head. His face is sallow, with dark circles under his eyes. I smile to myself, thinking that the bulge of fat round his waist must have stopped him fastening the bottom two buttons on his jacket.

Once he has introduced himself, Detective Inspector Alfio Romagnoli shakes my hand and asks, in heavily accented English, "Signora Farrell, or Signorina?"

What, I think, *has it got to do with him whether I am married or single?* Firmly, I reply that today we are all 'Signoras' in England.

He goes on, apparently not understanding what I've just said, "Welcome to Florence. You will not be lonely here. We Italians are verrry hospitable."

His broken English and the way he rolls his 'R's make me want to laugh, but I don't, reminding myself that I must sound even more ridiculous when I try to speak Italian.

Unaware of what's racing through my mind, the inspector holds out the keys to the flat, pressing them into my hand. "There you are: keys to your flat in our beautiful Firenze. Our forensic team have now carried out all their checks. I will see you again.

We must talk about your uncle. But not now; tomorrow morning. Rest and peace, Signora."

"*Grazie e arrivederci*," I gush, praying that he really will leave me in peace.

At that moment his colleague joins him. "*Buonasera*, Signora Farrell. I hope you had a good journey. I visited Manchester last January on a case. It's a dismal city and rainy most of the time, but I liked the people."

I find myself staring at him, unsure how I should reply, and wondering what information they have got on me. This new detective is around fifty, with dark brown eyes that are weighing me up. They are warm, seeming to sympathise with me. Unlike Romagnoli, he is fit and slim, his curly greying hair clean and shiny. Without more ado, he turns to his colleague, whispering something in Italian. Romagnoli's face darkens, and he announces that they have to be going, but will be in touch tomorrow morning for a statement.

The unnamed detective has crossed the entrance hall and is about to open the main door of the house when he turns back to face me, calling out a cheery, "*Arrivederci*, Ms Farrell."

As the door closes behind him, I could kick myself. There was something very attractive about him. Why didn't I ask him his name? And what's more, there could have been a hint of Scottish in his accent, bringing back a myriad of happy memories of Edinburgh and my trips to the Fringe Festival in August.

8

I stare at the polished mahogany door of Peter's flat, anxious to see what's inside. It's one thing to be told you own a property in Florence; another to actually see it for yourself. I feel like jumping up and down, like a kid opening her presents at Christmas, but manage to contain myself. I don't want Gabriele thinking I am bonkers.

Dangling a bunch of keys in his hand, he quickly selects one after another and deftly opens the three locks, making it obvious that he was a regular visitor when Peter was alive. Pushing the door open, he points to the burglar alarm. "Don't forget to switch this thing on and off when you come and go. Remember, the paintings are still inside."

He motions me through the hall into the sitting room, where I allow myself a discreet "Wow, Jesus. This really is special!" My eyes range over the spacious room, with sunlight flowing in through two French windows.

Gabriele is already moving briskly through the flat, throwing open one door after another. He makes me feel like a tourist on one of those package holidays where you sign up to 'do' Rome, Florence and Venice in just three days. His tone is apologetic. "Don't worry, tomorrow you'll have plenty of time to see the place at your leisure. This is the master bedroom, complete with an en-suite bathroom. On the left here, there's a guest room and a small bathroom. Then there's his study and the library next to it, full of books. They'll take some sorting! Here's the kitchen and scullery. Through there, the dining room, and there's a cellar in the basement. It's very well stocked, by the way. Oh, and here's the freezer room. I know, these chest freezers are enormous. Peter had this habit of buying and freezing masses of food. My theory is that it was something to do with his childhood experience of wartime rationing in England. He sometimes recalled how terribly hungry he had felt." Tears are welling in Gabriele's eyes as he draws to a close, "The flat must be about 250 square metres."

Back in the sitting room, I walk through one of the windows onto a tiny balcony to get a breath of air. I need to think about what I've just seen and heard. Running my fingers over the petals of the pansies and primroses neatly arranged in the window boxes, I wonder if Peter planted them. This display is certainly not Hamlet's 'unweeded garden'. Quite the contrary.

The comfortable but elegant sitting-room furnishings suggest that this is where he must have spent a lot of his time. Two large divans face each other, with a couple of armchairs at either end, one with a small table standing next to it, topped by a 1950s telephone. The large cushions of one divan sag, perhaps indicating the very spot where Peter enjoyed relaxing when he was at home. Separating the divans is a pinewood coffee table with a china bowl of shrivelled daffodils. And to complete the decor, a light wooden parquet floor, a stereo music set, three racks of magazines and newspapers, Persian carpets, and white walls, one covered with paintings. With growing excitement, I focus on the artworks, reading the artists' signatures – Warhol, Dalí, Picasso. The list I saw at Manetti's was spot on.

For a few seconds Gabriele lets me ogle, but the minute he speaks, his voice sounds stern. "As Manetti told us, the paintings have been left to us both, with the exception of one for Caterina. Once her evaluator has done her job, we'll need to set a date for the division sometime in the next three months. Remember what Manetti told us? In the meantime, you can work with Singh on the kitchen, bathrooms, cellar, office, etc."

"Why Singh?"

"He knows the place back to front and upside down. You'll see." Gabriele is smiling. "Besides, he lives on the premises, so without spending too much, you'll have a man to give you a hand for a few hours a day. You know, with the heavy things; the things you women find hard to manage on your own."

What he says makes sense, even if I don't much care for the 'you women' bit. Still, I remind myself, this is Italy, and men like Gabriele and DI Romagnoli seem to have sexism engrained in their psyches. On the positive side, some extra help will mean that I can head back to Manchester before too long. I decide to go along with Gabriele's advice and ask Singh if he has time, and what he wants for the job.

Gabriele is looking at the Picasso, his nose almost touching the sketch of a young man. "Quite something, eh?" His voice sparks with emotion. "It's a minor Picasso, of course, and a preliminary sketch for what became a major oil painting. Just the same, it's superb. Whenever I look at this young chap, he seems to be telling me something different. He looks utterly dejected, but each time I decide on a different reason for his unhappiness."

Immediately after, Gabriele's voice becomes matter-of-fact, as if he is attempting to stifle an unpleasant memory. His eyes run sadly over the furniture around us. "While you're busy with this lot, the evaluator will have a chance to complete the assessment of the paintings. I'm sure there's no need to tell you that this is where the serious money is."

Prior to my uncle's death I was struggling financially: a good

34

year here, a bad year there. Five years ago, at forty, I set up my own theatre company, but things have never been easy. I can feel my legs trembling. An idea has just struck me. I'll be able to relax and not worry where the next penny is coming from. I'll have my inheritance to fall back on.

Then my mind reverts to the clear-out, and my stomach tightens. Not because the job itself is difficult; rather, because of the bizarre tangle of relationships linking the people I've met here so far. Not least, the bond between Singh and Peter is niggling me. I ask Gabriele about their relationship and he replies, "Singh did a fine job of looking after Peter. I suppose you could say he was a kind of factotum." He hesitates, his expression turning sad, before going on. "He regularly cooked for Peter, and served his guests whenever he entertained."

"Did he care for Uncle?"

"Care... what exactly do you mean by 'care'? It's got several meanings in English, hasn't it?" Gabriele's eyes bore into mine, as if searching for an answer.

"Ten out of ten for your English," I exclaim, holding his gaze.

"The upshot of five years at Oxford, a PhD, and years working alongside Peter. Care... you might say Singh cared as a servant cares for an employer – formally, courteously. Still, I've never seen him drop his mask, not really. He certainly went out of his way to serve and assist your uncle, if that's what you mean. Peter paid him well, of course. To be honest, I don't think there was ever any real loving care on Singh's part, but you can judge for yourself."

I notice that Gabriele is glancing at his watch, implying that he must be off. I look at the time and am astounded to realise it is nearly 10pm. I've had nothing to eat all day and still have to check into my hotel. I have no intention of sleeping in the place where my uncle was murdered, and have booked into a small hotel about a mile away. I ask Gabriele if he'll call me a taxi, and a few minutes later I am speeding through the dark city streets.

Ensconced in my hotel room, I feel too tired to unpack. I simply pull a nightdress out of my case and get changed. Feeling more relaxed, I sprawl out on the double bed, stuffing a couple of pillows under my feet. I managed to order a couple of sandwiches and a glass of red wine at reception, and I am soon biting hungrily into one of the sandwiches. It's raw Parma ham, cheese and salad on Tuscan bread. Delicious!

It has been a long day and my legs are killing me. I snuggle down, dimming the lights and admiring the soft blue and gold-leaf pattern of the wallpaper. The period furniture gives the place an old-fashioned but friendly feel, and I am glad I've opted for what I hope is a genuinely family-run business.

Even as I am dozing off, I force myself to go over what has happened since I got here. This unknown world seems light years away from my circle of friends and acquaintants in Manchester. With my eyes closed, and sucking a sweet from the dish on the bedside table, I picture the faces of the people I've met so far. It's a game I often play, matching faces to voices, and afterwards adding the person's tiniest mannerisms and perfume. It's only then that she or he comes together in my head and begins to make sense. Could any of the people I've met today be Peter's murderer? Could any of them have hated Peter so much they decided to kill him? Could this scenario, like *Hamlet*, be a revenge tragedy, unfolding in 2000 instead of 1600?

I doze off with these unanswered questions, and Gabriele's tearful face as he spoke about Peter's wartime experience, in my mind's eye; Caterina's spicy perfume in my nose; the tip-tapping of her high heels and her excited voice in my ears, and the words she spoke scrawled all over the bedroom wallpaper: *Still, that's Peter all over. He was always a dark horse. I called him my unpredictable Albion.*

9

It's early morning, my first in Florence. I'm having breakfast in bed and thinking how odd it feels not to have to get down to the theatre when the phone rings. It's DI Romagnoli's secretary. They can't see me this morning, she says curtly; an urgent case has just come in. I tell her I am of course available any time they need me, and take a bite of my croissant, making the peach jam ooze all over the plate. A wave of relief engulfs me and I realise that I wasn't looking forward to going to the police station one little bit.

In a jiffy, I concoct Plan B. I open a street map of Florence and begin working out the quickest way to walk to Peter's. I rehearse my route in an assertive, encouraging voice, like a tourist guide, prompting myself to make a move. "Exit the hotel, make a right, then first left. After a minute, you'll come to Piazza della Santissima Annunziata; two minutes later you'll find yourself in Piazza San Marco. Go down Via Giorgio la Pira. After five minutes, you'll come to Via Alfonso la Marmora. Look for Number Sixty-Six. Now you're ready for the fray, Maria."

Gulping down the last of my coffee, I glance at the clock on the bedside table. It's 8.30, 7.30 in Manchester, and I remember that the *Hamlet* rehearsals are scheduled for this morning. I feel awful, but there's nothing I can do to help; the show's completely in Joanne's hands. Instead of phoning her, I decide to leave her to it and call her tomorrow. It'll give her a chance to settle into her new role and establish her authority with the actors. Instead I make a quick call to Jean to check she's at my place. "Hello there. How are you? Yes, I'm fine… And how are the cats? That's good," I say, feeling happy they're all right. "Sorry, Jean, I can't talk long. This call must be costing a fortune."

The second I ring off I bite my tongue, reminding myself that, for the first time in my life, I can relax about money. Once I've sold Peter's flat and paintings, I'll have enough money to chat to Jean any day of the week, at any time, for as long as I want.

On that note, I get out of bed and tiptoe to the window; I've forgotten to pack my slippers and the tiles are freezing. Pulling back the creaky wooden shutters, I peer out, curious to see what's outside. Last night when I arrived at the hotel it was already dark, and I haven't the foggiest idea what the neighbourhood looks like. Again, the Palazzo Pitti and the magnificent Boboli Gardens jump to mind, but the view outside the window is so very ordinary. Still, I tell myself, I should be grateful that the hotel is not located in some tourist hotspot and is thankfully very quiet. A high brick wall on the opposite side of the narrow cobbled street stares back at me. On the pavement, some old bikes are parked higgledy-piggledy in a rack. My eyes clock the graffiti daubed all over the wall: '*Fascisti, bastardi, bombe.*' This part of Florence certainly isn't in my guidebook.

Pulling the shutters to again, I take off my nightdress and have a quick shower. I'd better get down to Peter's flat – or rather, I correct myself, *my* flat. I pull on a practical outfit: some old jeans, a T-shirt and trainers. Hamlet's 'readiness is all' flashes to mind again. But stuff you, Hamlet. This morning I've got to make a start on clearing out a huge flat, and probably get myself really mucky in the process.

The morning air smells fresh as I emerge from the hotel. Following the map and armed with my guidebook, I veer right and make a quick left. A minute later, I catch my breath. In front of me, Piazza della Santissima Annunziata is already buzzing with tourists. On the left of the piazza, I marvel at the fifteenth-century loggia of the Hospital of the Innocents. At last my guidebook comes in handy, informing me that this was the first foundling hospital in Italy. I make a mental note to come back and have a proper look round, time permitting. I veer right, walking along the parapet in front of St Mary's Church. Two minutes later, I've reached Piazza San Marco; a far cry from its namesake in Venice. Here, dozens of local buses and tourist coaches are in fierce competition, trying to drop passengers off and pick others up. Hordes of holidaymakers are setting off on day trips, while other people, who look like commuters, are arriving in the city. Looking up, I see a street sign – Via Giorgio la Pira – then soon after, another sign indicating the Agrarian Department of Florence University.

After walking about fifty metres, I find myself skirting the botanical gardens I glimpsed from the taxi yesterday. I nip inside and visit one of the greenhouses, admiring the neat rows of flowers and plants carefully tended and labelled. Leaving the botanicals behind, I cross the street, curious to take a peep at the church I noticed yesterday. I try the door, but it's locked. A bronze plaque on the wall by the entrance informs me in English that this is an evangelical church, built by a Scottish architect for nineteenth-century Florence's Protestant community. I wonder whether Peter was a member. He and my father attended a Church of England grammar school, but none of my immediate family were practising Protestants. I've always had this hunch that the Catholic past of my Irish ancestors, the Farrells, makes any Protestant sympathy almost impossible for us.

I've reached Peter's flat in Via Alfonso la Marmora, and on impulse I decide I won't use the entryphone to call Singh. Pulling Peter's keys out of my bag, I push the biggest one into the lock. As I turn it, my hand quivers with apprehension at the thought of what might lie in store for me this morning.

Inside the hallway, I peer through the lodge window and see Singh shuffling towards me. His face looks weary, shot through with pain. His shirt is half unbuttoned and he's still in his slippers, his foot even more swollen. Thinking that this is probably the reason why he hasn't bothered to get dressed properly, I sympathise with him. "Hello! Are you all right, Mr Singh? You don't look very well this morning, you poor thing!"

"Gout. Today I can come clean with you. Every so often it attacks. I can't sleep when it does. But at least today I'm on my feet." He grabs a sandwich off the table and starts chewing it as if he is famished. His cheeks are still bulging as he holds up a teapot. "Fancy a cuppa, Signora Maria? Imperial gunpowder."

"I've heard of gunpowder tea, but never the imperial variety."

"It's the best. *Buonissimo!* Go on, try some. It was the professor's favourite. They sell it at the English shop just down the road. The owner stocks tea, food, clothes. Everything British. If you like, I can take you there one of these days."

Cradling the warm cup between my fingers, I settle down on Singh's bed-settee, sipping the aromatic brew. He's right, the flavour's excellent, and I muse about its name. It comes as no surprise when you taste it; the strong liquid works like a dynamo on my brain. Seconds later, I feel invigorated and get straight to the point, inquiring if Singh has time to help me for a few hours each day. He mulls over my proposition, then agrees. He'll be quite happy, he says, with the same hourly rate Peter used to pay him. He'll have to check with the building manager first, but he should be able to rejig his schedule and do the cleaning of the stairs and lift, as well as sort the post, from six to ten in the morning and in the late afternoon. That way he'll be free from ten until about one to give me a hand.

That sorted, I stand up, ready to get cracking. "How about making a start on the kitchen?"

"A woman's place," comes his solemn reply.

"Or in this instance, a man's," I joke, thinking that humour is probably the best way to deal with his sexist remark. "Or were there any women, or a particular woman, in my uncle's life?"

One of the masks Gabriele mentioned blanks Singh's face and he falls silent.

"Or were *you* the woman in his life? In a manner of speaking, of course. Gabriele told me you used to cook for Uncle on a regular basis."

By now Singh is hovering by the lift, showing his reluctance to go up to the flat. After dithering a little longer, he presses the button. "The arrangement worked well for many years. Your uncle relied on me. As he was going out, he'd leave me a coded message. It invariably started with one of three words: 'Italian', 'Indian' or 'English'." The lift door opens and Singh makes a courteous little bow, ushering me inside. "That meant the particular dish I was expected to cook. A number followed, indicating how many guests the professor was expecting. Then he wrote the time I had to set the table and serve pre-dinner drinks. He sometimes offered suggestions for the menu. However, if I found something particularly tasty at the market, such as porcini mushrooms, truffles or artichokes in season, he was delighted. I was forgetting the fruit, once again it had to be in season, whenever possible. I usually shop at the fruit and vegetable market just down the road from here in Piazza Sant'Ambrogio. It's got real character and excellent, fresh produce."

"You'll have to take me there. I love markets." However, clocking his deadpan face, I don't insist and simply add, "You sound as if you miss those evenings."

"No," comes Singh's blunt reply. "Those are the facts of my relationship with your uncle. It was a job."

"But tell me, don't you miss Peter?"

41

"Of course I do. He was a gentleman, honest and very straightforward."

I would like to continue questioning Singh. His description of Peter sounds so different from the countess's. I'd like to find out who Peter's guests were, what his relationship was with each of them, what else Singh knows about him. However, his lips are sealed, and I realise I'll have to wait.

Once inside Peter's flat, Singh makes a beeline for the kitchen, where he slumps down onto a chair, kicking off his slipper and cursing under his breath. He lifts his gouty foot as high in the air as he can manage and forces himself to wiggle it, but a loud yell tells me that the exercise isn't working and the pain just won't go away. Like the sitting room, the kitchen is spick and span, and furnished with exquisite taste. My eyes scan the pinkish-grey marble worktops and solid oak cupboards, the stylish designer kettle glimmering on a rose-pink hob, the shocking pink vintage fridge in the corner. A glass vase filled with violets stands in the middle of a table, the shrivelled flowers reminders of how many things and relationships suffered the day Peter died.

Singh does not waste a minute and sets about flinging open the cupboard doors and drawers. Magically, the kitchen turns into an Eastern bazaar as he pulls out and puts on display two sets of silver cutlery, an exquisite china tea service, and an impressive assortment of pots and pans of every conceivable size, shape and weight. I listen to him sing the praises of this and that pan, adding how much some of them cost. Singh's slow but self-assured performance makes it clear that for him the flat is home from home.

"Did Uncle ever cook for himself?" I pick up a hefty marble mortar and pestle, stroking the smooth whitish-grey mottled surface. "I love cooking Indian food, and back in Manchester I'll certainly use these to grind the spices for my curries. It'll be my way of remembering Peter. I'll think of him every time they release their flavours."

I throw Singh a smile, searching his face for a reaction. All I get is an impenetrable look, after which his eyes fix on the pestle in my hand.

"The professor certainly shared your passion for food; I mean, for eating it. He was 'a good fork'; *una buona forchetta*, as we say in Italy. He loved all kinds of pasta dishes, seafood, cheese, ham, salami, mushrooms. Still, steak was his favourite."

"Just like Dad. He didn't have a sweet tooth either." I chuckle. "Give Dad a well-cooked joint, roast potatoes, two veg, Yorkshire pudding and all the trimmings and he was as happy as Larry."

Suddenly I can see my father, standing at the head of the table on a Sunday when I was a girl. He's warming his backside near a blazing coal fire, a white apron wrapped round his ample midriff. He never in his life cooked or washed up – all that was left to Mum – but he tackled two weekend chores: carving the roast beef, and giving marks to that week's Yorkshire pudding. I loved the Yorkshire pudding game and would sit impatiently fingering the rim of my plate, desperate to have my say. And once Dad had pronounced his verdict, after slowly savouring a mouthful of the piping hot pudding, I got my turn. It was the only time of the week that Dad was really happy. He never liked his job as an English teacher, and would complain, "It's just a job that puts bread and a knob of butter on the table, Maria." On one occasion, I think we were celebrating somebody's birthday, and Dad had had a drop too much to drink when he confided, "When I was young I dreamt of a university career or something in television, but my degree from Hull put the damper on all that. If I'd gone to a decent college where the teachers challenged and inspired me, things would no doubt have turned out different. Dull Hull, that's where I ended up, while Peter was swanning around at Oxford. Make sure you find yourself something better than I did, Maria; something you're really passionate about."

Slipping out of my daydream, I notice a wry smile brushing Singh's lips. "On the practical side, the professor could just about cook himself a cup of coffee."

"Did you say cook?! Did it taste terrible? My dad's coffee was awful."

"It was like dishwater, and very un-Italian," Singh replies drily.

"His talents obviously lay elsewhere," I enthuse, hoping Singh will tell me something more about Peter.

"Of course – just look at that collection." The caretaker points through the open door to the paintings. "Then there are the books he wrote. You really have to read some of them. But not today; you look exhausted. Perhaps you should have a rest?"

Singh's admiration for Peter and the concern he's just shown me make me warm to him. On the spur of the moment, I decide I'll give him the pots, pans and china rather than ship them back to England. His face lights up the moment he hears my offer; then the mask drops again, but not before I catch an icy glint in his eyes.

"I won't be able to accept your offer. You've seen my place! There's not enough room to swing a mouse in there." Seeing me smiling, he adds resolutely, "And I do mean a mouse, not a cat, Ms Farrell. Still, it's most kind of you to have thought of me."

After a couple more hours of clearing out, I inquire what my uncle's favourite flowers were.

"The ones in the window boxes," Singh replies, glancing towards the sitting room. "Primroses and pansies in spring. Why do you ask?"

"I am going to visit Peter's grave and I'd like to take him some flowers. Isn't the cemetery just down the road from here? I'll enjoy the walk.

"*Buona passeggiata al cimitero*," replies Singh, adding that he'll teach me some Italian if I want. "Have a nice walk to the cemetery."

"See you tomorrow, Singh – *a domani*," I answer, smiling. "See, I am not a complete beginner."

10

I am standing by the gates of the English Cemetery, carrying a bag with three pots of primroses and violets. The din of traffic, speeding round the tiny island housing the cemetery in Piazzale Donatello, is atrocious. How on earth, I think, could Peter have chosen this as his final resting place? "May you rest in chaos," I exclaim.

Luckily, once through the gates and inside the high railings, it grows quieter. By the entrance, there's a small building whose blind is down. I am peering at a noticeboard outside the building when a youngish woman opens the door, a pair of gardening shears and a trowel in her hands. "Who are you looking for?" she inquires softly, in what sounds like an Australian accent.

"A recently arrived guest," I reply, tongue-in-cheek.

"Who might that be?" She pulls back her long brown hair into a ponytail, fastening it with an elastic band. "I'm one of the volunteers round here. I might be able to help you. I'm sorry but the shop and library are closed today. The lady who runs them is off sick." Holding out her hand, she introduces herself. "Pleased to meet you. I'm Maureen Kennedy."

It turns out Maureen came to Italy from Melbourne on a scholarship twenty years ago, and stayed. "Like so many expats here in Florence, I fell head over heels in love with the city. To survive, I teach English," she continues, growing animated, "but what I really relish is finding out about the lives and works of the well-known writers, artists and people buried here. As soon as I get a chance I spend hours in the library."

"Have you got time to tell me more about the cemetery?" I ask. "Mind you, I don't want to stop you from working."

"It'll be a pleasure," she says, smiling, evidently in no hurry to resume her gardening. "The adjective 'English' in the cemetery's name is rather deceptive. There are actually Swiss, Russians, Americans and Brits buried here. The cemetery was founded for members of the Reformed Church. That said, most of the graves belong to Brits and Americans. In nineteenth-century Florence their community was the largest. Walter Savage Landor, Fanny Trollope and Elizabeth Barrett Browning are among our well-known 'tenants', as I call them. You can find Elizabeth straight down that path, at peace, I hope, in what is a very impressive funerary monument."

"Sorry to interrupt," I butt in. I have the feeling that Maureen could go on for the rest of the afternoon if I don't stop her. "I've actually come to see Peter Farrell's grave. You see, I'm his niece, Maria, over on a visit from Manchester."

Maureen pulls up sharp on hearing Peter's name. She's obviously embarrassed and doesn't quite know what to say, so I break the ice.

"I suppose I'm not wrong in thinking you know all about what happened?"

"Yes, it was in the papers and on television. Absolutely shocking. When I saw you, I thought somehow it might be you. There was something about your face that reminded me of Peter. Your blue eyes are just like his. I've... sorry, it's a simple past tense now – I first met your uncle ten years ago. He sometimes talked about his niece in Manchester. But come on, I'll take you to see his grave."

As we weave our way through the gravestones, passing an occasional cypress tree, Maureen complains about the many plots that are overrun by weeds, the shortage of gardeners, and the collapsed tombstones lying sprawled and crumbling in the earth around us. "Peter was a great conversationalist," she beams, "and had a real passion for the international community in Florence. He felt closely connected with these people who, like him, like me, had chosen to make their home here. He always said when his time came..."

Maureen halts mid-sentence, pointing to a pinkish-grey marble tombstone surrounded by vases of wild flowers. I smile as it strikes me that Peter's final resting place perfectly matches his kitchen furniture. I can feel tears welling in my eyes, and quickly pull the pots of flowers out of my bag, setting them down near the other vases. Kneeling next to Maureen, I listen as she reads aloud the writing etched on the marble stone:

Peter Farrell
Born Manchester, 1st April 1927
Died Florence, 2nd April 2000

My heart pounds as I read the lines immediately below Peter's name and dates. The allusion to death in Hamlet's celebrated monologue has never chimed so powerfully:

To die, to sleep;
To sleep: perchance to dream: ay, there's the rub.

"Did Peter choose this epitaph?" I ask my new friend.

"He did. About a year ago. It was the day he reserved his plot here. He handed me the quotation. It's now filed in our archives. He actually talked about Shakespeare's *Hamlet* several times over the years. He felt close to Prince Hamlet, and identified with his tendency to think so much about things that in the end he fails to act. He also confessed that, like Hamlet's father, who probably had a terrible relationship with his brother Claudius, he'd experienced a dreadful rift with his own twin brother, Edward."

"Did he tell you anything more about my dad?"

"No. When I said Peter loved talking, it was about things in general. He very rarely talked about himself. But he did mention his religious beliefs once. He was an agnostic. He just didn't know what would happen after death, so 'To die, to sleep… to dream, ay, there's the rub' sums him up to a T. Like the Danish prince, he wasn't certain about Heaven or Hell, or about anything, come to that."

11

I am enjoying my usual breakfast of coffee and croissant at my hotel when I get a second phone call from DI Romagnoli's secretary. They want me down at the station for questioning in about an hour.

The call leaves me feeling uneasy, and I let my half-eaten croissant fall back onto the plate. I stare glumly at it, wondering what's in store for me. Wrapping the croissant in a napkin, I tell myself it might come in handy if the interview drags on too long or, worse, they decide to detain me.

In Romagnoli's office, I find him sitting at his desk, enveloped in a cloud of smoke. A long, narrow neon strip on the ceiling throws a garish light on the room's occupants. It could be ten in the morning or ten at night and the room would look the same. I can feel my eyes stinging and am tempted to shout, *Put that cigarette out, can't you, Inspector, and show some consideration for me and your colleague?*

The inspector's gaze holds mine as he mutters a curt "*Buongiorno, Signora*", while the eyes of his unnamed colleague, seated at a small table in the corner, stay glued to a paper in front of him. I look quickly around the office, asking myself what it can tell me about its occupant. An old Venetian blind at a tiny window is only a quarter open and askew. On the windowsill, a shrivelled rubber plant with three yellowy-brown leaves defies the laws of nature by clinging on to life in circumstances in which any other plant would have snuffed it. Shelves of neatly arranged files, white, cream, brown and grey, cover the walls to the left and right of me. The decor seems to signal a degree of immobility and fatigue.

Romagnoli beckons me to take a seat in front of him. "*Prego, Signora Farrell.*" On this cue his colleague nods in my direction, acknowledging my arrival, after which he hastily returns to his reading.

I panic at the prospect of the interview, worried that I won't understand what the detective is asking me, and I am heading for the door when a young woman comes in. Seeing my frightened face, she introduces herself. She's Vivien Newman, a police interpreter, originally from Surrey. Catching me fidgeting nervously with the strap on my bag, she pats my hand, insisting that there is really nothing to worry about. It's just a routine interview and she'll be interpreting. It really shouldn't take too long.

As if in a well-rehearsed scene, Romagnoli takes down and opens a large grey file, while his colleague takes his cue and gets to his feet to set in motion the spools of a tape recorder. Vivien sits beside me, ready to translate the questions and answers.

Once everything and everybody is in place, the inspector begins. "I've been told you never had any contact with Peter Farrell. Can that be correct?" Without giving me time to reply, he goes on. "In Italy families stick together. You know exactly who your uncles are, and your aunts, cousins, nephews and nieces. You usually see them regularly – say, once a week, if you live locally. Or, if they are farther away, you see them at Easter, Christmas, or during the summer holidays."

I start to explain that this is most likely a cultural difference between Italy and England, that close family ties mean far more to Italians than to Brits, but I draw a blank.

"No letters, no phone calls?" he repeats, shaking his head.

"Nothing," I confirm, while admitting that there was quite probably a specific reason for this in my uncle's case. "You see, Peter cut himself off from his family fifty years ago. Or perhaps my father cut him off. I simply don't know." A skeleton in the cupboard flashes to mind, but luckily I manage to bite my tongue before the skeleton gets a chance to slip out onto Romagnoli's desk. I feel pretty sure black humour wouldn't go down well with him.

Leaning towards me in a bid to establish eye contact, he switches to more personal matters. "According to my information, you are unmarried; indeed, have never married. And you work as a stage director. Is this correct?"

These questions strike me as a waste of time, but there is little I can do in the circumstances. I glance at Vivien, hoping for some moral support, but her eyes shift quickly away. Determinedly, I meet the inspector's gaze and launch into a description of my life as a single woman, my job in Manchester, my hopes for the future. Puzzlement, surprise and last of all pity dart across his face as I end by confirming that I have never been married or had children. He pauses for a second before cocking his head to one side and shrugging his shoulders, as if to say that I am a truly lost soul.

In response, I change tack. "But you have to understand, Inspector, I would have loved to meet Peter and get to know him, but I never dared to. You see, he was the black sheep of the family. And even when my dad died, I didn't want to infringe on Peter's privacy."

Romagnoli shakes his head again. "Privacy? No, this was your uncle, Signora; no need for privacy."

"You should understand, he was my only uncle, and now he's dead and my father and mother have passed away, there's just me and my two cats left in Manchester. I have, you should know, already been to visit Peter's grave at the English Cemetery. It was very moving, very emotional."

My outpouring of familial affection and grief has just the effect I am looking for. My interlocutor's eyes soften and a smile crosses his lips. After glancing at his watch, he informs his colleague that I can leave.

An hour after my arrival at the police station, the unnamed detective leads me along a bustling corridor towards the exit, then downstairs to a waiting taxi. His eyes light up for a moment as he opens the car door for me. "*Arrivederci*, Signora Farrell. I'll no doubt see you soon."

I throw him a quizzical look and launch into an "*Arrivederci, Ispettore*" in my broken Italian. As the taxi gathers speed, I wonder what exactly he meant by that. *I'll no doubt see you soon.*

12

It's early morning and I've just had breakfast. Signora Franca and her husband Carlo, the hotel proprietors, and their two children are lovely. We've come to an arrangement that they will leave my breakfast ready in the dining room, so I can have it at whatever time I like.

Back in my room, feeling ready for action after a strong black coffee and a couple of croissants, I phone Manchester. I need to find out from Jean how the cats are doing. "Are they eating? Crikey… Make sure Richard gets enough food; Henry will shove him out of the way and wolf everything if you don't. Henry is a charmer, but he's also a certified glutton! And please, Jean, give them a hug from me."

I then phone Joanne with something urgent. Even if they are well into rehearsals, I am not sure she's gathered the full significance of Hamlet's stabbing of Polonius. Recently I've been thinking a lot about murder and my take on Hamlet's character has undergone a sea change. "Don't forget, Joanne, that anybody, and I mean anybody, can become a murderer. You, me, anybody else we know. As the play opens Hamlet is just any old university student at Wittenberg. Well, okay, I know he's a prince, so he's privileged and all the rest. But when he kills Polonius – yes, even if he probably doesn't mean to, because he doesn't realise it's Polonius hiding behind the arras – at that moment the prince turns into a murderer. Chilling, eh? You need to get Benedict to build this into the role. He can do it if he works at it. He's got the necessary depth and sensitivity… That's precisely why I cast him in the part, see. After Hamlet has pulled his rapier out of the corpse and smelt his bloodstained hands, it dawns on him that he's no longer the innocent young man he was a minute earlier. Benedict has got to show this change and these emotions through his body language and vocal timbre."

As I hang up, my thoughts turn to the people I've met so far in Florence, and again I ask myself the question I asked soon after I arrived. Could any of them be Peter's murderer? Gabriele Foschi? The countess? Singh? Respectable people who have turned into criminals due to motives still unknown to me. With that conundrum racing through my mind, I drag myself out of bed. I must get down to Peter's flat.

Singh and I still haven't progressed beyond the kitchen. Clearing out the food cupboards is proving a nightmare. Just like his artworks, Peter spared no expense in this department; huge supplies of gourmet food are stored in every cupboard and on several shelves. Singh has just returned from a shopping expedition, with some crates, and we set to work filling them with bottles of ten-year-old Modena vinegar, a couple of Parmesan cheeses, twenty litres of pure virgin olive oil, five jars of dried porcini mushrooms and three jars of prize Piedmontese truffles. Some of this, I decide, will certainly be going back to Manchester.

"When the professor needed a break, he'd take himself off on what he called 'a food and wine jaunt'," Singh explains as he fills a crate with olive oil. "He used to set off the minute it was daylight. Professor Foschi and Countess Caterina usually joined him, and they'd visit a farm, a wine cellar or an oil mill. In early autumn they'd make a trip to buy rice, mushrooms, truffles. *I tartufi erano una sua passione*. He adored truffles."

I notice that every so often Singh is in the habit of switching to Italian whenever he wants to underscore something and teach me some Italian.

"And in November they had another never-to-be-missed ritual. The professor hired a van to bring back the olive oil he'd had made in Pontremoli. These bottles, here in the crates, are his special oil. It's delicious! In spring he bought cheese and fresh ricotta; in summer, kilos of fresh apricots, peaches and plums for jams and preserves. The three of them would make a day of it. They loved sampling and buying the local produce. Then at midday they'd eat out at a local restaurant or trattoria. Here, have a look at this. It's one of the professor's notebooks, where he jotted down his impressions of their days out."

Going over to a shelf above the fridge, Singh takes down a notebook. There are about thirty, each with a bright cover and a handwritten label indicating the year; another example of Peter's meticulous method of storing and filing things. Singh tells me that Pontremoli was Uncle's favourite place for eating porcini, after which he reads from the diary. "Listen to this…"

15th October 1998, Pontremoli, Trattoria della Posta, Lunch
Tagliatelle and porcini, the best I've ever tasted! A perfect wedding of porcini, butter, parsley, garlic and home-made pasta. Mouth-watering! Service unfaultable. Salvatore is the best chef in the area.

I watch Singh flicking through the pages of a second notebook.

"And just listen to what he says about the same restaurant a year later…"

20th October 1999

The tagliatelle and porcini are not a patch on last year. The chef not only skimped on the parsley; he added it too late for it to give the dish its full flavour.

Salvatore's been given the boot. It's a real pity! He's a lovely man, while the new chef's as thick as two short planks, as Mam used to say. The waiter let it slip that the present chef can't tell a porcini from a toadstool. God help us! This trattoria used to be a safe haven when Salvatore (no pun intended) was around!

Just the same, we had a great time because in the evening Salvatore invited us to his home and cooked us a superb meal.

Listening to these diary entries, it occurs to me that even though Peter had been in Italy for fifty years, he never forgot his Lancashire sense of humour and lived life to the full. He evidently loved variety since he mixed with people from all walks of life: a countess, a university professor, a caretaker, a local historian, and a chef called Salvatore. I suddenly realise that these snippets of information, gathered from different people, are helping me piece together an identikit of a man I never met.

The entryphone rings and I run to answer it. A man's voice, in accented English. "Detective Sergeant…" He pauses, then starts again. "Detective Sergeant Gianni Celentano. May I have a word with you?"

His voice sounds familiar and I feel a buzz of excitement as I tell him to come upstairs. Seconds later the doorbell rings. It's the good-looking detective, now with a name attached to him. His 'I will no doubt see you soon' as I left the police station evidently meant 'two weeks'.

"I've called, you see…" He is looking slightly awkward. "I mean, I've got a few questions I need to ask you."

I attempt to hide my own embarrassment by trying out some of the Italian I've learnt in recent weeks. I now know that in Italy if you use somebody's title, you usually get a more positive reaction than if you address them as plain 'Mr' or 'Mrs'. So, making my invitation sound as grand as possible, I say, rolling my 'R's to achieve momentum, "*Buongiorno, Inspector. Venire dentro casa mia. Benvenuto!* ('Hello, Inspector. Do come in and welcome!') Come through to the kitchen. Singh's in there. He's giving me a hand with clearing out Peter's stuff."

"*Benissimo*. It's good to hear you're learning Italian." Celentano smiles. "I was wondering whether you have remembered anything else about Professor Farrell that could help our investigation. I am aware, of course, that you never actually met the deceased, nor were you in Italy when the murder happened, but I need to double-check. There might be something your father, or some other relative, told you."

"Nothing, I'm afraid," I remark, wondering why Romagnoli hasn't called me down to the station for a second interview rather than sending his colleague.

Then Celentano adds, "I hope you are coping with things here in Italy. Even the intricacies of an Italian post office can be a nightmare for an outsider. And then—"

"I'm doing fine," I reply, cutting him short. "Singh knows all about that kind of thing."

On impulse I grab a jar from one of the crates. "Here, I'd like to give you these porcini mushrooms, *Inspector*. Give them to your wife and family as a present from me."

It's the detective's turn to look embarrassed. Avoiding eye contact, he takes the jar and studies the label. He has no wife, he confides. "She died not long ago, leaving me to bring up our son, Tommaso, single-handed. And although I love mushrooms and know a fair bit about them, I can't possibly accept a gift while on duty. All the same, thanks for the thought." And, putting the jar firmly on the table, he hoists himself onto a high stool near the cooker.

Realising that he looks like he's planning on staying, I keep on with my work, weaving back and to, with Singh dragging his feet behind me. I can feel Celentano's attentive gaze following me around, and to break the silence, I ask him how he learnt such good English.

"I lived and worked in Glasgow while attending a training course and then stayed on with the international squad. Some people say I picked up a Scottish accent during my time there. What do you think?"

"That's exactly what I thought when we first met!" I reply, complimenting him again on his English.

"I can give you a couple of good recipes for the porcini you've inherited," he continues, changing the subject, seemingly not wishing to dwell on his life abroad. "I grew up in the Maremma; that's Southern Tuscany. It's much wilder and less touristy than Florence. Like many of my family, Tommaso included, I am a forager, and in autumn it's mushrooms and truffles in the woods. Once we've gathered enough porcini or whatever, I usually make a risotto for the friends and relatives who come with me. Washed down, of course, with a full-bodied red wine that's typical of my region."

"I think I've got some of that." I point to a couple of bottles of Peter's Sangiovese on one of the shelves. "Is it a good one? I've absolutely no idea." Clocking Celentano's enthusiastic nod as he reads the label, I decide to offer him a drink. "To this year's mushroom season! May you find some real beauties!"

He puts his nose in the glass, smelling the wine and muttering an approving "*Eccellente*, but no, I won't. I'm on duty."

He is smiling now, and launches into another episode of his family history. "Mushroom gatherers have been in my family for around five generations. I was born and brought up in a hilltop village on Monte Amiata, where the staple diet of our forebears was mushrooms and chestnuts. While there are many varieties of mushrooms, some edible, others poisonous, I can spot the good ones a mile off. Still, in every season there's always some fool who gets poisoned, but never anybody in my family, *tocca ferro*, as we say in Italy, which I suppose translates as your 'touch wood'. The exact time of year for the season depends on the weather. It might be October, sometimes November. The amounts of rain, fog, damp and sun are important."

"But tell me, how did you come to be a detective, rather than an agronomist, or a lumberjack, or something of the sort?"

Celentano's laughing now. "It might sound strange, but my walks in the chestnut woods looking for porcini and truffles were excellent training for my present job. My childhood and adolescence in the Maremma were fundamental. That's where I learnt to tell the sharks from the angels."

"What do you mean?"

"It's complicated to explain in English, but I'll try. To survive in the woods you need to know what you're doing. From your father and mother, aunts and cousins, you learn all sorts of things; little tricks and precautions. In my village, I met everyone. The mayor, the lawyer, the chemist, the doctor, down to the shoe repairer, the butcher, and farmers galore. They're a bizarre assortment of folk characterised by every shade of good and bad. A village is like a classroom. I find it much more interesting than the city, where social classes, professional people and tradesmen tend not to mix so much."

Before leaving, Celentano hovers for a moment by the open lift. Lighting a cigarette, he blows a chain of smoke rings in the air and his eyes hold mine. "I'm sorry, Ms Farrell." He looks awkward, "I am very sorry but… I want to tell you. I shouldn't, but I will. We've made hardly any progress on your uncle's case; no breakouts. It's very frustrating." He sees me smiling. "Isn't that what you say?"

"Not exactly." I smile back, realising for the first time how difficult phrasal verbs like 'break in', 'break out' and 'break through' are for Italians. "I think you mean 'breakthrough', and you're right: I am praying you'll have one before too long."

"Rest assured, even if this is a difficult investigation, we are trying very hard. Trust me."

13

Once Celentano has left, Singh, who until now hasn't had a bad word to say about anyone, lashes out. "A difficult case, all right! You saw him; how he sat there for over an hour, idling the morning away. He should stay in the woods up that mountain of his and snooze there. Nothing will come of their investigation. Trust me!"

Singh's deep-seated hostility towards the police surprises me. After all, the case is bound to be a hard one to crack. Peter was presumably not part of any criminal gang, and led a respectable life, mixing with respectable people. This must make it particularly difficult for the police to make any headway. I notice Singh still shaking his head, scepticism painted all over his face.

"After the initial coverage, there's been nothing in the papers," he complains bitterly, "and very little media attention. Know what I think? They have written the professor off."

He seems to be painting a deadlock of negativity, and I hear myself blurting out, "You're the one who found the body. You must have seen what the murderer or murderers did to Uncle. Tell me about it, please."

"As I told you, the police have—"

"Didn't you just tell me to forget the police?" I retort. Celentano struck me as genuine and well-meaning, but he himself admitted they're getting nowhere. "I am the professor's only surviving relative. That must count for something."

Singh is staring at me again, the muscles in his face twitching, his lips moving slightly. His reluctance to relive his horrific experience prevents the words from getting out.

Indignantly, I insist, "I have every right to know how Peter was murdered."

When Singh finally speaks, his voice is almost inaudible. He hesitates, weighing every syllable. "If that's what you want. It was a Monday morning and he was due out at nine for a meeting. At 9.30 he still hadn't come down, which was very strange for him. He was usually very punctual. I took my keys to the flat, got the lift up, rang the bell several times and waited. There was no reply. I tried the handle. The door was unlocked. That was most unusual. You've seen the alarm and the three locks on the door. His flat is like the Bank of England.

"I could feel my heart thumping as I went through to the sitting room. It was perfectly tidy; everything as it should be. I went into the bedroom. One of the wardrobe doors was open. That was strange. Peter would never have left a door open like that. He was such a tidy person. He wasn't there; nor had the bed been slept in. The bathroom door was ajar, so I went in."

Singh's face has grown earnest, one hand half-covering his mouth, the other stroking his paunch. He pauses, reluctant to finish, then unexpectedly picks up the thread. "It was only when I saw the professor's keys lying on the bathroom tiles that I realised something was terribly wrong. I went berserk, rushing from one room to another. I went back to the bedroom, flinging open the wardrobes, then I ran into the master bathroom and the second bathroom. I took the lift again, after which I forced myself to walk down the stairs leading to the cellar. He wasn't there.

"I returned to the flat, went through to the kitchen, made myself some coffee and ate the remains of some strudel I'd bought the day before. I was feeling queasy and hoped it'd settle my stomach. I told myself I'd have to call the police, and started sorting out what I'd tell them. Then I remembered the freezer room, next to the kitchen. Come and have a look, Maria."

Opening a door next to the fridge, he leads me into a tiny room, nodding at me to sit down on the only chair.

"Your uncle has – *had* – these three big freezers. That morning I opened this one nearest the door, not dreaming for a moment… It was jam-packed, and I realised that the plastic boxes and bags from another freezer had been crammed inside. That was very peculiar. I opened the second freezer and discovered what had happened."

As Singh pulls open the huge freezer, my head starts spinning.

"Don't worry." His voice is reassuring. "It's completely empty now. That day, in the centre here, I saw a large black plastic bag, bulging with something inside. Using both hands, I pulled the plastic tight over the topmost part of the bag and I could see the shape of a forehead, a nose, a chin."

"Jesus Christ! Did you recognise him?" I ask, shivering with cold, even though the freezer is turned off.

Singh nods, his eyes staring into the empty freezer. "Yes. It was him; his nose and chin."

"Did the murderer or murderers steal anything from the flat? Were they burglars, perhaps, whom Peter caught red-handed?"

Singh shakes his head. "I'll tell you exactly what I told the police in my statement. As far as I know, and I've checked very carefully, only two ties are missing. What's more I know exactly which ones. Peter kept them in his wardrobe according to when he'd bought or received them. You've realised what a stickler for tidiness and order he was. The first tie on the first rack was his old grammar-school tie, while the last one on the second rack was a present from somebody – don't ask me who – for his last birthday.

It was me who phoned the police, Signora Maria. And a quarter of an hour later they came down here."

I thank Singh and tell him I'll have to be getting back to my hotel. Stuffing a bottle of Uncle's wine and a wine glass into my bag, I make a beeline for the door.

A gruesome image of Peter's body in the freezer has lodged itself in my mind. My father's identical twin has been brutally murdered, and even if it is totally irrational it feels like Dad's body has been desecrated too. Once again I can see my dad's corpse, lying lifeless in the hospital bed where I saw him for the last time ten years ago. His ashen face looked so peaceful. At last he was free from the cancer that killed him. The memory of that time still hurts, and I need to be alone and mull over what is going on.

On my way back to the hotel, I stumble on a deli with an impressive display of Italian food in the window. My eyes hook on the way the dishes are set out; the meticulous attention to shape and colour. As an antidote to Singh's description of Peter's murder, this foodies' paradise seems just the job. My imagination wanders to the programmes you see on British television about Italian food and cookery. You know, the ones in which an attractive chef by the name of Giorgio or Jamie takes you seamlessly through the motions of making a mouth-watering pasta dish in the setting of a Tuscan farmhouse kitchen.

Once inside the shop, a dish of lasagne catches my eye. A portion has already been cut out and a mixture of olive oil, béchamel sauce and ragout oozes from the pasta layers onto the white porcelain. I can't resist. The man behind the counter smiles encouragingly, his expression inviting me to go for it. I try to explain what I want, using my rudimentary Italian coupled with sign language. I point at the lasagne, then at some buffalo mozzarella, a mixed vegetable dish, a hunk of Tuscan bread, a pot of panna cotta, and a helping of fruit salad. Menu complete, I pay up, telling him I hope to be back soon. The man beams at me, pushing a second pot of panna cotta into my hand. *"Per lei, Signora inglese, buon appetito!"* ('For you, English lady, enjoy!')

I went into the shop feeling brain-dead; I come out astonished by the man's unexpected generosity. I walk along, swinging my bag of food, aware that a little bounce has returned to my stride. The people I've met so far in Florence seem to love the English and everything English, though I've still not quite worked out why.

Back at my hotel, I kick off my shoes and sit on the bed, making preparations for supper. I arrange the various plastic boxes around me, place the glass and bottle I've brought from Peter's on the bedside table, and switch on the television. What looks like a quiz show is in full swing. A brash male presenter fires the questions, assisted by two not-so-young bleached blondes. The pair are sporting clingy, sequinned dresses, with plunging necklines showing off their ample breasts. Every so often they teeter round the studio on high heels, the first woman marking up the score, while the second brings on the guests and flirts with the quizmaster.

My thoughts are soon travelling far from this grotesque farce. I imagine I am back in Peter's freezer room, staring at his body in the icy box, and force myself to try and understand what makes his murderer tick. Has he or she – I refuse to rule out that the culprit might be a woman – taken revenge on Uncle for something terrible he did at university, in the art world or in some other field I know nothing about? Did the murderer, a former student perhaps, think to herself, *You failed me three times in three consecutive exam sessions and I am going to top you, Professor Farrell?*

Or is it worth my while to investigate other possible motives? Shakespeare's Iago springs to mind. I directed *Othello* last year and I can still remember the play almost line by line. Early in the story, Iago claims he despises Othello because the latter has just given Cassio the promotion he, Iago, thinks he's entitled to. However, as we rehearsed the play, I realised that this explanation does not hold water. In the end Iago seems to engineer the deaths of Othello and Desdemona, two decent people, for no rational reason, but propelled by some kind of overriding antipathy towards his fellow human beings. I shudder as I think that Peter may have had the misfortune to come across such a person, and remind myself that, if this is the case, it's futile to try and uncover the killer's motives. At the end of Shakespeare's tragedy Iago declares, 'Demand me nothing. What you know, you know. From this time forth, I never will speak word.' His deeply disturbing revelation lets the audience know that, if they have any sense, they won't waste their time trying to figure out what makes him tick.

Shakespeare grappled with evil throughout his writing career, not just in *Othello*, but in *Macbeth*, *Richard III* and *Hamlet* too. Even so, he appears to make little headway when it comes to fathoming the inner workings of the criminal mind.

"What you know, you know." I repeat Iago's words aloud, making my voice heard above the noise of the recorded studio laughter and applause. Translated into modern English, Iago warns us all, *Don't kid yourselves; I'm never going to disclose the real reason I ruined the lives of Othello and Desdemona, leading a newly married man to smother his innocent young wife and then kill himself when he realises he's made a horrendous mistake.*

Before falling asleep, I recall how Shakespeare gives Iago his comeuppance. This 'hellish villain', as Lodovico calls him, is tortured: his body probably stretched and broken on the rack; a much-used and dreaded device at the time. An idea comes to me. Why don't I endeavour to catch Peter's murderer and make sure they get their comeuppance? I could take the part of Hamlet, whose ingenious mousetrap device manages to 'catch the conscience of the king'. But then I'm assailed by doubts. I feel ill-equipped to take on such a challenge.

14

Gabriele has arranged a meeting at his favourite tea shop. He has, he confides, "a little treat in store". By 10.30, armed with my street map, a bit dog-eared after many a walk around Florence, I navigate a web of deserted alleys, heading for the address he's given me. I have deliberately planned my route, taking in what Italians call the *vicoli*; the dark, sometimes dank, narrow lanes generally ignored by tourists. In contrast to the rafts of slick bars, classy opticians and upmarket boutiques, I stroll along an unbroken line of run-down tenements and boarded-up shop windows and doors, their fronts daubed with colourful graffiti and words in Italian I don't understand.

My thoughts stray to last night and the decision I've left pending. I can feel the heaviness of the closed shutters and rusty pipes sapping my energy. In this place, into which hardly any light filters, I find myself confused and unsure. I only get halfway through Hamlet's famous line 'To be or not…' when I pull myself up short, telling myself to get real. Here in Florence I am not experiencing vicariously the emotions of an old tragedy, but the real thing.

A few minutes later, emerging from the alley, I catch sight of a line of glowing lamps on the corner of Via Ricasoli. There are five of them forming the lower part of a tabernacle, with a single wooden crucifix underneath. At nose level, there's a marble slab with a slit in it. Above the slit I read the word '*Elemosine*'. Flicking through my pocket Italian-to-English dictionary, I find the translation: 'charity'. I repeat it aloud: "Charity", remembering how my religious education teacher defined it as love of God, but also love for a neighbour or friend. Allowing my gaze to merge with the lamps' flickering flames, I pause gratefully. The quiet sanctity of the shrine seems to be inviting me to concentrate on what is important. Yes, I will start my search for the murderer out of this strange love for an uncle whom I never met. I'll need to enlist some help, though. My Italian isn't good enough for me to handle the case single-handed. I'll ask Gabriele. He'll probably agree, if he and Uncle were as close as I suspect. Pulling two thousand-lire coins out of my purse, I shove them through the marble slit and head for the tea room.

I am nearly twenty minutes late when I reach our meeting point near the cathedral, which turns out to be an elegant cake-shop-cum-café-cum-tea-room. I'm anxious that Gabriele might have got fed up of waiting and headed off home. But I needn't have worried; the minute I walk through the door, he comes over to greet me, with Phoebe making her usual fuss. This time, though, she circles around me, sniffing at my trainers in a show of recognition.

Once we're ensconced in comfy armchairs, my companion runs through the list of cakes, tarts and pastries on the menu, explaining the words he thinks I might not understand. "I would highly recommend this *torta di fragola*, strawberry tart; or this *millefoglie*, literally, 'a thousand leaves'," he adds, smiling.

We are soon arguing about which one to choose, even though a glance at the cakes on display suggests it would be hard to get it wrong.

"This strawberry tart is delicious," I enthuse, savouring my first mouthful. "The shortcrust pastry is first-rate, and these strawberries… wow! Perfectly sweet. That's the difficult bit, you know; getting the fruit syrup just right. I wish I—"

"What did you expect?" Gabriele interrupts, his tone revealing a mix of surprise and irritation. "You're sitting in one of the best tea rooms in Florence. It is a solid family firm. Look at the decor – 1920s and still pristine. I love it, and it was one of Peter's favourite haunts for a cuppa and a cake. Just think, we're only a stone's throw from the cathedral. *Your* cathedral, Maria: Santa Maria del Fiore."

"Mine and another million women whose name happens to be Maria!" I joke. "But really, it's astounding that the place isn't mobbed by tourists. I suppose an invitation here is one of the bonuses of having you as a friend."

Gabriele seems flattered that I am enjoying his treat, and I keep up the patter a little longer. I need to keep him in a good mood, since very soon I will drop the bombshell about my decision to investigate Peter's murder, hopefully with his help.

"You know, in England they're just not into it. I mean, the real thing; the authentic Italian cappuccino." I look hard at the perfect cocoa heart floating on the whitish froth of the coffee in front of me and add, "They pretend they are, and spend huge sums on coffee every year. New chains with Italian names are forever opening upmarket cafés with annoyingly long menus listing dozens of cakes, pastries and drinks. But even if you pay through the nose, the coffee is often rubbish. It doesn't taste bad, but there's too much froth. Still, it's probably not the coffee beans, but the staff, who aren't properly trained to use the espresso makers. At least, that's my theory."

It's Gabriele's turn to laugh. The expression 'pay through the nose' strikes him as bizarre. "Why can't it be the throat or the ears," he queries, "or some other bodily orifice?" He moves his chair closer to mine, warming to the fun.

I stick my fork into the cake and give an over-the-top woeful sigh. "Ah well, if I'm not careful, I'm going to put on weight in Florence. I'll be the size of a house before I know it. Ever heard that expression?"

I look at Gabriele, but he's swivelled sideways and has his eyes fixed on a young man sitting at a nearby table. When he turns back to face me, his voice sounds serious. "No danger of that, Maria; you do plenty of walking. How many hours a day do you exercise?"

"Usually a couple, and mostly in the evenings when I've finished at the flat. It takes my mind off all that's happening. Last night I sat by the fountain in Piazza della Signoria, gazing at the stars all those miles away."

"And I bet you took a peep at Michelangelo's *David* in his birthday suit," Gabriele quips mischievously.

"Of course I did – all twenty feet of him!"

"Don't exaggerate. He's only seventeen feet tall."

"Joking apart, stargazing helps me put Peter's murder into perspective. Listen, there's something I have to ask you. It seems to me that the police are not making much headway in investigating Peter's case. The detective who came round to the flat the other day to ask me a few questions hinted as much."

"Or is he interested in you?" Gabriele throws me an inquiring glance.

"I don't think so. He's just very kind."

"Be careful, Maria; you'll soon be a fairly wealthy woman and you're a youngish forty-five." He adds, laughing, "And you're English. Many Italian men have a soft spot for wealthy English ladies."

"Well, now you mention it..." I keep up the banter. "But listen, I've got something to ask you. I need – how can I put it? – your assistance."

Gabriele's face tightens. "Assistance? With what exactly?"

"I've decided to investigate Peter's murder."

It's some time before he answers. He just sits there, swirling the froth on his cappuccino and peering into the cup.

"Well, come on, what do you think?" I can't stand the silence any longer. "Do you or don't you want to find out what happened to Peter?"

Gabriele takes another slurp of coffee, before pulling a handkerchief out of his pocket and wiping the beads of sweat trickling down his forehead. His face has grown red and flustered. "Of course I do, but I don't think we should go meddling in such things."

"Meddling? Am I hearing right? We're talking about Peter Farrell, my late uncle, and your close friend and business associate."

Gabriele's eyes avoid mine. "We should leave it to the police. Anyway, I honestly don't know if I'm capable. It's really not my thing. Give me a painting or an exhibition to curate any time."

"Do you think it's my thing? My job in theatre, doing admin and directing plays, doesn't exactly equip me for detective work. In rehearsals we might discuss how we can represent death onstage. The other day I was talking to Joanne, my assistant. We were trying to decide whether we should show the audience Hamlet's bloody corpse after Laertes has stabbed him with his poisoned sword, or do the scene with no mangled bodies strewn on the stage. That's about as near as I come to murder in my job. However, in this case, it's the real thing, and I just don't see that we've any choice in the matter, unless we decide to just sit around and do nothing. But don't you see, we could be waiting until the cows come home? Know that expression?"

Gabriele shakes his head. "I'm not saying I don't want to investigate Peter's murder. I sometimes wake up at night and it's as if he's still alive. His death seems so unjust. He still had so much he wanted to do. If this hadn't happened, we'd have been in Paris this weekend to buy an important painting; a deal we'd been negotiating for months. We'd said we'd—"

"So, you two were an item?" I blurt out, for the first time putting into words what I've been thinking.

"What do you mean, an item?"

"That's colloquial English for a couple."

"We were business partners, Maria, a strong team, untouchables. And when we decided to buy a painting that interested us, we nearly always pulled off the deal."

"Weren't you lovers, then? It's just… the way you talk about him…"

Gabriele's face crumples, and he makes an attempt to say something, but the words stick in his throat.

I continue. "I suppose I always sort of knew that Peter might have been gay. It was one particular photo; it must have been taken at the twin's birthday party when they were about ten. There's a group of boys dressed up as soldiers. They look high on testosterone and are levelling their toy guns at the camera. Peter stands out like a sore thumb. He's in the front row, and the only one of the group sporting a school blazer. He's wearing his scarf like a noose and pointing his gun at himself, a faint smile puckering his lips. He was definitely not one of the lads."

"Listen, can you keep a secret?"

"Never; not kept a secret in forty-five years," I joke. "Come on, of course I can."

Gabriele lowers his voice so that the young man at the nearby table can't hear. "We had sex the first evening we went out."

"So what?" I shrug.

"Well, aren't you surprised?"

"Certainly not. Don't forget, I was clubbing in the late '60s. There was free love and a crazy music scene, especially in Liverpool. I just can't work out why you didn't tell me sooner."

"I'll try and explain. Initially, I didn't consider the relationship as anything special. I was seeing somebody else at the time. I couldn't wait to leave for England to start my PhD, so I wasn't looking for anything lasting. I was very lucky to have Peter as a teacher, because a few years after he quit teaching to devote himself to his art business and art-history research. He was an amazing tutor; passionate about his subject, but not in a stuffy sort of way."

"So, he wasn't actually a professor according to English standards?"

"No; in Italy even secondary-school teachers are called '*professori*'. And in Peter's case, after he left his teaching job, the title stuck.

"Anyway, one evening he invited me out for what turned out to be a euphemistic drink. He bewitched me. Know that old song? It was one of Peter's favourites: *Bewitched, bothered and...* how does it go?"

"*Bewitched, bothered...*" I repeat, apologising because I can't remember the rest either, while thinking that Peter must have lived in a time warp.

"Peter introduced me to so much. We went to concerts, to art galleries, for walks at night. We had endless conversations and arguments about everything! Art, of course, but we also talked about philosophy, psychology, the Etruscans. We had an amazing time. After a few weeks we'd fallen for each other. Corny but true. That was another of Peter's words. His English had sort of calcified in the early '50s when he came to live in Florence. And that love changed, but lasted until the day he died. I feel so very lonely, Maria, still I have to keep this hurt inside." He quickly changes tack, as he wipes the tears from his eyes. "But know what? He never wanted to visit England again. Not even later, when I was living in Oxford. He insisted I came back here to see him."

"Did you never ask him why he cut himself off from England and his family?"

"Of course I did, but he would never tell."

"I remember the countess called him a dark horse. Is she right?"

"It seems to me that he had no choice. He simply had to keep some things secret, not least our relationship. Officially, to the outside world, we were close friends and business partners.

The people we knew accepted and respected us on those terms. Peter belongs – sorry, I must remember to say 'belonged' – to a generation of men who never came out. He was dogged by a prudery that didn't allow him to relax about his sexuality, and I went along with his need for privacy. It was the age thing too; there was a thirty-year gap, remember.

"But all right, Maria, if you want a helping hand, here you are." Gabriele holds out his hand, smiling. "We can work together."

"I really appreciate that."

"I owe it to him, my very best friend and companion. Apart from everything else, Peter probably saved my life. The night he died, we'd been out with Caterina to a restaurant to celebrate his birthday. After the meal, he and I had agreed we'd go back to his place, but as we left the restaurant and Caterina was about to head off, he asked her for a lift home. He wasn't feeling too well; indigestion or something. He told me he'd see me the following day. If he hadn't felt ill, I'd have been by his side as he walked into his flat that evening."

I feel relieved to have found an ally in Gabriele, and rummage in my bag for a pen and paper. We need to decide on a plan and act on it. Putting on my glasses, I jot down some notes:

Peter Farrell, born Manchester, 1st April 1927; died Florence, 2nd April 2000.
People we need to speak to…

I raise my eyes and catch Gabriele looking nonplussed. I suppose he finds my managerial mode disconcerting, so I try to reassure him. "I'm sorry, but my mind functions best if I draw up a carefully conceived plan. It must be the years I've spent running a theatre. It's tough, and if you don't keep on top of things, you go under. To start our investigation, we need a rationale and a list of people we should interview. People who might be helpful. Can you think about this for tomorrow? But for now, just tell me the name you would put at the top of the list. In other words, the person or persons who in your opinion might be most helpful."

His reply comes instantly. "Actually, she asked me last night if I would invite you to lunch at her place tomorrow. How's that for speed and efficiency?"

"Who is 'she'?"

"You've already met her."

"Countess Guiccioli?"

"Yes, she was your uncle's closest friend… after me," he adds playfully. "Caterina hails from one of Florence's oldest aristocratic families. She was unusually quiet at the solicitor's office the other day. She's normally far more talkative. You'll soon see! When she's on her second glass of wine, she'll start banging on about her family tree, most of which she's dreamt up. Or at least, that's my theory. She'll almost certainly let slip, in a rather heavy-handed fashion, that she's related to four popes and – wait for it – Dante."

"Four popes and Dante?"

"I was expecting a 'Wow!' Dante Alighieri. Never heard of him?" he asks scathingly.

"The name rings a few bells," I quip, laughing. "Dante's *Inferno* – Hell, all mayhem breaks loose, right? Roman Catholic sin and guilt, crime and punishment, that kind of thing?"

Gabriele's nostrils twitch. He is evidently irked by my flippancy. I catch him tapping an unlit cigarette on the table, and then he grows angry. "You Brits are so ignorant. Sorry, darling! It must be something to do with living separate from the rest of Europe on a tiny island in the middle of the North Sea. If you go to school in Italy you learn that Dante is our *Sommo Poeta*, our Supreme Poet, and the first to write a great masterpiece in Italian rather than Latin. But you also hear about Shakespeare and study his major plays, as well as reading the odd passage from Milton, Pope and Swift, not to mention Goethe and Tolstoy. In contrast, you lot generally haven't a clue about European literature, not to mention our national treasure, Dante Alighieri, born and brought up just down the road from here."

"I promise I'll read him while I'm in Florence," I reply defensively. "But right now, tell me more about Caterina."

Gabriele lights his cigarette, walks over to the nearby window, opens it and stands eyeing the passers-by on the street outside. Keeping his back to me, he replies calmly, "She was very close to Peter; so close that people sometimes thought they were lovers or married. She was a regular guest at his dinner parties, the life and soul of the spaghetti. The three of us spent a fair amount of time together. We used to go on trips, with her behind the wheel of her old Alfa Romeo. Neither Peter nor I can drive." Suddenly he spins round to look at me, his eyes sparkling with good humour again. "Can you drive? It'll come in useful if we're going to work together. And of course, Caterina knows everyone worth knowing in Florence."

"What exactly was in the relationship for her?"

"I like that. You got straight to the point. It must be your English pragmatism. And I totally agree with what I'm pretty sure is going through your head: disinterested friendship does not exist. Am I right? If you were being cynical—"

"Or realistic?" I cut in.

"—you might say that years ago, Caterina was Peter's passepartout; a stellar card stamped with her name and family crest. Through her, he managed to climb to the highest echelons of Florentine society; the very place he wanted to be."

"Was he a bit of a snob?" What I've just heard worries me. "We don't suffer snobs lightly in the Farrell family."

"In his youth he was undoubtedly very ambitious and just had to get to know those people," Gabriele volleys, "if his – and later *our* – art business was to take off. That's pretty obvious." As he stresses 'our', I notice a hint of smugness spreading over his face.

"Okay. That was the appeal of the relationship for Peter, but what was in it for her?"

"That's more difficult. I suspect she relished having a companion like Peter – witty, intelligent, cultivated. The things that were missing in her marriage. She married into money, since like many aristocratic families today, hers had fallen on hard times."

"Tell me about her husband."

"He died about five years ago. He was a leading orthopaedic surgeon and the only heir to an important pharmaceutical company. He could have just sat back and enjoyed life, but instead he was a workaholic who spent most of the year travelling the world, attending international conventions where he entertained the delegates with accounts of his pioneering methods for inserting nuts and bolts into his patients' hips. That meant he didn't see very much of Caterina. You might be wondering what was in the marriage for him. Certainly an important title and the prestige that went along with it. Caterina's sixty-five now."

"She doesn't look it." Remembering our first meeting, I feel taken aback. "I'd have guessed she was in her mid fifties."

"She'd be flattered. And – this is a very emphatic 'and' – she still enjoys a little romance. Her gardens, though, and her charity work, into which she's channelled a lot of energy in recent years, most definitely beat everything else."

"I don't know if I buy that. I mean, I'm passionate about my job, but I'm still on the lookout for the right man."

"I'm sure she was too, for many years, even if she was married to her always-reliable husband, and enjoyed the company of Peter and a cosy circle of friends."

"But what about passion?"

"Here's what Peter told me on that topic only a couple of months before he died. 'Caterina,' he whispered, 'still indulges in… well, you know; every now and then, she enjoys a little romance. They're usually powerful men, intelligent and attractive. And to think that many years ago, she had an affair with one of her gardeners.' Seeing me looking surprised because the match seemed highly improbable, he continued, 'Go on, Gabri, have a guess who I'm talking about.'" Gabriele pauses, an impish grin on his face.

"You see, I couldn't for the life of me think which gardener he was referring to. She employs three and they're all pretty attractive. Then he put me out of my misery. 'Alfonso Guidi, darling.'"

"A lover, like Lady Chatterley's Oliver Mellors?" I ask.

"Not quite, but I see you've read your Lawrence, Maria."

"Of course," I retort. Gabriele managed to trip me up over Dante, but I am determined he isn't going to score with Lawrence. "And not just his novels, but his poetry, travel journals and plays too. And by the way, have you ever seen his paintings? They are seriously underrated."

Our meeting over, I stand outside the café, watching Gabriele weave his way along the crowded pavement with Phoebe trotting by his side. For a second, I imagine a tall, elderly man, rather overweight, walking beside them, an old leather briefcase in his hand. Like a shot, I force myself to blot the figure out and focus on my plan. Tomorrow I have an invitation to lunch at Caterina Guiccioli's.

15

It's ten o'clock and I am heading to the flea market close to Piazza Sant'Ambrogio. Singh has told me the place is worth a visit, and I left my hotel a couple of hours before my lunch appointment at Caterina's to have a mooch round. The market is already abuzz, and I wander round the stalls and small sheds, taking a look at the mountains of bric-a-brac. One of the traders is soon trying to sell me a matching blue-and-white china teacup, saucer and small plate. Florentines have a long history as traders, and the woman certainly knows her job. Showing me the stamp on the bottom of the cup, she swears the set is authentic 1930s and by Richard Ginori, one of Italy's leading china makers. *"Autentico, Signora, un autentico Ginori, giuro!"* ('I swear, madam, authentic Ginori!')

I am about to hand over twenty thousand lire, when I remember the piles of china in Peter's kitchen. "Sorry, I'll have to think about it; I'll be back later," I tell her sheepishly, clocking the disappointment on her face.

In the midst of the animated haggling and trading going on all around me, I recall my first meeting with Caterina Guiccioli.

Compared to the down-to-earth grittiness of the patter of these market people, it strikes me that she's living on a faraway planet. I can still hear her too perfect English, so different from how most people speak today. I wonder again what she meant when she called Peter 'a dark horse' and 'my unpredictable Albion'. If she wants to, she can no doubt tell me more about my uncle. Then I remember her invitation to lunch. I'd better make for the cake-shop-cum-tea-room where Gabriele took me, and buy a cake and some wine.

Armed with a strawberry flan and a bottle of spumante, I find Gabriele and Phoebe waiting outside the main entrance of Caterina's house, which turns out to be a magnificent Renaissance palace. I feel glad I've purchased these small gifts, since this isn't the sort of place you'd want to turn up empty-handed. However, the minute Gabriele catches sight of my carrier bag, he goes berserk. "When you visit the aristocracy," he exclaims, "you just take yourself. There's no need for presents."

Showing him the contents, I say playfully, "A drop of spumante and some cake never hurt anybody, did they?"

But Gabriele refuses to listen. "You might take flowers, if you really want to, but with gardens in three different properties, Caterina has enough to last her in this life and the next."

Without saying a word, I stuff the cake and wine into my thankfully large handbag, and he presses the bell.

In the courtyard, I pause, astounded. Here is a secluded world hidden from the eyes of most visitors to Florence. The scent of jasmine lies heavy in the air. Bees are buzzing and a couple of flamingos strut across a perfectly mowed lawn, kept lush by water jets from a Baroque fountain. High on a ladder, a gardener is busy lopping branches off a palm tree. Is he, I wonder, Alfonso Guidi?

A woman emerges from a door at the far end of the courtyard. She's wearing a plain green blouse, a denim skirt and tattered sandals, her greyish hair hanging loose over her shoulders. For a second I take her for the cleaner. Then I realise it is the countess, without a spot of make-up and evidently in her 'at home' attire. She is soon leading us up a wide staircase, chatting to Gabriele in English. Once again I'm amazed by how fluent they are, and I can't resist asking them why they choose to go on speaking English between themselves even now Peter is dead.

"I suppose it makes us feel like the old fart's still around," Gabriele jokes. "And who knows, he might show up again any minute."

We are standing at the top of the stairwell, opening onto a veranda, with a view of the green lawn below. Opening a door, our hostess ushers us inside her apartment. In the sparsely furnished vestibule, a Venetian chandelier shimmers in the sunlight. On the left are a Japanese table and a matching chair, where she sits down to pull off her gardening shoes and socks. As she does so, she cries out to the by-now-familiar Madonna, saints and an animal or two for an instant miracle to relieve her aching feet. I catch myself digging my nails deep into the palms of my hands; I am not looking forward to the formalities of having lunch here one little bit.

A door opposite swings open, and a maid beckons us in. The long, narrow room has high windows on one side, while a line of Old Master paintings is arranged on the sober damask wallpaper opposing them. With a dismissive wave of her hand, the countess strides past them, muttering, "Just my old popes, kings, lords, the occasional lady, and of course Dante. But don't worry, Ms Farrell, I'll show you round later."

We've reached our hostess's sitting room, decorated with long wall tapestries, four easy chairs, two settees, a grand piano, and a bar at the far end. The cabinets and shelves are chock-a-block with top-notch English china – Wedgwood, Mason's, Coalport. Seeming to forget all about me, like a mischievous schoolgirl, the countess grabs Gabriele's hand, and they slump down onto one of the divans. She's soon cuddling up to him, giving his tie a coy tug.

He responds, stroking her hand and making a solemn promise to organise a trip out to the country before not too long.

Seeing the easy-going way she treats her friend, and her casual clothes, I begin to relax. In contrast to the austere surroundings and the stern faces in the paintings, the countess's behaviour is open and warm.

She's coming towards me now, a hesitant smile on her lips, her hand stretched out ready to take mine. "I'm so very sorry about Peter. I know I told you at Manetti's, but I want to say it again. Please have a seat, Maria. May I call you Maria? I'm Caterina."

I just manage to say that's fine by me, when a Siamese cat leaps onto the back of the divan the minute I sit down. Perched there, it weighs me up, and I can feel myself tensing, waiting for it to pounce. Compared to my good-natured cats in Manchester, this one looks feral.

Seeing me on edge, Caterina tries to reassure me. "Don't worry, dear. Like the rest of the clan, Sammie is quite harmless. You'll probably see another three of these chaps prowling around the place before the morning's out. Their motto: 'Here's me, looking at you, stranger.' Mind you, they're the same with every newcomer, so don't imagine you're anything special. Settle down and relax. There's Prosecco on the bar over there, some nibbles, and mint water. Help yourself! Take a leaf out of Gabri's book! He's already halfway through that glass of mint cordial. But the odds are, he'll be enjoying something stronger later in the day."

With Sammie still threatening, I find it impossible to relax, and walk over to the piano. I've caught sight of a photo in an ornate silver frame. It is Peter, looking decidedly older than in the photos belonging to Dad. A second later Caterina joins me and picks up the photo, peering hard at Peter's face. "This was taken in 1951 when he first came to Florence." I detect a hint of nostalgia in her words. "He was young, blond and dashingly handsome. He was not long out of Oxford, twenty-four and so skinny. It's incredible when you think that he weighed a hundred kilos at his last medical. Well, in those now rather hazy but certainly delightful days, I was just finishing high school and my mother hired him to give me English lessons. She was always unconventional. When I was growing up, French was a must for any upper-class young lady wishing to find herself a suitable husband. It was a leftover from the war, I suppose. Mussolini abhorred the English and everything to do with them – sorry, Maria! Anyway, instead my mother said, 'Caterina, you really must learn English.'"

"Your mother and all the people I have met so far in Florence seem to have drowned their hatred," I say, recalling how kind everybody has been since I arrived.

"I suppose we have," she murmurs thoughtfully. "We may even have gone to the other extreme and begun to idealise the English."

The way Caterina clips her words, slipping in the occasional old-fashioned noun or turn of phrase, reminds me of the Queen Mother.

Her voice grows excited. "My girlfriends used to swoon every time they saw Peter. And I was no better. I fell for him the minute we met. He could have had his pick of any of us. It took me quite some time to realise he wasn't interested in me and never would be! Well, you know, we were so naive in those days. Just the same, once I'd got over my disappointment, my romance with England blossomed. Even though English isn't my mother tongue, it's a language I love. I suppose it reflects the part of me I like best. It makes me feel free, you see, from all the Italian stuffiness attached to being a countess." Noticing my puzzled expression, she adds, "Still, it's probably difficult for you to understand, seeing as you've always lived in England. Like many English people, I imagine you can't speak any foreign languages properly."

I go on the defensive and correct her. "It depends, you know. I learnt French at school and since then I've visited France several times. I once took a play of mine to the Avignon Festival, and only last September I was back in Paris for a friend's first night. At the moment I'm learning some Italian. Whenever I go out shopping or for a walk, I listen carefully to what people are saying. I'm determined to pick it up."

She stares at me quizzically, as if she doesn't know exactly what to make of me. I obviously don't fit into one of her little boxes. Having put the photo back on the piano, she shakes her head and prattles on about herself again. "As I said, I was a rather naive teenager. Like most girls of my background, I went to a convent school, where even the mention of sex or bodily functions was taboo. Like my mother and grandmother, I had a good education which unfortunately failed to equip me for the real world." Chuckling, she adds, "Mind you, I've managed to make up for that since."

Seeing me still hovering by the piano, her tone sharpens. "Even though this is a palace, Maria, please don't stand on ceremony!" She throws a weary glance at the tapestries, the china and the grand piano. "Unfortunately, I can't do much about all this stuff. I inherited it. My apologies."

She is smiling as she grabs my arm and leads me back to the picture gallery. I can hear peals of laughter, and a second later two Indian boys come pelting in, a uniformed nanny at their heels.

"They've just flown in from New Delhi for hospital treatment. You'd never dream he was ill, would you?" Caterina catches the smaller boy by the arm and gives him a big hug, whispering to me, "Ravi has a serious heart condition. And at his age, poor mite! This is his big brother, Amitav. He's come over to keep Ravi company. Listen, boys, this is my friend, Maria Farrell. Off you go now, the pair of you, and have something to eat."

Halting in front of each portrait, Caterina fills me in on the popes, royals and aristocrats lining the walls. "Most of them are distant relatives. Look at him – that's Dante Alighieri. It was painted in the sixteenth century when he'd been dead for more than two centuries. Just the same, it's the painting I treasure most. He was my great-great-great-great – I never quite get the number of 'greats' right – uncle."

"You must have been doing a fair bit of research on your family tree. The results sound incredible. I'd like to find out more about mine one day," I remark, doing my best to butter her up, while remembering Gabriele's remarks about her dubious claims to this illustrious relative. Like him, I have my doubts that she can actually prove a direct line over more than six hundred years.

"Well, yes, I'll have to show you the evidence when we've more time." And with that, her eyes revert to the portrait hanging next to Dante's. "This puffy-faced individual with the shifty eyes, dressed in exquisite purple silk, is Pope Boniface VIII. He was partly to blame for sending Dante into exile. Dante was given a choice: he could either pay a huge fine, or suffer death by burning if he chose to stay in Florence. The Florentines were such barbarians! And remember, politics was a very dangerous game. You had to be either White or Black; a member of one faction or the other. Dante had the terrible misfortune of being a White Guelf at a time when the Black Guelfs were in power. This meant he was thrown out on his heels! After 1302 he never saw Florence again; he had to live in exile in Verona and Ravenna. Truly horrible places; so provincial!"

I stare at Dante's gaunt face, thinking that Verona and Ravenna don't strike me as so terrible. He appears to be looking straight back at me, his eyes searching mine. He's dressed unpretentiously in a grey cloak, with no necklace, brooch, ring or hat. The gravity and simplicity of his mien remind me of a churchman. Here is a man, according to Caterina, with very different principles from the well-heeled popes and bishops, got up in their swanky clothes and expensive jewellery, who share the gallery space with him.

Suddenly, Caterina's hand tugs at my sleeve. "But do you want to see the real thing, Maria?" Seeing my baffled expression, she continues, "I mean Giotto di Bondone's portrait of Dante; probably the only one painted during the poet's lifetime. Giotto was an absolute genius, and a friend of Dante's. I am convinced he managed to capture my great-great-uncle's rebellious streak more than this unknown artist did. Unfortunately, the fresco's faded rather, but it's still worth seeing. It's only a five-minute walk to the Bargello Palace from here. If we hurry, we will just about make it before lunch. I'll put on some clothes and we'll be off."

Her invitation reminds me of what it means to live in the centre of Florence. Florentines like Caterina take it for granted that they can see the finest artworks of the Renaissance any day of the week. From childhood, they rub shoulders with Giotto, Botticelli and Vasari in the city's many galleries.

We set off, leaving Gabriele grunting that he'll stay put. With Peter, he's been to see the Giotto at least a dozen times. He'll enjoy a quiet drink and a read of the paper, he chuckles, pouring himself his first glass of wine of the day.

16

For our trip to the Bargello Palace, Caterina has put on some make-up and brushed her hair, and is wearing a purple-and-grey silk dress, whose layered skirt billows as she walks. She looks stunning. As her gaze falls on my jeans and T-shirt, she whispers, "As soon as I get a chance, I'll show you a good dressmaker's. I've been going to Signora Giuliana's for years. You can't go round Florence, Maria, wearing baggy trousers and a T-shirt."

What can I say – *I'm a grown woman, and don't you dare tell me what I should or shouldn't wear?* But, on second thoughts, she might be right. Some new clothes might not be such a bad idea.

As we walk along, Caterina bumps into a few people she knows; this is very evidently 'her' part of town. Her more leisurely pitch earlier this morning has given way to a pithy spiel. After diving down a gloomy alley, we come into a square, where an impressive whitish-grey marble church stands at the far end. "Santa Croce, Maria – well worth a visit. It's a splendid example of early Gothic architecture. There's also a cenotaph to Dante inside. His remains, though, are in Ravenna. But, sorry, we can't go in there today. You'll have plenty of time while you're here."

As we head down Via Giovanni da Verrazzano, a narrow street flanked by tall grey buildings, Caterina continues. "This is a very special part of Florence for me. It's where Dante lived and worked. Just think – he would have walked along here most days. And just round this corner there's the tiny church where Beatrice Portinari, the woman he loved all his life, is buried. You should remember that in Dante's day Florence was only the size of a pocket handkerchief. Everybody worth knowing would have known each other and lived in this area. They were undoubtedly a very select group of people. I certainly couldn't live in any other part of Florence."

Caterina's snobbery makes me seethe. Still, I keep silent. I daren't give her a piece of my mind if I want to enlist her help to find Peter's murderer.

We're passing by what looks like a theatre. "That's the Teatro Verdi. You might like to meet the people who run it, but another time. Just five minutes and we'll be at the Bargello."

Standing in front of the heavy iron bars on the windows of a medieval palace, my guide shows no sign of letting up. I'm feeling at the very end of my tether, given this overload of information, and am on the verge of telling her so.

"This is the Bargello Palace, once the Palace of the People; actually the first government building in Florence, built around 1250. It was here that Dante held the position of Prior; one of the six most important men in government. Later the building was used as a prison. Just look at those massive bars over the tiny windows. Today it's the National Museum."

Once we are inside the museum's cramped entrance hall, Caterina buys two tickets and pushes one into my hand. She leads the way through room after room filled with cabinets displaying jewellery, armoury and china. "No time for these either. Sorry!" she apologises, glancing at her watch. "We can't keep Gabriele waiting for lunch."

I'm about to flip after her umpteenth, 'Sorry, there's no time', when her footsteps slow down, and I breathe a deep sigh of relief. This whirlwind tour might just be concluding, since Caterina is looking relaxed and her face lights up as we enter what could have been a chapel. "We're here at last, Maria!" she exclaims, pointing triumphantly at the frescoes on the walls. "That's Giotto's *Last Judgement*. Look up there! Can you see it? That gruesome scene of Hell?"

I scan the fresco, catching my breath at the horrific sight of the sinners hurtling down into the void.

Oblivious to my shock, Caterina switches to more mundane matters. "As you can see, the painting is in urgent need of restoration. But sadly, it's the same old story. The Italian government has no money to do anything about it, so it's left to deteriorate."

She makes for the far end of the chapel, where, judging by the marks on the wall, at one time there was an altar. Pointing to a spot high on the wall, she asks, "Can you see him? Concentrate, Maria."

I crane my neck, scrutinising the area of the fresco she is indicating, until I locate a figure whose face resembles the image of Dante I saw in Caterina's gallery. Dressed in a red tunic and hat, he stands out from the other figures, who are wearing yellow and blue.

Caterina's eyes are still fixed on Dante as she adds, "Giotto painted Dante in around 1300, when he was already an important figure in Florentine politics. That red cloak shows that he's been elected to the Council of Priors. And just look at his nose – I think you call it an aquiline one, don't you? Or is it a hawk nose? Anyway, it's got a huge bridge. I am convinced that Dante was blessed with a nose like that; it's so distinctive. And what's more, it must have come in extremely useful for sniffing out the crime and corruption he so abhorred."

I check out Dante's stoical expression again, feeling admiration for the man. He seems to have chosen a quiet form of resistance which gives absolutely nothing away. His long, white fingers and beautiful nails grasp a book. The painter has chosen a pale blue background void of any realistic detail, suggesting a specific place. He's created a spatial vacuum that increases the mystery surrounding Dante.

I suddenly wonder whether Dante has the same effect on the woman standing next to me as he does on me. If so, Caterina isn't telling. She tugs at my sleeve, her eyes darting towards the exit. "Time to be heading home, Maria."

In the dining room, Gabriele is sitting at an exquisitely laid table complete with a damask linen cloth, a porcelain dinner service, and silver cutlery, each item stamped with the Guiccioli family crest. The moment we come through the door, he turns to face us, a glass of wine in his hand, toasting our return. While he's anxious to find out whether I enjoyed the Giotto, in the next breath he complains that he's starving. "Caterina," he chides, "is always late."

Despite the lavishly decked table, I am relieved to see that the atmosphere remains informal. The maid brings in a couple of bowls of mixed salad, and platters of cheese, cured ham and salami, arranging them carefully on the table before disappearing and leaving us to help ourselves.

Our hostess beams. "Now do tuck in. I've spent my entire life trying to prevent this place from turning into a museum. It could have easily ended up as a second Bargello. And all this clutter! I quite understand if you don't believe me, Maria. However, when my parents died, I really did throw out tons of stuff."

By now Gabriele is visibly tipsy, and slurring his words. "I can vouch for that. Peter and I gave her a hand with the clear-out. I had a bad back for weeks after."

Sipping the delicious red wine, I decide I'd better broach the reason for my visit. "It's very kind of you to have invited me, Caterina, but I'll get straight to the reason why I am here."

She looks taken aback. "So this isn't just an enjoyable social occasion for you? I invited you here so we could get to know each other better and have a chat about my dear friend Peter."

"Well, actually, I did come to discuss Peter. You see, I've made up my mind to try and find out who murdered him. I need to ask you a few questions."

Her jaw drops a mile, and she sits to attention, holding her fingers pressed together as if in prayer. When she speaks, she pronounces the words hesitantly. "Do you really think that's a good idea? Such things are best left to the police, aren't they?"

I explain that I need to feel like I'm doing something to get to the bottom of Peter's murder, since the police, try as they might, don't seem to be getting very far. Caterina lights a cigarette, glaring at me and seemingly warning me not to take my plan a step further. Thankfully, Gabriele comes to my rescue, revealing that he intends to give me a hand. She throws him a stern, reproachful look, and for the first time since I met them, they switch to Italian, their voices growing steadily angrier. Their heated exchange lasts for a few minutes before Caterina gives in and nods to indicate that she is willing to help.

My heart thuds, and a lump has lodged itself in my throat. Caterina has switched on the green light, but I can't get the words out. It's only natural, I tell myself. After Singh, Caterina is only the third person I've questioned about the murder. Fidgeting with my glass, I beg my voice to come back, and eventually it does. "Caterina, do you remember how, at Manetti's, you called Peter 'a dark horse' and 'my unpredictable Albion'? That description has been niggling at me ever since. Is there anything you know about him that could help us get to the truth about his death?"

In reply, she picks up a bottle of wine from the table and points to the label. "It's 1999 and pretty special. And look here, it's got its own label, featuring a castle on a hill. It was Peter who sketched that." Her voice turns mysterious as she gently fingers the drawing. "The castle is just outside Florence. You'll see it, Maria, before too long."

Holding the open bottle under my nose, she invites me to smell the bouquet. "Exquisite, isn't it?" She pours herself another glass.

I repeat my request for help, determined to get her talking, and this time she complies.

"You want names, telephone numbers, addresses of people, I suppose, even though I was just about to tell you more about Dante and how he's affected my life. He was a man of impeccable ethics who hated the way his fellow Florentines had grown money-mad. You see, they had this insatiable hunger for material things. You saw how simply *he* dressed – no ruffs, no brocades. On top of that, he was a writer, a poet, and also an outstanding politician and soldier. Had he lived today he would certainly have taken charge of—"

"Can we perhaps talk about Dante next time we meet?" I cut in firmly.

"Sorry, Maria, all right. Back to your investigation. Gabriele won't want me to tell you this, but I think it's my duty." She pauses again, glancing at him, before going on. "I said Peter was something of a dark horse and unpredictable, and I stand by that because he sometimes did things that were completely out of character. I mean, he associated with people who were – how can I put it? – a tad on the shady side. I really don't know much more than that."

Gabriele, sitting next to her, gives her a sharp nudge, but she is adamant she's going to tell me, and whispers, "I'd never tell the police about these contacts. I would never run the risk of tarnishing Peter's reputation, you see. However, you strike me as an intelligent young woman."

Seeing my embarrassment – she hardly knows me, and here she is singing my praises – she adds, "I'm not being patronising; I'm in deadly earnest. I know I've only just met you, but the moment I saw you I trusted you. Well, you are the niece of one of my dearest friends."

She pauses, a sad look on her face. "Here's my advice. You must meet a man called Angelo Verza; a fisherman on Lake Trasimeno in Umbria. We – Peter, Gabri and I – used to visit him from time to time. Peter had a passion for Etruscan artwork, you see."

Her last words strike me as strange. "But wasn't he into twentieth-century art? The paintings in his sitting room…"

"Of course. The splendid collection he shared with Gabriele is all modern stuff. Still, Etruscan antiquities were another of his 'things'."

I don't have a clue about Etruscan art. This time, though, I have no intention of being called an ignoramus, and decide I'll make a joke of it. "What on earth has a fisherman called Angelo, living by some lake in Umbria, got to do with Etruscan art?"

Caterina promptly brushes my question aside, replying drily, "I would suggest you arrange a meeting with Angelo. His name means 'angel', by the way. He'll live up to that, you'll see. Gabri's got his phone number and address. I haven't the foggiest who else you should talk to. Remember, though, before you meet Angelo, to find out all you can about the *tombaroli*."

She scribbles down the name on a scrap of paper and hands it to me. I begin guessing what the word means – "Tombs? Death? Graves, maybe?" – when Gabriele blows his top, saying I'd better not start meddling with things I will never understand.

However, Caterina insists. "If Maria's to get anywhere, she's got to meet Angelo and discover more about the *tombaroli*. And by the way, Maria, I'll give you a couple of bottles of wine for my earthbound angel."

There seems to be a huge contradiction in what she's just told me. In one breath she mentioned shady characters; in the next she called Angelo an angel. I could ask her to explain herself better, but decide against it. I want to get down to Lake Trasimeno and meet the man for myself. But before that, I've got to find out who or what exactly the *tombaroli* are.

Gabriele and I are crossing Caterina's courtyard on our way out, when a lively aria fills the air. It's Mozart's *Non più andrai* from *The Marriage of Figaro*. A man of around sixty approaches us, his sturdy, suntanned arms effortlessly propelling a wheelbarrow piled high with twigs and dead flowers. His eyes glint in the sunlight, and the minute he catches sight of Gabriele, his broad face opens even wider in a huge smile. For a second time he belts out the opening line: "*Non più andrai, farfallone amoroso...*"

"Bravo, bravo!" cries Gabriele, boisterously singing the aria in English for my benefit. "*You'll no longer go astray, my beloved wanderer...*"

A second later the two men are hugging and whispering something in Italian. Keeping his hand on Gabriele's shoulder, the gardener throws me a quizzical look, before turning back to his friend and their discussion. I understand very little, except that Gabriele's voice has grown serious. With no sign of the conversation ending or Gabriele introducing me to his friend, I butt in, telling him that I need to be getting back to my hotel to make some phone calls. Gabriele appears not to hear me, and I notice him lightly fingering the sweat on the other man's shirt. In response, the gardener grabs a sprig of jasmine and holds it under Gabriele's nose. The two seem reluctant to part, their hands clasped tight, locking the jasmine between their palms.

Caterina's maid has opened the main door, and we have stepped out onto the pavement when Gabriele gives me a little nudge, asking me if I understand who the man is.

"You could have introduced me," I say, irritated at the way he gave me the cold shoulder while coming on to his friend. "Where are your manners? Anyway, I bet he's Alfonso Guidi, Caterina's number-one gardener."

"Correct!" He chortles, ignoring my irritation and sniffing at the jasmine in his hand. "Nice chap, eh, and a fine singer?"

"At least now I understand what Caterina and you see in him. So what's the story between you two?"

"What do you mean? Italian men know how to show our feelings, unlike you Brits. We appreciate male beauty. Take Michelangelo's *David* in Piazza della Signoria. It's superb. In Britain I don't think there are many naked statues in public places. Am I right?"

Seeing that I'm still fuming, he adds gently, "I'm very fond of Alfonso. We're good friends. What's peculiar in that?"

"Mm. I was thinking," I say playfully, ready to gauge Gabriele's reaction, "I might invite Alfonso to landscape my garden in Manchester. I'll soon be coming into some serious money and will be able to afford to get my garden back in shape. Since Mum died, it's turned into a wilderness."

"As you wish, darling." Gabriele's tone of voice contradicts his gracious consent. "Anyway, if we take Caterina's advice, tomorrow we'd better head off to Lake Trasimeno where you can meet Angelo. I'll come to your hotel at around noon."

As soon as Gabriele has left, I make for the Basilica di Santa Croce. After the eventful morning at Caterina's, I need some peace and quiet. At the entrance I buy a pamphlet, from which I learn that Santa Croce is the largest Franciscan church in the world and, as Caterina mentioned, a masterpiece of neo-Gothic architecture. I marvel at the high open-timber roof of the splendid building, and its long aisle dotted with funerary monuments. Moving from one to the other, I slowly read the names of the famous people buried here: Michelangelo, Galileo and Machiavelli, each housed in his own impressive monument.

After a while I wander out into the sunlight to visit the finely wrought cloisters with their well-trimmed lawns. As I stroll round one of the perfect green rectangles, my thoughts grow crystal clear. The quiet seems to be inviting me to process the events of the day so far. While centuries ago the Franciscan monks must have cottoned on to the benefits of walking in silence while meditating, they only dawn on me this afternoon. Listening to the regular crunch of my footsteps on the gravel, I go over what happened between Gabriele and Alfonso. Italians are masters of body language, their skill in this far surpassing your average Brit's. I had witnessed the playful intimacy between the two in Caterina's courtyard, but couldn't help suspecting that the scene hid a much more complex relationship.

And how far, I wonder, can I trust the people I've met so far – Gabriele, Alfonso, Caterina, Singh, Manetti? Machiavelli's celebrated motto from *The Prince* springs to mind: 'The end justifies the means.' And in this church, I am standing squarely on Machiavelli's stamping ground. I've just visited his funerary monument, and the man himself lived down the road.

My thoughts turn to the big money involved in Peter's estate. It must have looked like a tempting prospect for the people in his inner circle. Have any of them, I wonder, anything to do with his murder? But if they had been after his money, the murderer or murderers would surely have stolen the paintings. Then something even more disturbing strikes me. Here I am, an outsider who's had the good fortune to come into the bulk of Peter's inheritance, just because I'm his next of kin. Why me? Why didn't he leave everything to his partner, Gabriele? He and their other friends might well see me as a threat; about to do them out of a considerable part of what they believe they are entitled to. I probably need to be more careful how I tread. Like ruthless Machiavels, they might be scheming to get rid of me.

As I leave Santa Croce and its beautiful cloisters behind and make for my hotel, I recall how, before I left Manchester, I tried to comfort Joanne by quoting Hamlet's line, 'The readiness is all.' I can hear myself now, repeating the words for my own sake. To get anywhere with this investigation, I will have to stay focused. And, recalling Hamlet's words again, I will need all the readiness I can muster.

17

It's morning the day after our lunch at Caterina's, and I make for the local library. I want to see if I can find out about the *tombaroli* before my trip to Lake Trasimeno to meet Angelo. I pull Caterina's note out of my pocket, showing it to the librarian at the desk. He makes no reply, but his surly eyes stare back at me as he nods me in the direction of the adjacent reading room.

The place is bustling with people of all ages – studying and writing at the spacious wooden desks; consulting books, newspapers or magazines; or simply standing in queues, waiting for information.

I join a queue, and ten minutes later my turn comes. Trying out my Italian on the librarian behind the counter, I do my best to tell him that I want some information on the *tombaroli*. He seems embarrassed, avoiding eye contact and whispering something to a colleague. It flashes through my mind that perhaps Gabriele was right; I shouldn't be interfering in such matters. Once the man has conferred with his colleague, he issues instructions in an icy voice, pointing me to some filing cabinets.

I check the files and find three articles with references to the *tombaroli*, and request them. Once they have been delivered to my desk, I attempt to read them, but can only make out the odd word. I'll just have to ask Gabriele for the information I need.

With an hour still to kill before meeting Gabriele, I saunter along a busy street lined with fashionable boutiques. One in particular takes my fancy. There's a mannequin in the window, wearing linen pants and a stunning silk-and-lace blouse. Remembering Caterina's advice to get myself some decent clothes, I open the door and walk in. In the full-length mirror by the door, I glance at my reflection and have to admit that my jeans and T-shirt do very little for me. My dark blonde hair and pale skin look spent, making me think that it really is time I treated myself. The sales assistant is busy in conversation with a customer, so I nod in her direction, asking if I can have a browse.

A few minutes later, I hear a voice behind me. "Signora, Signora, I'm Anita. I was wondering how I can help you."

"I'd like a new outfit, please."

Soon I am trying on linen pants and blouses, while paying attention to Anita's advice. Her golden rule: coordinate the different items of any new outfit *in modo armonioso*, which sounds far more exotic than the English 'mix and match'. I soon discover that the young woman has an excellent eye for colour and style, and seems to know intuitively what will suit me. A little later, I take a second look at myself in the mirror, this time scrutinising the slim-fitting pants and long-sleeved blouse I am wearing. They are both lilac, and the silk blouse has a geometric pattern in smoky grey.

Weighing up the outfit, Anita cannily produces a smoky grey shoulder bag with a lilac handle and a silver clasp. "*Vedi? Quasi perfetto!*" ('See? Almost perfect!') She smiles. Facing me, she points at the ceiling, then at my bare feet. A second later, from a nearby cupboard, she whips out some grey high-heeled shoes. Magically, they seem to launch me skywards, making me look slimmer and taller.

I feel a buzz of satisfaction as I pay up and walk out of the shop in my new rig-out. Throwing a rapid glance in the mirror by the door, the person looking back at me makes me think that I will no longer stand out like a sore thumb among the fashion-conscious Florentines. Not a bad thing either, for my investigation, if I can manage to merge seamlessly into the woodwork.

At noon I find Gabriele waiting for me in the hotel lounge. Unusually for him, he is wearing jeans, a T-shirt, a hooded fleece and trainers, with a capacious backpack slung over one shoulder and a map in his hand. As I teeter towards him on my high heels, I notice his eyes scanning my new outfit and his head shaking disapprovingly. A second later, his gaze latches onto my shoes and he wags his finger. "Those shoes are totally unsuitable. And those clothes!" he groans.

"What do you mean? I love them. It's my Florentine look. I went to Anita's on—"

Without allowing me to finish, he volleys, "Muddy fields and cow dung, most probably. Open countryside. Get the picture?"

Feeling peeved that I won't be able to show off my new clothes, I return to my room, where I change back into the T-shirt and jeans I swore to Anita would stay in my case until I return to Manchester. "Come on! Off we go," I let fly, with a note of forced bravado, as Gabriele and I saunter through the hotel lounge and make for my little car. "Your limousine is waiting, Professor Foschi; step inside."

"*Benissimo, Signora*. Let's hit the road and head south out of Florence," he laughs. "Then it's Arezzo, Cortona, Lake Trasimeno. If all goes well, we should be at our destination in less than two hours."

In the passenger seat Gabriele spreads the map out on his lap and starts navigating. After a few hiccups – a wrong turn down a one-way street, the glimpse of a tourist coach that has knocked a poor girl off her bike – we reach the motorway and drive south. All around, trees are in blossom, and I roll down the window to let the warm air and a tantalising whiff of the scent fill the car. I start reciting Robert Browning's poem, *Home-Thoughts from Abroad* – "*Oh, to be in England, now that April's there…*" – but quickly grind to a halt as I wonder how Browning, who was living in Florence at the time, could possibly have felt homesick for rainy England on such a beautiful spring day. Still, I tell myself, this isn't the right time for such trivia, and I force myself to focus on the road ahead.

A sly glance at Gabriele tells me he is daydreaming. "A lire for your thoughts!" I say playfully. "Hey, you may as well know: my trip to the library was rubbish. The only articles I found were in Italian and too difficult for me. So, before we get to Angelo's, you need to fill me in on the *tombaroli*."

His expression turns serious. "How about beginning with a little game of deduction? At Caterina's you mentioned tombs and graves, I think?"

"Yes, and death."

"Add the word 'thieves', and you're almost there."

He begins filling me in on some background, showing his knowledge of the Etruscan civilisation, "Italy boasts some of the finest antiquities in Europe. The regions of Tuscany, Lazio and Umbria are particularly important. Etruscan civilisation flourished in these parts from the ninth to the second centuries BC. The Etruscans were magnificent artists and craftsmen who produced an impressive range of useful but aesthetically first-class vases, jugs, jewellery and religious objects in terracotta, bronze, silver and gold. We're fortunate in that the religion the Etruscans practised meant that wealthy families wanted these beautiful things to be buried along with them in their tombs. The upshot: many of these artefacts have survived intact."

As he pauses to light a cigarette, I butt in. "Okay, all well and good, but what do these guys actually do?"

"In Italy corruption is widespread, and tomb thieves are one category of embezzler. These people excel in locating and excavating the ancient Etruscan tombs. But once they've got their hands on the goods, they need to sell them."

I am flabbergasted. Here is a world I knew nothing about, and Gabriele's explanation sets me wondering how Peter, and very likely he, could have got mixed up with the *tombaroli*. Before he gets too carried away, I decide I'd better ask how he came to be involved in the racket. "How about a cappuccino in the first bar we come to? That way we can have a breather, and I can take some notes. I need to concentrate on the next part of your story."

"The next part? What do you mean?" He sounds baffled.

"How exactly did Peter and you, I suppose, get involved with the *tombaroli*? There must be some connection if Caterina insisted we come down here."

I notice his fingers fraying the edges of the map. He stares at his nails and his words start coming in fits and starts. "In England you have a much clearer sense of right and wrong than we do – at least on the surface. The concepts of 'legality' and 'illegality' are more clear-cut and distinct. In Italy they're – how can I say? – more fluid. May I use that adjective? The tomb thieves generally lead – how can I put it? – a double life. They work as bank clerks, bakers, garage attendants from nine to seven while—"

"And fishermen, maybe?"

"Yes, and fishermen. But you see, as well as holding down a daytime job, they have this second job they keep secret. The locals usually know about it, but pretend not to. Nor would these people ever call themselves *tombaroli*. If you ask them what they do, they say they're collectors who, of course, are looking to sell what they find. That's where people like Peter and me come in. We've got the contacts to make the deals happen, not just in Italy but globally."

"But isn't that illegal?" Gabriele's disclosure makes me wonder why he is willing to explain all this to me.

"Yes and no. From a certain point of view, it is. Let's take a specific item – the terracotta mug we sold just before Peter was murdered. It represented the head of a young African boy, and was nearly three thousand years old. A real beauty! And guess what? A tomb thief we know had found it in a neighbour's chicken run. That mug had never existed from the perspective of the taxman or anyone else in the modern world. For all those centuries it had been on first-name terms with a load of hens. So we, or anyone else for that matter, didn't lift it out of a museum or steal it from some stately home. All we did was facilitate its move and give it a new home. Eventually, it ended up somewhere in North America, where its new owner is bound to treasure it. If you are responsible for such a transaction, you're bringing people happiness. Peter and I were the middlemen who set up the connections. You just pick up the phone, write a letter (or, today, an email), and other people take care of the rest."

His words make perfect sense, but the logic strikes me as bizarre. He seems to forget that he and Peter could have taken the mug to the curator of the nearest archaeological museum. I strongly dislike the idea that my uncle wasn't too morally scrupulous. Remembering the librarian's icy look earlier on, I am determined not to let Gabriele off the hook. "I imagine you and Peter weren't – or aren't in your case – in this business to be Good Samaritans. There must be substantial financial rewards to be had."

"Well, yes and no," he replies, a wry smile crossing his face. "The money can be first-rate, but also erratic. There can be a whopping great treasure trove one day, then the next, bugger all, as Peter used to say."

"So you both enjoyed the sometimes-lucrative earnings and the lifestyle they presumably brought. And all this happened while keeping the police and the taxman in the dark."

"Yes, that's about it. Still, don't you go climbing on your high horse, St Maria. Over the years Peter and I channelled a substantial part of our earnings from the Etruscan business into our modern art collection. So, if you accept and sell his paintings, then just like us – me, sorry, I was forgetting again – you'll be sharing a bed, so to speak, with the tomb thieves."

Gabriele throws me a defiant look. He has just issued an unambiguous warning not to poke my finger any deeper into what strikes me as a murky business. I shudder at the thought that Peter, whom I considered a pillar of society, was involved in this. I pause, thinking hard, and have to admit that Gabriele is right. If I accept the paintings, at the very least I'll be turning a blind eye to an illegal trade in valuable antiques.

With my conscience pricking me, I decide to let the matter drop for now and fire my next question. "And what about Angelo? Why does Caterina want me to meet him?"

By now Gabriele is looking exhausted. He has evidently made a tremendous effort to explain his position and he's had enough for today. "As far as I know, Angelo's just a small fisherman operating in a very big lake. In any case, I'll leave you to find out about that when you meet him – if, of course, he has anything he wishes to tell you."

18

It's just after one and Gabriele points to a lane on the right. I make a sharp turn off the main road and a second later we are driving along a dirt track without a house or a soul in sight. The track fizzles out and my friend tells me to park the car; we need to walk the rest of the way. We're stumbling along a path when a lake comes into sight. In the distance, two dots are wading out in the water. As we approach, a man and a woman come into focus. The woman, slightly taller than her companion, is walking beside him, scanning the water. Suddenly she bends down and pulls something that looks like a box out of the lake. She shows it to the man, who grabs it and carries it to the lakeside, where she puts it into a large bag.

Gabriele shouts at the top of his voice, "*Angelo, Angelo, ci siamo!* Angelo, Angelo, we're here!"

Looking round, the man ambles towards us, giving Gabriele a warm hug. There is something about his relaxed gait that reminds me of that French expression 'to feel perfectly at ease in one's skin'. Around fifty, he's dressed casually in shorts, a rumpled shirt and ragged sandals. His sturdy build, rugged features and swarthy complexion suggest that he spends most of his time in the open air. The woman, who has long blonde hair and an athletic build, joins us. I notice her red nose; perhaps from too much wine, or just an overdose of sun. Angelo introduces her as Gerda. She's come over from Germany on holiday and is staying at his place, he says, giving her a peck on the cheek.

The minute Gabriele introduces me as Peter's niece, Angelo's face turns sad. "I was so sorry," he mutters, throwing me a gentle smile. "I hear news... Oh, *mio Dio*! Sorry, my English... Gabri, you tell Maria, please. Here, come and sit down, you two."

Once we are settled in the shade of a large tree, Angelo asks Gabriele to translate what he says into English. "I was listening to the radio when I heard the news of Peter's murder. It came as a terrible shock to me and my mother. I never saw Peter very often, but his visits were always a pleasure. He was a real gentleman. You know, we had some good times down here. Whenever he came, I'd grill some fish and we'd drink Caterina's red wine. It's first-rate! I'd do a barbecue and he'd muck in with whatever needed doing. There was something very ordinary about him, even though he was so brainy, and he could talk the hind leg off a donkey when he got going." He winks at Gabriele. "I had a lot of time for Peter."

I suddenly remember I have some of Caterina's wine in my bag, and hand over the bottles to Angelo. His face lights up and he waves one at Gerda, asking if she fancies a drink. First, though, they need to go and fetch today's catch.

Gerda giggles as she and Angelo race back to the lakeside, looking like two young hares rather than middle-aged people. Gabriele and I follow at a slower pace, no less anxious to find out if there's anything for lunch. The pair are now wading in the lake again, where Angelo casts about for the net he's put out. The minute he finds it, he and Gilda each grab a corner and, tilting back on their heels, give it a mighty tug, trying to heave it clear of the water. It refuses to budge, and for a second there's deadlock before Angelo takes over. Nudging Gerda to one side, he gives another strong pull, and this time the net slides onto the shingle, spewing out scores of wriggling fish. "Hallelujah! And what have we got here, Gerda?" Angelo crouches down and sifts carefully through the haul. "Come on, tell our two friends what I've taught you."

This makes me cringe; he sounds so patronising. Gerda doesn't seem to mind, though, and kneels down beside the net, scrutinising the fish. After a moment's hesitation, she reels off the names of the different species. She knows them in Italian, English and German, and keeps glancing at Gabriele and me, as if to solicit our approval. Angelo picks up an eel and beckons me to take a closer look. I wince; it looks so disgusting. Seeing my reluctance to touch it, Angelo takes Gerda's hand and makes her stroke the slimy creature. Once again, she does as she is told, and Angelo rounds off the day's lesson by asking me, "*E' un grande capitone*; a big, juicy eel! You don't like it, do you, Maria?" The eel flops to the ground, moving a little longer before lying stiff and motionless. "It's only twenty centimetres long," Angelo remarks dismissively, "but next time, don't worry; I'll manage something bigger and more succulent."

His words send Gerda off into peals of laughter. The size and shape of the fish are evidently a private joke between them. "Yes, it's really not big enough," she remarks coyly. "I like my eels long and hard."

The game over, Angelo makes a start on the barbecue, lighting a charcoal fire while Gerda ferries some bags from a nearby shed to a sandy patch by the lake. Next comes a blanket, then a plastic table, paper plates and plastic cutlery. The exceptions to the picnic ware are some crystal wine glasses with delicate pale blue stems. We can't possibly drink Caterina's wine out of paper cups, Angelo snorts; it's got to be Venetian crystal. While he gets stuck into cleaning and descaling the fish, Gabriele and I enjoy a drink to the tune of Gerda rattling on about the fabulous time she is having on the lake. Every so often her eyes dart in Angelo's direction, making it clear that he is the reason for her unbridled enthusiasm. Then she dishes up an assortment of mouth-watering antipasti, piling our plates with aubergine, artichokes in oil, black olives, sun-dried tomatoes and home-made bread. Coming close to me, she confides, "You know, these are his mother's specials. He absolutely worships her. That's why he has never married; at least, that's my theory. I can't cook for the life of me, can you, Maria? And know what? I've discovered it's a deadly sin in Italy if a woman can't make a meal with at least three courses."

I laugh, tucking into the starters and telling Gerda about my special Indian meals which usual consist of about five different dishes. I ask her jokingly, "What do you think? Will I manage to get myself an Italian husband while I'm in Florence?"

Laughing, she quickly sets me right. "Never, Maria – Indian food will never do the trick; only good, wholesome Tuscan cooking will do."

She offers me some more wine, but I stick to just one glass. I want to remember anything Angelo might tell me – if, of course, it's worth hearing. I notice he's positioned a glass and a bottle of wine on a stool next to him and is silently enjoying a quick slug in between cleaning one fish and the next. *If he tells me anything*, I think wryly, *it will be in vino veritas*.

Under the pretext of giving him a hand with the fish, I go and stand beside him, beckoning Gabriele to come and translate. "Any idea if Peter had any problems? Is there anybody who might have wanted him out of the way? Somebody local or farther afield who might harbour a grudge against him?"

Pointing his knife in my direction, Angelo throws me a quizzical glance, seeming to wonder if he can trust me. As he goes back to cleaning and gutting his catch, I notice him plying the knife with evident skill. It makes me wonder if he'd be capable of performing a similar operation on a human being. His smile is gentle and he has the warmth of an angel, as Caterina suggested, but this might just be a clever camouflage.

Once he's finished with the fish, Angelo gestures to Gabriele to interpret again. "You put me in a difficult position, Maria," he replies after a pause. "I was fond of Peter; he did me many a good turn. Not for nothing, of course – he was a wily old fox. But the least said on that count, the better."

I clock the description of Peter as a 'wily old fox' and am about to ask our host to expand on that when Gabriele begins gesturing impatiently and speaking slowly so I can understand him. Angelo, he insists, should get to the point and tell me all he knows if he wants to help us find Peter's killer. He can trust me not to tell the police anything about what he might disclose. After all, I am Peter's niece and would never want to damage his reputation.

Washing the blood off his hands and knife, Angelo begins in a whisper, with Gabriele translating again, "To be honest, Peter did have a spot of bother about six months back. He decided not to tell you, Gabri; he didn't want to worry you. He came down here with Caterina. He was edgy and exhausted – he was very worried about some phone calls, you see. He couldn't sleep, he was so worried. The caller had apparently told him to leave off the fish round here, otherwise he'd be in big trouble."

Seeing my puzzled expression, Angelo explains, "In our business the competition is fierce, whether it's national or international. In the past I've been plagued by anonymous callers, and that's why Peter thought I'd know how to handle the matter. The caller usually kicks off by suggesting that you supply him with fish for his restaurant or hotel. That's the coded language they use. After this, they ring off with, 'Well, if you ever have any surplus on your hands, and provided it's the real thing, hatched or reared locally, here's my number. And make sure you contact me and nobody else; otherwise, you know the consequences.' Luckily, I've never needed them. I've relied on Peter and, in more recent years, Gabriele. They've always taken the really good stuff off me."

The smell of burning fish makes Angelo jump to salvage the smouldering pieces. Soon after, he proudly dishes it up. "Here, Maria, try this. I hope you like it. Mind the bones! It couldn't be fresher. You saw it wriggling around in that net only a few minutes ago."

I sink my teeth into the charred pike. While beneath the burned skin, the moist flesh smells tempting, the flavour is nothing special. Seeing my face fall, Gabriele whispers that lake fish is usually pretty tasteless. The water in this particular area doesn't help; it tends to be shallow, muddy and awash with reeds. Still, there is no way I can tell Angelo I don't like it; I'll have to grin and eat up. I need to keep on the right side of him, and that means leaving him in no doubt that I appreciate his cooking. Luckily Gerda has just plonked some lemon-and-oil dressing on the table and I grab it, drowning the fish in it. Covered in the dressing, it looks and tastes much better. As I eat it, finishing every morsel, I quiz Angelo about the mysterious caller.

"That's a tricky one," he replies, slurring his words. "From sources, er… Sorry, I can't say any more. Almost certainly it was a former university colleague of Peter's."

"Are you sure?" I murmur, incredulous.

"Possibly," says Angelo, reluctant to divulge the person's name.

"It's Mario Giovanelli, isn't it?" Gabriele snaps.

"Yeah, possibly!" Angelo pushes another forkful of fish into his mouth.

"Giovanelli's in the business, too," Gabriele confides. "He and Peter were never exactly pals, but I don't think he would have…"

Then it's our host's turn to snap. "I've told you all I know, Maria, and if you've any sense, you'll follow it up. But what I suggest now is a little nap, considering the – how can I put it? – the fortifying lunch we've just had."

After all I've eaten, it is a relief to get my head down and stretch out on a blanket on the grass. As I doze off, I can still taste the wine and food. The fish has turned stale and bitter, and even the antipasti have lost their flavour.

In a flash I stare, mesmerised, as a cone of strawberry, chocolate and pistachio ice cream drips temptingly before my eyes. Night has fallen and I am strolling under a starless sky. I am back in Manchester, engrossed in another Arts Council application. I have thousands of pounds in the bank, but I have no intention of stopping work and am actually planning a new theatre company on a grander scale than my present set-up.

Suddenly the sound of voices jolts me awake. Rolling onto my side, I realise it's Gerda and Angelo, talking to Gabriele. On the table in front of them is a black object, the size and shape of a large loaf. Gabriele is on his feet, staring hard at the object. He picks it up, holds it in the air, turns it round and points to something on its side. The conversation grows animated, suggesting that they are haggling over a price. "*Cento milioni*," Gabriele kicks off.

"*No, no*," Angelo says firmly.

"*Centoventi milioni*."

"*No, non basta*."

"*Centotrenta, ultima parola*."

"*No, non basta*," Angelo concludes firmly.

Gabriele's offer of 130 million lire is evidently not enough, and a silence ensues. The two men have failed to clinch the deal, and, like lightning, Gerda gets up. She picks up the object, wraps it in what looks like bubble wrap and stuffs it into a red metal box. Is it, I ask myself, the same box she pulled out of the lake some hours ago? It strikes me as incredible that such an insignificant-looking object can be worth thousands of lire. I suddenly feel uneasy. While Gabriele brought me down to Angelo's claiming that he could probably help us with our inquiry into Peter's murder, this visit might also have been a pretext to do some business. Peter's death has evidently not put a stop to Gabriele's dealings with the tomb thieves.

I must have slept for another few hours when I hear Gabriele calling my name and laughing that the wine knocked us both flat out. Looking round, I realise that we are alone. Gabriele tells me that Angelo and Gerda had to dash off some hours ago; Angelo's mother has apparently had a fall.

I don't relish the prospect of driving back to Florence in the dark, but we've no option. Without more ado, Gabriele and I jump into the car and hit the road.

19

Professor Mario Giovanelli had just given his Wednesday lecture in his usual classroom at a private university in the suburbs of Florence. He'd been teaching on Wednesdays, at that time, in that same plush classroom, ever since he was appointed to the Chair of Etruscan Studies twenty years before. In Italy top professors are allowed to organise their own timetable, and Giovanelli was no exception. He'd opted for 5.30 on Mondays, Wednesdays and Fridays, giving himself ample time for a leisurely siesta and an afternoon read before driving down to the faculty from his villa in Fiesole in the hills above Florence.

That day's lecture had been uneventful. The twenty or so international students had quietly jotted down notes as he trotted out the facts, as he saw them, concerning Etruscan funerary utensils. Giovanelli's self-confident, albeit monotonous, teaching style depended on the fact that he'd given the same lecture at least twenty times before. Just the same, he didn't anticipate criticism from the students. The present generation was much more passive than his own. He and his companions had been passionate about society and politics, quick to question a teacher's authority and methods. Instead, today's 'herd', as he called them, were generally laid-back. Their sole aim: to graduate as soon as they could, with flying colours.

Once his hour-long slot was up, he stuffed his lecture notes into his briefcase, took off his reading glasses and pulled a packet of Marlboro out of his pocket. He was craving a smoke, and headed downstairs. He walked quickly through the central quadrangle, throwing a disdainful glance at the cigarette butts, plastic cups and stirrers strewn over the gravel. After that, he tut-tutted at the dozens of students sprawled on the wooden benches, chatting, smoking, snacking and drinking. But of course, they didn't give a hoot about the middle-aged tutor rushing by.

Giovanelli wanted quiet, and made straight for his usual spot: at the top end of a narrow alley in the farthest corner of the complex, where hardly anybody ever went. Once he reached it, he settled on a low wall and lit up. He began thinking about the faculty meeting the following morning. It was into these, at this stage in his career, that he channelled most of his energy. After sitting on the barricades during the 1968 Student Movement, by fifty he'd turned conservative and was now top dog in the art of public speaking. At the moment he was fighting tooth and nail to implement a reform. This would increase his and his colleagues' workload by about thirty per cent, without increasing their salary. He'd spent the weekend writing a paper outlining the draconian measures he was proposing. What, you might wonder, lay behind his reforming zeal? The answer was straightforward. He'd given himself five years to become chancellor. If he could muster support for his proposal, he hoped the university governors would pull the necessary strings.

He was on his second cigarette, coughing and clearing his throat, preparing himself for the fray. He imagined his colleagues in the austere meeting room of Senate House listening to his speech. He could see the faces of his supporters silently egging him on, while his adversaries prayed he'd have a heart attack.

Suddenly he sensed somebody coming up behind him, and before he could react, a huge hammer smashed into the back of his head, knocking him instantly unconscious, after which a sharp object pierced his flesh and zigzagged rapidly down his back.

Robin, who had been watching Kim's every move, turned away as Giovanelli slumped to the ground in a pool of blood. He felt revolted and began to run off, but Kim grabbed his arm, pulling him back and making him finish the job. Armed with a knife and cleavers, Robin reluctantly set about making several cuts in the corpse, according to the instructions Kim had given him earlier. In minutes the job was finished, and the killers quickly pulled some clean clothes, water and a couple of sponges out of a bag. Once they had cleaned themselves up and changed, they strolled casually through the complex, making for the exit.

An hour later, Rinaldo Caprino, a university cleaner, walked quickly down the alley, hoping he could manage a nap before his shift started. He froze as he saw a body lying there. The victim's head was spattered with blood, as were his open jacket and shirt, revealing his chest and stomach. His shoes and brown leather briefcase lay close by, and a couple of cigarettes and a lighter were scattered on the grass. Caprino gingerly approached the corpse and was horrified to realise that it was Professor Mario Giovanelli.

His eyes fixed upon a neat incision running straight through the belly button, besmirched with blood. Caprino scrutinised Giovanelli's palms. There was an incision in each of them, going from the top of the middle finger to the middle of the wrist. The sight of this bloody, battered corpse made his stomach heave, and he was violently sick. For a few seconds he stood staring at his own vomit on the grass. He had to force himself to make a move, and slung his coat over the body.

He raced to the emergency phone in the adjacent quadrangle, and in no time shrieking sirens, accompanied by the sounds of running feet and muffled voices, responded to his call. Seeing his distress, the first paramedic to arrive on the scene wrapped a blanket round him and gave him a tranquilliser. There was nothing to worry about, he reassured Caprino; he'd be all right. Caprino fell unconscious, and didn't remember anything about the murder until he woke up after a very long sleep.

20

I have to goad myself to concentrate on the road ahead, my eyes scanning for signs saying, 'Cortona'. I just have to get back to Florence and get to bed. The heavy lunch and the mysterious scene at Angelo's have taken their toll. A string of disconnected images races through my mind: wriggling eels; a bottle of wine; a little black object worth a small fortune; a man with an arrogant smile on his face, most probably Mario Giovanelli; and Angelo's own gentle smile.

My eyelids are closing and my head moving slowly forward when a sharp nudge in my side jolts me awake. Gabriele has seen me nodding off, and saves us from what might have been a nasty accident. "Come on, Maria, let's talk." He sounds shaken after the near miss we've just had. "You decide the subject and I'll keep you awake. We can't have you snoring behind the wheel at this time of night. You've absolutely got to get us back to Florence."

"Dante Alighieri," I murmur sleepily.

"That's a massive subject. Can't you be more precise?"

"Okay, here goes. Who was he and why is he still so big for so many Italians? And why is Caterina obsessed with him?"

To my left, I notice the occasional car tearing by; to my right, an occasional glimmer from a nearby village illuminates the dark fields. A thought haunts me. I have got to stay awake and keep the conversation going.

"The paintings of him I've seen so far have certainly helped me to visualise the man, even if I don't feel like I really know much about him." In my mind's eye, I can see Caterina's portrait of Dante in her private gallery, and Giotto's fresco in the Bargello Chapel. "I suppose it's the training I've had as a stage director; I need to be able to visualise things. When you think of Shakespeare, there's that painting we find reproduced everywhere in Britain: the Chandos portrait. In schoolbooks, hanging in tourist information offices, in reproductions – it's all over the place. In truth, William doesn't look like much to write home about. He's just passable: his hairline's receding; his eyes are medium-sized and dark. He's dressed soberly, with the exception of a fancy lace collar and a single earring. Still, once you've seen that picture, you feel he could be any dude you might meet at your local pub and have a drink with."

Gabriele smiles, and a look on his face tells me, *Watch out. You're losing the plot.* Then he points to the town of Cortona, faintly visible, on the nearby hilltop and asks how I rate the fresco of Dante in the Bargello Chapel.

"It was worth a visit. He looked stoical, I'd say. Still, tell me what you think. You're the art specialist."

"If you ask me, in that fresco he looks more defiant than stoical. He's gaunt; the strain of his political role has taken its toll. At the same time, if you look close, there's a hint of a smile touching his lips. Didn't you notice? Still, like all geniuses, he leaves you with the feeling that you'll never fathom him, not completely. He remains mysterious, enveloped in darkness."

"Like you, Gabriele," I blurt out, surprising myself.

"Really?" Out of the corner of my eye, I catch his eyes, curious and challenging. "So, I'm in your 'mysterious genius' category, am I?"

"Don't know about the genius, but certainly the mysterious."
I laugh, popping some chewing gum into my mouth. "Here! Have
some; chewing might help keep us awake."

It occurs to me that I hardly know the man sitting beside me.
I know nothing about his family or background, his wider circle
of friends and acquaintances, except for Peter, Caterina, Alfonso
and Angelo. And here we are working together on something as
sensitive as a murder inquiry. I run over his way of talking and
behaving, his tics and mannerisms. Right now, one hand is rapidly
tapping his knee, while the fingers of the other grip a cigarette.
It must be his third since we left Angelo's. He's obviously feeling
anxious but, I tell myself, that's hardly incriminating behaviour.

"What would you like to know about me?"

"Everything! The truth is, the pair of us have been thrown
together by this investigation."

"You did the throwing, Maria," Gabriele retorts, a hint of
recrimination in his voice.

"Sorry, but there was really no time to think about it. I felt –
and I stand by this – that I had to act quick. But it means we're
not a strong team."

Gabriele's lips tighten. He looks offended, and I try to explain
what I mean.

"You see, I'm feeling isolated and unsure. It may sound clichéd,
but sometimes it feels like I'm walking on quicksand."

"Are you saying you want to call it a day?" His tone turns
aggressive. "Are you backtracking; do you now want to leave the
inquiry to the police?"

"I'm simply telling you what I'm feeling. Take the tomb
thieves. I now understand you and Peter better. I mean, your way
of living in between."

"In between what?" he asks, bewildered.

I try to spell it out. "It strikes me that you lead a double life
in which legality and illegality overlap. One day you're a teacher,
attending a faculty meeting or teaching a fine arts class; the next,

you're doing a business deal with a buyer in New York for a Warhol, say, or you ring a dealer in South America about selling him a choice item of Etruscan antiquity. Am I right?"

"Very perceptive, Maria. Especially for somebody who claims she doesn't know me well." Gabriele lights up again, eyeing me warily, as if anticipating that there might be more questions in the pipeline.

The sparring match has woken me up, and I press my foot down hard on the accelerator, making the car take a massive leap forward. A split second later Gabriele's hand grips my arm, his fingers pulling at my sleeve. He's imploring me to slow down, and only when I ease my foot off the pedal does he stop tugging. Out of the corner of my eye I catch him leaning back in his seat and relaxing, and I decide to seize this opportunity to shift the conversation back to Dante.

"You remember how I mentioned Dante's *Inferno* and mayhem when you asked me if I'd ever heard of him? Tell me more about the *Inferno*, in a nutshell."

Gabriele takes a last drag on his cigarette before stubbing it out. "That's a tall order, Maria: the *Inferno* 'in a nutshell'. Anyway, it is the first instalment of the *Divine Comedy*; later Dante wrote *Purgatory* and *Paradise*. In the *Inferno* he invites his readers to take a walk through Hell. The imagery is so graphic that most Italians remember it even if they can't always recall the exact details of the story. This is reinforced by the masses of paintings everywhere in Italy that represent Dante's *Inferno*. You'll find several illustrated editions of the book in Peter's library. It's worth having a look at them! Over the centuries this masterpiece has inspired a raft of artists, who have interpreted it in all sorts of ways."

"You're rambling. Stick to the point."

"Okay, in a nutshell, Lady Never-Give-Up," he quips playfully, "if for instance you say, 'Canto 3 of the *Inferno*' – 'canto' is like saying 'chapter' in English – your average Italian will shout back, '*Ignavi!*' I suppose you can translate that as 'the Neutrals' or 'the

Apathetic'. They're the folk, according to Dante, who go through life never taking a stance or expressing a strong opinion about anything. Florence is full of them. The leisure centre where I go is throbbing with them."

After thinking about this widespread state of apathy, I reply, "The *Ignavi* or the Neutrals in England would probably say something like, 'Things aren't so bad.'"

"That just about sums them up. A bomb could go off and they'd plunge into the pool, whining, 'It's not so bad.' Italy can swing in different political directions, and they'll still be mumbling, 'Things aren't so bad.'"

"If I've understood you right, what Dante claims is still relevant today. Perhaps by now the *Ignavi* are a Europe-wide phenomenon."

Gabriel listens carefully and then corrects my pronunciation. "Try saying the 'gn' again. *Ignavi*. I know it's difficult. You have to rub your tongue against the back of your palate if you want to say it properly.

"What's more, it's not just the Florentines. From north to south this country is awash with people suffering from the same chronic apathy. Every night they indulge in a nauseating diet of television sleaze – quiz shows, chat shows, reality shows, game shows full of nauseating platitudes.

"In the *Inferno* Dante sets out to tackle the degenerate society of his day. For each crime, he invents what he calls a *contrappasso*, or an eternal punishment. In the case of the *Ignavi*, he assigns them a place at the gates of Hell, in eternal pursuit of an elusive banner, symbolising their search for ever-shifting self-interest. At the same time, they are stung by wasps and giant hornets; a putrid mix of blood, tears and pus, streaming from their naked bodies—"

Gabriele breaks off in mid-sentence. His mobile is ringing. As he takes in what the caller is saying, his face turns grave. Hearing him pronounce a succession of yeses and nos, steadily more seriously, I have a gut feeling that something terrible has happened, and pull into the next lay-by.

He turns to me; his face pale, his eyes distraught. The chancellor's assistant has just informed him that an emergency meeting has been scheduled for 9am the following day. There's been a murder on college premises, and it's one of Gabriele's colleagues. The following morning he has to report immediately to the university.

21

DI Alfio Romagnoli and DS Gianni Celentano had just been assigned a second murder case; the victim, Professor Mario Giovanelli.

Twenty years ago Romagnoli had managed to secure a transfer to Florence from his home in Palermo. He had been adamant that he would work in a city in central Italy, where the Mafia would hopefully not play such an important role in daily life. For many years, his move had paid off. Unlike some of his colleagues, he'd been lucky. He hadn't been assigned to any of the more challenging cases, such as that of the Monster of Florence. Now, with two murder investigations on his desk, he was beginning to feel like his luck had run out. While Peter Farrell's murder hadn't attracted as much media attention as he'd hoped, the papers and television were soon buzzing with the news of the murder of this second university lecturer. The fact that Giovanelli had been killed on college premises likewise provided some tasty pickings for the journalists. They went to great lengths to describe the spot where the murder had been committed, and spiced this up with any university gossip they could find. Romagnoli suspected that the two murders had been carried out by the same person, and kept returning to the idea that the culprit would probably strike again.

Once he and Celentano had gone through the usual procedure at the crime scene, they wasted no time in calling on Giovanelli's widow. When the doorbell rang, Ilde Giovanelli had flour all over her hands. Even if it was ten in the evening she was still hard at work. She'd been making fresh tagliatelle, with the help of her cook; a predictably buxom woman dressed in navy-blue overalls and an immaculate white apron. Before setting off for the faculty in the late afternoon, Mario Giovanelli had told her he would be back late, since he was meeting a colleague for a drink, and had given her instructions to start preparing a lavish supper for the following evening. He'd invited his closest allies, and over supper he meant to detail his plan of action for the coming months.

Ilde had never worked outside the home. After graduating with a first-class law degree, she'd devoted herself to her husband and his career. Three children had come along, but even they had taken a back seat compared to Mario. Luckily her gamble had paid off and the family enjoyed a privileged lifestyle, secured by his sizeable salary and the extra money that poured in occasionally. This money, always in cash, came from people he referred to as his 'fellow collectors', about whom she preferred not to know too much. His was a man's world, and she had chosen to stay in the quiet of her home. Whenever she felt bored – and this happened fairly regularly – she organised a coffee morning, or a visit to an exhibition with some women friends. Whenever things got really dull, she took herself off on a shopping spree. Florence boasts some of the finest upmarket boutiques in Italy, and Ilde was a regular customer. Life had jogged on pleasantly enough until that evening.

The doorbell was ringing, and she came as near as she ever did to swearing. Thinking that it was her husband, she yelled the old-fashioned oath "Capperi!" ('Capers!') You really are late!"

Unhooking the small chain securing the door, she pulled it ajar and saw a man standing outside, saying that he needed a word with her. This unexpected intrusion made her jittery, and she ran her fingers through her hair, leaving a myriad of floury specks behind. Then a hand proffering a police badge appeared through the gap in the door. Realising she had no option but to open up, she snapped, "You'll have to be quick, though; I'm making some fresh pasta."

Romagnoli and Celentano walked into the hallway, and the former got straight to the point. "Good evening, we're looking for Ilde Giovanelli? Is she in?"

"It's me. No, I'm not the cook. Appearances can be deceptive." Ilde replied, rubbing the flour off her hands. "What did you want?"

"I'm afraid it's serious, Signora. It's your..."

"My husband? One of my children? Is he... is she... are they all right?"

The cook crept into the room and weighed up the police inspector who was talking to her employer.

"I'm afraid it's your husband, Signora. It happened late this afternoon, straight after his lecture."

"A heart attack? Tell me!" Ilde sank onto the divan.

"Somebody attacked him," the inspector said. "When the paramedics got to him he was already dead. I am so very sorry."

The cook ran to her grief-stricken employer and, for the first time in twenty years' service, gave her a hug. Ilde did not reciprocate, but slumped deeper into the cushions. Her head bent, she stared at the large emerald on the gold ring on her finger; a present from her husband. A client had apparently paid a fabulous sum for something Mario had done him. In that moment Ilde forced herself to consider a question she'd never dared ask before: how had Mario come by the extra cash? It had worried her in the past, but the spoils had been too tempting and she'd blotted out her suspicions. In her present state of confusion and despair, she could see some of the unnamed characters who'd drifted in and out of Mario's life and hers. Had one of them murdered him?

Romagnoli cut into her thoughts, inquiring whether her husband had had any enemies. Ilde started murmuring under her breath before she managed to reply. Then she heard herself saying offhandedly, in words that took even her by surprise, "The usual backbiting of university life… Faculty feuds, that sort of thing. University tutors can sometimes point daggers at each other's throats – metaphorically speaking, of course." She bit her tongue, suspecting that she might have overstepped the mark. "At fifty, Mario, my husband, was very ambitious and on the way up." She paused unable to stop sobbing. "So naturally, he made an enemy or two. No, I wouldn't suspect any of his colleagues. No, Officer; they attack each other with words, not with daggers. They are decent people. I'm sorry, but I need to rest."

As the front door closed behind the detectives, Ilde recalled the terrible wrangling twenty years earlier when Mario had been trying for a post at one of Florence's prestigious private colleges. One colleague, whose name she didn't know, had, for reasons Mario had never explained, done his level best to turn the faculty against him. Her husband had suffered the pangs of Hell – he'd started smoking and had never kicked the habit since.

Soon after, equally mysteriously, he'd come up trumps and been appointed to the position he so wanted.

22

Back in the hotel reception, Signora Franca throws me a worried look, asking if I am feeling all right; I look so pale. I tell her it's been a long, eventful day, and in response she whips out a dish of tiny sweets and a soft drink from behind the desk. She is remarkably kind, and for the umpteenth time, I thank my lucky stars that I stumbled upon this hotel.

Once in my room, I collapse on the bed. I need to relax, so I listen to Sting's 'Fragile' on my player. The news of this second murder has left me deeply disturbed. As I sing quietly along to the music, the lyrics about our fragility chime perfectly with my sense of unease and uncertainty.

I doze off, but at three in the morning, I suddenly find myself wide awake. Try as I might, I can't get back to sleep, so I jot down some thoughts in my notebook about yesterday's events: my visit to the lake, Angelo's skill as he cleaned and gutted the fish, and his tip-off concerning Mario Giovanelli.

I force myself to consider what my next move should be. Gabriele and I will have to call on Giovanelli very soon. I'll ask

Gabriele to give him a ring and arrange an appointment. We'll have to invent an excuse, though. We could perhaps say that I am a journalist over from the UK to write an article and do some interviews on university life in Italy and, given Giovanelli's key position in the faculty, I'd like to interview him.

I have just put my pen down and am nodding off when the phone rings. It is DS Celentano. He needs to speak to me. "At this time of the night?" I ask, looking at my watch. "Don't you realise it's just gone 4am?"

"It's urgent, I'm afraid. I'll be at your hotel in fifteen minutes. Can you come down and open the door?"

I listen to the song again, and the line, saying that nothing comes of violence, sends a chill racing through my body. I start pulling some clothes on. I wonder if Celentano is coming to tell me about the murder, and, if so, why it is so urgent that I know about it right now?

I open the main door of the hotel and see Gianni waiting on the pavement. His expression instantly conveys how serious the situation is. Whispering to him that we must be careful not to wake the proprietors, I motion him inside, inviting him to sit down on one of the divans. He is soon outlining what has just happened.

"I'm sorry, but a second professor from Peter's former university was murdered late yesterday afternoon. His name was Mario Giovanelli, and he was a specialist in the Etruscans."

My heart sinks the minute I hear that name, and I can feel my stomach tightening. Fortunately, Celentano does not seem to notice my reaction and goes on.

"We've already spoken to his widow, who, as you can imagine, is devastated. I suppose you are wondering why I am here. News of the murder will be in all the papers and on television tomorrow morning, so I thought I'd better let you know before that happens. And, even more important, you must be careful. You see—"

I pull him up short and say, very slowly, trying to get a grip on my racing thoughts, "Thanks for coming here at this unearthly hour. In fact, I already knew there had been a murder at the university. Gabriele Foschi told me, but he didn't know who the victim was."

I am debating whether I should tell Celentano what Angelo said about Giovanelli's links with the tomb thieves when he adds, "As there are two victims connected with the same university, it can't be ruled out that we are dealing with a double murder. The person or persons who killed your uncle may have killed for a second time. I suggest you take a few precautions, Ms Farrell. Don't go out alone at night, and in the daytime make sure you let somebody know where you are going and who you are meeting. Feel free to phone me, or one of my colleagues, at any time. Here's my mobile number. If you haven't got a mobile, you should get yourself one."

We sit in silence for a few seconds, his gaze holding mine. Up to now I hadn't realised just how dedicated he is to his work. I've misjudged him, and feel immensely grateful for his concern. Perhaps I should make a clean breast of things and tell him about my decision to investigate Peter's murder. On second thoughts, I'd better not; not just now. He looks exhausted, and I venture, "You're looking tired, Gianni. May I call you Gianni?"

He nods his consent, throwing me another long look. "But only in private, remember."

I nod back. "Isn't it time you called it a day and got some sleep?"

"No way; I've got to get back to the crime scene. There's still plenty going on there."

And with a wave, he goes off into the night.

23

I'm enjoying breakfast in the hotel dining room, and reading about the murder in the morning paper. In the kitchen, I can hear Signora Franca, Signor Carlo and their eldest son, Marco, discussing it. Franca's voice has an unusual tremor that conveys her fear, while Carlo mutters something about what Florence is coming to and how something so awful could have happened in broad daylight on university premises. I imagine similar conversations going on all over the city as it dawns on the locals that there's a murderer or murderers in their midst.

After Gianni left last night, I returned to my room and lay awake in the dark, my head throbbing, with the mounting fear that the murderer might indeed strike again; Giovanelli's death has left me unsure what my next move should be. I want to meet his widow, but it seems only right to give her a chance to get through the agony of the coming days.

I decide to turn the spotlight back on Peter and make a thorough search of his office. By eight o'clock I have finished breakfast and got my things together, and am heading off for his flat.

The office at the far end of the flat, like the sitting room, has two French windows, making it incredibly light. On the balconies, the primroses and violets which greeted me when I first arrived are dead; a reminder that it is late spring.

I settle down at the cherrywood desk in the centre of the room. The high-backed chair, complete with a soft red velvet cushion, feels comfy. On the desk, a black leather-bound diary lies open at the page for the 31st March, two days before Peter's death. *The 1st April and his birthday*, I think grimly, reading the entry in his neat handwriting:

Very soon, another birthday and another April Fools' Day. Now for some fun! I've ordered a giant chocolate fish for G. from our favourite cake shop. He'll love it, or at least I hope he will. And there's a surprise for him! I've asked them to hide a gold chain in one of the seven little fishes inside the big fish. A very fishy fish for my love.

Compared to my father, Peter must have gone through life with a smile on his face. While Dad took life seriously, even morosely at times, Peter evidently loved a practical joke. I imagine him giving Gabriele the fish, and then waiting, a mischievous grin on his face, for him to find the gold chain.

My gaze falls on a cluster of photos in frames at the back of the desk. There's one of Peter's parents – my grandparents – in their garden picking apples. Peter and Gabriele on deckchairs – in the early '80s, judging by Gabriele's youthful appearance. Peter and Dad, at around ten, armed with nets, fishing rods and baskets, ready to set off on a fishing expedition. They look grumpy, like they've just been scrapping. In another photo the twins are on a platform at what looks like Manchester's Piccadilly Station, which was called London Road Station in the 1940s. They are clutching tiny suitcases, suggesting that this was probably the very day they were evacuated to Scotland. Dad's face is grim, while Peter is smiling, seemingly unaware of the tragedy unfolding around him.

Opening the left-hand desk drawer, I discover several bundles of letters, each tied with a red ribbon. I take them out, thinking that I'll start reading them, and in the process I uncover another black-and-white photo at the bottom of the drawer. This one is of my dad and me. The date scribbled on the back is 1958, so I was three at the time. I look closely at my cheeky smirk, my straggly pigtails and my nursery school uniform. I loved that uniform, and especially the silk tie with its yellow and turquoise stripes, which made me feel a cut above the other kids in our neighbourhood. His cousin Edith must have given this photo to Peter. I wonder why he didn't have it framed like the others? Perhaps he didn't want to see Dad and me together. Then I gaze at the photo for a second time. The man standing next to me, holding my hand, is the spitting image of my father, but looks happier than Dad ever did. What's more, he's dressed in an expensive tailored suit and a smart overcoat and scarf. Dad certainly never had an outfit like that. My eyes remain hooked on the image. The man by my side must be Peter. Until now I believed that Uncle had never set foot in England after graduating from Oxford. What brought him back to Manchester? What went through his mind each time he looked at us together in this snap? I suddenly understand why Peter used to talk to Gabriele and other friends about me. He actually met me when I was small. Did he ever consider picking up the phone or writing me a letter to tell me about our meeting all those years ago?

"Drop it!" I tell myself sharply. "These are things you'll never know."

My eyes roam to a small table with a computer, near the high windows. There are only a few books in the office. Peter kept most of them in his library in the adjacent room, and in a bookcase in the sitting room. One shelf holds his diaries, arranged meticulously in chronological order. The first one is dated 1951, the year he arrived in Italy. The sheer number of them is daunting; one a year from 1951 to 2000.

My mind starts racing. The photo of Peter and me was taken in 1958. I pull down the diary for that year and flick through the entries. On the 2nd September, I find what I am looking for.

My last day in Manchester. How I loved Mam; how I'll miss her. Thank God, the funeral is over. For the entire week, the atmosphere with Edward has been hellish. The only sunshine is Maria, his little daughter. She's a real cracker. I can see myself in her when I was a child. She's so full of fun. I feel so sad to be leaving her and Manchester behind.

My discovery knocks me for six. I look at my watch and realise that it's lunchtime, but this new evidence has taken my appetite away.

I take the lift down and go for a stroll. Wandering aimlessly along Via Alfonso la Marmora and as far as the cathedral, I try my best to remember that one occasion when Peter and I spent time together. Still nothing emerges from the dark abyss of my memory. I return to the flat exhausted and throw myself onto the divan.

I'm sound asleep when the doorbell jolts me awake. It's Gabriele. As he comes in, he stares anxiously at me. "You look strange, like you've just had a terrible nightmare," he mutters, a frown puckering his brow.

"And you're on cloud nine by the look of you," I quip sarcastically, quickly concealing the photo I left on the table and deciding not to tell him what I've found. I nod at the diaries. "I was just thinking I should read these. There may be some important clues here."

Gabriele doesn't listen, and instead fills me in on the details of Giovanelli's murder. I don't let on about my meeting with Celentano, and let him talk.

"I suppose you already know that the victim was a colleague of mine: Mario Giovanelli, the man Angelo advised you to talk to. Anyway, at university the atmosphere is definitely strained. Since the murder, people in uniform have been searching and prodding in every conceivable corner. Yesterday evening, they apparently refused to allow Giovanelli's junior research assistant back into his office, despite the fact that he had left his car and house keys in there while he nipped out for a coffee. And our chancellor, who is usually in full control and known in the faculty for the cheesy grin he's able to turn on in the direst of circumstances, looks thoroughly dejected."

Changing the subject, I volley, "Have you seen the sheer number of these diaries? There's so much stuff in this office. Isn't it better to go through life untidy? If you're a neat freak, as Peter undoubtedly was, you can hoard so much more. Nothing sprawls. I don't know where to begin."

"I think you've done quite enough for today. We both need to switch off for a while," Gabriele says firmly. "Let's go for a drink and forget everything. There's a friend of mine, a gallery owner, just arrived from New York. Doris Gainsborough's a very old friend of Peter's. She, Peter and Caterina got on like a house on fire. I saw Doris yesterday and she's invited us both over."

"I'm not in the mood, sorry. There's so much to do here, and Giovanelli's murder has really shaken me," I reply, opening another diary.

"Maria, put that back on the shelf. It'll only be for a few hours. What's more, you'll get a chance to see one of the most fabulous hotels in Florence."

"Where's she staying?" I ask, curious.

"It's where royalty and the mega-celebrities set up camp when they visit Florence. Doris is used to the very best. Her father was a multimillionaire. Today she owns one of the leading art galleries in New York. Of course, she doesn't need the money; the gallery is a hobby. Anyway, whenever she's in Florence, she expects friends to turn up at six for drinks. She hates drinking alone."

"I'm almost persuaded. Can I wear my new outfit? Will it pass the test on this occasion?" I ask playfully, remembering how Gabriele said that my linen pants and silk blouse were unsuitable for the trip to Angelo's.

"Your new outfit is perfect. I've got a feeling you've been yearning for a touch of glitz since you came to Florence. Am I right? Not the loud, gaudy variety, but pure, untainted glamour. Behind that dogged determination you've shown of late to catch Peter's murderer, I detect a woman who enjoys some fun. Go on, get dressed and I'll be at your hotel at a quarter to six."

Back at my hotel, I take my lilac pants, silk blouse and high heels out of the wardrobe. I shower, wash and blow-dry my hair. A couple of squirts of my favourite perfume and a touch of glittery grey eyeshadow followed by some lip gloss and I'm done. I peep into the long mirror, looking at my reflection. My little black dress can certainly stay in my case until I'm back in Manchester.

As I breeze through reception, Signor Carlo cries, "Wow! *Buona serata*, Maria. Have a lovely evening."

24

Gabriele and I climb the steps leading to the luxury hotel reception. It's two minutes to six and my friend checks his watch anxiously. Doris, he whispers, is a stickler for punctuality.

The hotel is stunning. A white marble statue in a fountain towers in the entrance hall. It's a sea god, surrounded by fish frolicking in the water. Two are soaring upwards; another, its face resting on the rim of the fountain, appears to be grinning at us as we walk by. In all directions, water jets spray from the fishes' mouths, conjuring up a delightful spectacle. This hotel, Gabriele informs me, was originally a Renaissance palace; and of course, the exquisite oriental carpets, antique furniture and frescoed hall ceiling hail from that time.

A uniformed steward accompanies us to Doris's exclusive suite, leading the way through a spacious sitting room, where some guests are lounging near a magnificent fireplace. Here the decor is a carefully arranged blend of old and new: antique furniture and prints of historic Florence jostle with brightly coloured abstract acrylic paintings reminiscent of Rothko's work.

Taking the lift to the fifth floor, we exit onto a private landing leading to Doris's secluded suite. The minute the lift door opens, a woman's voice can be heard. "At long last you're here, Gabri. It's late. How dare you? Don't you realise it's four minutes past six?"

We find ourselves in a sitting room with an adjacent patio, where Doris is seated, waving a newspaper at us as we approach. The view from the patio of the white-and-grey marble facade of Santa Croce strikes me as a stunning picture-postcard shot. Doris is small and slim, around seventy, with bright red hair and lashings of red lipstick. Her sapphire-blue silk dress, jacket and matching slingback shoes, diamond necklace and ring, shout dollars and loads of them. From her opening line, her lively banter cheers me up.

"Gabri, I've not seen you in ages! Thank God, somebody's turned up this evening. I was beginning to think I'd have to break my rule and drink this bottle all on my own." She gestures dismissively towards a bottle of champagne on ice, surrounded by dishes of olives, canapés and nibbles. "How's life treating you, ugly face?"

"Hi, Doris, nice to see you! You're looking terrible!" Gabriele gushes, rushing over to kiss her. "This, as I told you, is Maria; Peter's niece."

A smile spreads over Doris's face, turning her many wrinkles into furrows. "Come on, sit down, the pair of you. Nice to meet you, Maria. At last I can have a drink. Gabriele, pour us a glass. Is champagne okay? It's no use waiting for the waiter. The one they've assigned me moves like a slug. It took him an hour to lay the table. Gabriele has told me all about you, my dear."

I nod, wondering what exactly he has told her.

Doris wags a finger at him. "Isn't he the ugliest guy you ever set eyes on, Maria? Nothing's right with him, eh? Big nose, blackheads, uneven teeth and the first signs of a midlife paunch. Only visible to a highly trained eye like mine, of course."

For a moment I scrutinise Gabriele, who has sat down next to Doris. As usual he is perfectly groomed, and he's not got an ounce of surplus fat on him. I decide I'll invent a role for myself in their game, and mime extreme revulsion.

Seeing my antics, Doris enthuses, "Maria! I can see you're a professional. There's no way we can compete with you."

"Tell Maria about your latest Botox job," Gabriele shouts, keeping the banter going. "I heard it cost you a million bucks, Doris. You're looking ninety-one, not a day older – congratulations, darling. That must be quite some treatment you've had.

"She doesn't look bad for seventy, does she?" he whispers as soon as Doris has taken herself off to find an ashtray.

"It's worse than America in this country," Doris declares, coming back with a large ashtray half hidden under her jacket. "Even here they've caught the anti-smoking bug. What's the owner thinking of? I'll kill him. Doesn't he realise smoking helps me chill?"

Seeing my bewilderment, she explains, her voice turning serious, "I've a love-hate relationship with Italy. I was only five when I first sailed here with my parents, two brothers and our nanny. We came on one of those transatlantic liners. Very grand! And with Florence, it was love at first sight. I still adore the place, but there are some things about it that drive me crazy."

Producing the ashtray, she thumps it onto the table and lights a cigar. Her voice has grown subdued and a slight twitch pulsates under her left eye. "Sorry, Maria, you must think I'm mad but if I don't let off steam, I explode. It's a law of physics, or so they tell me. You see, the smaller you are – and look at me, I really am a dwarf – the louder the explosion. Inside a tiny body, the air is more compressed. Gabri knows all about it."

"A nuclear missile on the warpath against the entire universe, that's Doris," Gabriele remarks sardonically.

"And too decrepit and advanced in years to change in the slightest, you jerk."

She gives him a hug, chuckling, before returning to me. "I do love him, Maria. But seriously, I'm so deeply sorry about Peter; he was a very dear friend. We met in the early '60s, the first time he and Caterina visited New York. We clicked immediately, even if we were like chalk and cheese. I loved his English accent, his English good manners. And he loved New York and the artists I introduced him to. The three of us used to hang out in the café at the Museum of Modern Art, smoking cigars. You'd never get away with that today. He was a great talker, but very opinionated in those days. We rowed like cat and dog. Thank God he mellowed with age.

"At the time, Andy Warhol was his idol. I was never a big Warhol fan myself. Nor was Caterina. We actually ganged up on Peter from time to time. And once, I've just got to tell you, I slapped his face and yelled, 'Andy's no artist. His art's fake.'

"Peter didn't speak to me for a year after that. And when he did call, it was to tell me he'd managed to buy himself a Warhol. 'I've bought one, Doris. So there! And just listen to my forecast: you're going to live to regret your "down Andy" campaign.' He sounded like a spoilt child taunting his best school pal. Give him his due, though, he managed to score a Warhol before their prices hit the roof. He must have made a tidy few dollars on that deal."

I note the admiration in her tone. Here is one dealer in awe of another's intuition.

Her eyes are riveted on me again. "You know the painting I'm talking about? It's next to the Picasso in his sitting room. But why am I rambling on like this? I wanted to show you this. It's really shocking." She hands Gabriele the paper that's been lying on the table in front of her. "Even though I guess you've already seen it. It's terrible – a colleague of yours murdered, Gabri."

Gabriele tells her that we already know, and that he was summoned to the college for an emergency meeting the morning after it happened. Then he asks her, "Did Peter ever mention Mario Giovanelli to you?"

"I really can't remember. My memory's not what it used to be…" Doris replies, sidestepping the question and finishing mid-sentence.

Still Gabriele insists. "You should know, Doris, that Maria and I are working together to try and find Peter's killer. His murder might well be linked to Giovanelli's. Maria knows about the tomb thieves and can be trusted to keep quiet. You can talk openly about anything you think might be of help in our inquiry."

Doris is taken aback, and listens carefully. I can hear her humming softly to herself before she speaks. "On the phone one day, just before he died, Peter mentioned some threatening letters he'd received, telling him to quit dealing in Etruscan antiquities. And listen carefully – he told me he suspected Mario Giovanelli, a former colleague, who was also a dealer."

Seeing Doris's reluctance to continue, Gabriele encourages her to go on.

"And there's something else, closer to home. I had a spot of trouble myself earlier this year. I was being followed. When I went home in the evening or left my apartment to take a taxi, I sensed there was somebody waiting out there on the street. It was scary. I live alone, you see, except for my housekeeper, who finishes at eight in the evening. Anyway, one night somebody took a potshot at the car I was travelling home in. The bullet just missed the rear window where I was sitting. Just a fraction to the left and that would have been me finished. There and then my son hired a private investigator, one of the best in New York. I don't know exactly what the man did, nor do I want to, but he put a stop to whoever it was. My guess is that an American dealer in Etruscan antiquities is at the bottom of this. Whoever it is wants to get his or her hands on the entire market in Umbria, Lazio and Southern Tuscany. This," she brandishes the newspaper, "together with Peter's murder, means the person is prepared to kill."

Doris's revelation comes as a surprise. Evidently, she too is involved in the *tombaroli* business. She has also confirmed my suspicion that there is a distinct possibility that the two murders are related and connected to the tomb thieves.

At that moment a waiter appears, carrying a tray with a letter on it that he hands to Doris. She reads it slowly, her face turning ashen. "Jesus! Listen to this. 'Ms Gainsborough, we wish to inform you that Mario Giovanelli was a medium-sized fish in a rather big lake. He has been disposed of, but you should know we intend to continue our operation. Our advice: be careful how and where you tread.'"

I shut my eyes, hoping to block out the thoughts overwhelming me. If the writer of this letter is the murderer, he or she is acquainted with Peter's circle of close friends.

A second later, a hand grabs mine. It is Doris's, her defiant eyes telling me to pull myself together. "Come on, Maria, snap out of it. And here, have another drink. I survived World War II, remember, so the likes of these rascals don't scare me. Chin up and prepare for action and retaliation."

Having issued her instructions, she very deliberately folds the letter and pushes it back into her bag, along with the newspaper. Lighting another cigar, she sounds calm and in control. "Now, let's change the subject. Gabriele, have you had anything interesting in recently? I've a client in New York who has been hounding me for weeks for something special. Money's no object. The guy's an Italo-American heart surgeon whose only daughter is getting married. He's already purchased a penthouse for the girl in Manhattan, but now comes the difficult part. He needs to furnish the place before the wedding next month. He's seen an Etruscan jug I sold to his best friend and wants something similar, but even bigger."

Suddenly it all makes sense. Etruscan antiquities – vases, burial urns, mugs, jewellery – are like shots of adrenaline for Doris and Gabriele. They are addicted, and will not stop dealing until someone stops them. Sadly, it looks like there is somebody out there who has every intention of doing just that.

We are on our second bottle of champagne when Caterina shows up, sporting an emerald-green tunic and flowing trousers, an armlet with dangling crystals, and a sequinned bag slung over her arm. She's just bought this Indian outfit, she gaily reveals, to celebrate Doris's return to Florence. Doris doesn't seem to give a hoot about her friend's new outfit, but pulls out the threatening letter, pushing it into Caterina's hand. Sitting beside her, Caterina pores over it. Once finished, she says firmly, "Get yourself a bodyguard, and do it right now. That's my advice."

On hearing this, Doris lets rip. "That will be my second in six months, *mia cara*!" ('My dear'.)

It's now Caterina's turn to leave us dumbfounded. Sipping her drink, she begins by asking Gabriele, "I suppose you've told Doris about Giovanelli's murder?"

"We didn't need to," he replies, "she had already seen it in the paper."

"But they didn't say how he was murdered."

"No, of course not!" Gabriele replies, "the police only ever disclose such details when the trial begins."

For a second, Caterina pauses, before pulling a letter out of her own bag. "An anonymous caller brought this to my house a few hours ago. The details it contains about Giovanelli's murder are shocking. The killer mangled the body, making a neat slit from the chin right down the body. He then made neat incisions in the victim's palms. Yes, it's truly terrible – the body was gaping wide open. Only a skilled butcher or a surgeon could have inflicted these injuries."

These horrendous details make me shudder, and I just sit there, lamely holding my glass of wine.

But the next minute, Caterina's voice is jubilant. "Well, it's Dante, pure Dante!"

"What the heck do you mean?" Gabriele holds his friend's gaze.

"You evidently weren't paying attention, Gabri. The injuries described here tally almost perfectly with one of the punishments Dante describes in the *Inferno*." Caterina sounds euphoric.

Gabriele is silent, deep in thought, before thumping his glass on the table. "Blast! Why didn't I get there first?"

"You should pay more attention to what I tell you," Caterina gloats.

Doris, who's been silent for a while, enters the fray. "Why bring Dante into this, Caterina? He died centuries ago, and the person who killed Peter and probably Giovanelli is still around."

"That makes what I'm thinking even scarier," Caterina confides. "Giovanelli's murder very nearly matches the punishment Dante advocated for the Sowers of Discord. You look puzzled, Maria. According to Dante, they are the sinners who divide people in times of war. They split entire families and households apart. As a punishment, their bodies are cut into two perfectly symmetrical parts."

"Canto 28," Gabriele chimes despondently.

"That's right, Gabri. You've woken up at last. I don't know enough, though, about Giovanelli's character to say whether he fits that bill."

"Absolutely," Gabriele replies bitterly. "Over the past year he managed to divide the faculty over a crazy scheme he dreamt up. Peter was long out of it, of course, but I found myself on the front line, fighting Giovanelli tooth and nail. The reform, as he euphemistically called it, would have meant more work for my colleagues and me, with no extra pay."

"It all seems a bit far-fetched to me, but you both sound convinced, so go for it," Doris mutters. "Still, I can't see why you're looking so depressed, Caterina."

"I'm just so very sorry Dante's not around. He'd have been able to help Maria with her investigation. He was like a sniffer dog, capable of spotting sinners and evildoers a mile off."

As Caterina pours her third glass of champagne, I catch Gabriele winking at me, warning me to expect more Dante.

"If Dante had been born in 1965 instead of 1265, he'd have been a leading figure in our government," she remarks tipsily. "He had real ambition, you see. By the age of thirty he was already a Prior and a powerful man in Florentine politics. You saw him in the Giotto fresco, Maria. Today he'd have got stuck in and tackled the criminality in this country. I am absolutely certain of it." Seeing Gabriele shaking his head cynically, she snaps, "Well, that's what I think, Gabri."

"For once I agree with you, Caterina – I mean, about what Dante wanted to do." Now it's Gabriele's turn to look dejected. "But don't forget what happened to him. In 1302 Pope Boniface and his cronies sent him into exile on charges of conspiracy, corruption and embezzlement. Absolute baloney! Today they'd have arranged for him to crash his car in dodgy circumstances, or something of the sort, wouldn't they?"

"Perhaps, but this doesn't detract from his absolute honesty," Caterina replies firmly. "Dante loathed the greed and corruption he saw everywhere. Florentines were making piles of money, thanks to the wool trade and banking. The city was expanding rapidly, and the nouveau riche demanded new types of housing, higher and more luxurious than ever before. They demanded shops, too, stocked with exquisite clothes, jewellery and furnishings. Dante's fellow citizens were show-offs, flaunting their new-found wealth and power. He hated the sham of it all. You saw him, Maria, in my painting; dressed so simply compared to the popes and bishops in the paintings on either side of him."

"Jesus!" I whisper. "The man had guts. And even in exile he kept on writing about evil and corruption. He refused to be silenced."

Clocking my admiration, Caterina throws me a warm smile. "That's true of his *Inferno*, but in the *Paradise* instalment of the *Divine Comedy* he explored the concept of good. Both good and evil were never far from his mind. However, if present-day society is going to get itself out of its current mess, we need to tackle the corruption and criminality in many areas of life. Take these two murders on our doorstep. One of them was a person very close to us. Peter's loss is still excruciatingly painful."

Calling the waiter to empty Doris's ashtray, Caterina orders a bottle of wine. I can feel her eyes boring into me. "As a newcomer to Italy, it must be difficult for you to understand such things, Maria. Are you following?"

Before I can answer, it is Doris's turn to climb on her high horse, and this time she is galloping. "The waiters here can't even manage the simple task of emptying an ashtray. *Che puzza!* What a smell!" She is yelling and pinching her nostrils against the stench, making it evident that she has completely forgotten that she and her friends are to blame.

Caterina has just rolled another cigarette and is making the cloud already floating above us even thicker. She takes a drag, choosing her words carefully. "Of course, when Mussolini governed the country, we were blessed with a strong, efficient leader. My father used to say that *Il Duce* made things work. Efficient trains and well-serviced roads, things like that."

Gabriele, who's been smoking quietly, hits the ceiling. "Not again! How many times have I heard you say that?! That's enough of your Fascist crap, Caterina. You always, and very conveniently, forget the death squads and castor oil that *Il Duce*, as you so fondly call him, prescribed. And you, Doris, can take yourself back to New York if you don't like the room service round here."

"No, Gabriele, I'm not saying I want Fascism back. Whatever will Maria think of me?" retorts Caterina.

I decide I'd better keep out of their quarrel, but throw Gabriele a warm smile, encouraging him to keep up his attack. I want to understand better how Caterina's mind works.

I needn't have worried; she has no intention of letting the matter drop. "You see, in Italy we really need somebody – on the left or the right, it really doesn't matter what their politics are – to get things back on track."

"You're so naive, Caterina. The truth is, you have never understood a darned thing about politics," Gabriele retorts.

"But I do know a thing or two about Dante's *Inferno*," she volleys, a twinkle in her eye. And on that note, she springs to her feet and heads off home, without saying goodbye to any of us.

I take her departure as a cue to make a move. I am feeling exhausted.

As the taxi drives by the cathedral, I make a note in my book in capital letters. There seem to be two lines emerging in my inquiry. On the one hand, the business of the tomb thieves; on the other, our Florentine man. And one thing is certain: I need to read Dante's *Inferno*.

25

The next morning I do something very Italian before going to Peter's flat to dig out his translations of the *Inferno*. I decide to have breakfast in a bar near my hotel. I drop into the first one I come across which doesn't look too touristy, and by that I mean there are no menu boards in English or any other foreign language on display outside. From the minute I walk through the door, I enjoy a fantastic Italian lesson free of charge. As the locals come in for their espresso or cappuccino, I manage to get the gist of their brief conversations about last night's football match, the rising cost of car insurance, their children's latest school reports, etc. Disappointingly, nobody is talking about the murders, which reminds me that life goes on as normal for ordinary people, even if there might well be a double murderer in their midst.

The apricot jam croissant I've chosen (or *brioche*, as it is called in Italian) turns out to be delicious, and I make a mental note to come to this place more often. I flick through the local and national papers to see if there is any more news about the murders, but there is none, and I am soon telling myself I had better get a move on. I pay up, reluctantly leaving the gossip and banter going on all around me, and head in the direction of Peter's flat.

Once there, I set about searching the library and find a good number of books by and on Dante, spread out over three shelves. One shelf contains the illustrated versions of the *Divine Comedy* that Gabriele mentioned, including a volume illustrated by the French artist Gustave Doré. His sublime landscapes and Michelangelo-style nudes are terrific. I soon come across an English translation of the *Inferno* by Henry Wadsworth Longfellow, annotated in Peter's neat handwriting. Clutching the book, I go through to the sitting room and sprawl on one of the divans, reading the first lines aloud.

Midway upon the journey of our life
I found myself within a forest dark,
For the straightforward pathway had been lost.

The English sounds rather old-fashioned, and I just can't get into it. No fault of Longfellow's, though; the American writer translated Dante more than a century ago in a style that was doubtless fitting the Victorian age. Frustrated, I force myself to make a move. I want to read a translation in more contemporary English; one I can get my teeth into. If Dante is rated the greatest poet in the Italian language, there must be a vibrancy and an urgency in his great masterpiece that I have yet to discover.

I suddenly recall Gabriele mentioning an Irishwoman called Deirdre, who runs a second-hand stall selling English and American books on the road flanking the River Arno. Apparently, Peter was a regular customer. I grab my bag, telling Singh I'll be away for a couple of hours. I want to give her a try.

There's a long line of bookstalls when I reach the Arno, making me wonder whether I'll manage to find Deirdre. I needn't have worried – her bright red hair and pale, freckly skin make her easily recognisable. She is already at work, carrying a pile of books from a nearby van to her stall. The minute I tell her I'm Peter's niece, she stops in her tracks and gives me a hug, saying how much she misses him. She arrived late this morning, she moans, and is suffering the after-effects of a very late night out.

While she keeps toing and froing between the van and the stall, I browse through the books already on display – Shakespeare, Emily Dickinson, Thackeray, Ken Follett. Reading snippets here and there, out of the corner of my eye I notice Deirdre bringing another stack of paperbacks in my direction. Then her mobile rings, prompting her to perch the pile of books on the edge of the stall.

"Saved," I cry, catching a book tumbling from the top of the pile. It is Niccolò Machiavelli's *The Prince*. "Hi there, I might take this one."

Dierdre immediately cuts her conversation short at the prospect of a sale.

"I mean, even if it's not exactly the book I am looking for." Her face falls a mile, so I add, "You may be able to help me."

When I tell her I found Longfellow's translation of Dante's *Inferno* rather dated, she dismisses all Victorian men as fuddy-duddies and heads back to her van. A few minutes later she's back with a nondescript paperback edition. The translator, a friend of Deirdre's and a fellow expat, has self-published. I flick through the well-thumbed pages, with the scribbles of a previous owner in the margins. The translator has rendered Dante's Italian in modern English, giving it a decidedly contemporary flavour. I read the opening lines aloud, with Deirdre whispering, "You should have been an actress, Maria!"

> At midway on my walk through life
> I found myself in a dark wood.
> I had wandered off the right path,
> Far, very far, from the light.
> It's so hard to describe that wood.

It was a rough, unwelcoming wilderness
That makes me tremble even now when I remember it!
The thought is so awful that death is scarcely worse.
But since my topic is the good there,
I'll also describe the other things I found.

This time the more contemporary language carries me into Dante's dark, gloomy wood, and I can identify with his loneliness and distress at finding himself in a place so different from his native Florence. He seems to suggest that he has set out on his journey without knowing exactly where he is and where he will end up. The translation has a pithiness that brings Dante's verse to life; extraordinary when you think that the *Divine Comedy* was written centuries ago. But when exactly? I skim the introduction and discover that the work is dated to about 1307. Dante, though, has set the beginning of the story at Easter in 1300, seven years earlier.

The date hits me like a meteor. The events described in the *Inferno* unfolded seven hundred years before Peter's murder in April 2000. In the Kabbalah, the number seven is deeply significant: as a prime number and therefore impenetrable, and as a key number in an esoteric system. What's more, this is the first year of the new millennium and there have already been several deeply disturbing forecasts. I shudder as an idea hits me. Might Caterina be right about the connection between Dante and the recent murders? At this crucial turning point in history, has somebody decided to unleash Dante's punishments in order to tackle the corruption in Italian society? By 1302 Dante was wandering around the country in exile, making it impossible for him to mete out the retribution he had envisaged to his fellow Florentines. Now somebody in the present – and this thought makes me quake – might have got it into their head to carry out his harsh punishments.

"How much do you want for these two?" I ask Deirdre, as casually as I can, holding out *The Prince* and *Inferno* at arm's length, together with a thousand-lire banknote.

"You must be joking – four thousand lire," comes her curt reply as she takes the books off me and puts them firmly back on the stall.

"You're never going to sell this *Inferno*, you know. How many people in Florence will want to read Dante translated by an unknown author? I'll give you two thousand lire for both books. Go on!"

I try pushing the money into Deirdre's hand, but she brushes it aside. Shaking her head, she says assuredly that there is no shortage of English-speaking tourists and residents who'll jump at the chance.

We've reached a stalemate when a well-dressed man with greying hair and a winning smile butts in. "Go on, Deirdre, let the lady have them," he recommends, wrapping his arm round the shoulders of the beautiful woman by his side. "Take the money. Never look a gift horse in the mouth. Here today, gone tomorrow."

His advice does the trick. Deirdre grabs the notes, shoves them in her pocket, and asks the man to mind her stall for five minutes; she's starving and desperately needs some breakfast. I watch her race along the road and promptly disappear into the first bar she comes to; then I shove the books into my bag, throw the man a grateful look and say goodbye. Absorbed in reading a passage from a book to his companion, he looks up for a second, but makes no reply. I leave them to it. I can't wait to get my nose into Dante.

My journey through Hell lasts several hours. Until now I had the idea that Dante wasn't for me; he was some austere Catholic poet whom only Italians could truly appreciate. Who, after all, in contemporary society, needs Dante's punishments to tackle corruption and evil? Today people in England use expletives like 'Go to Hell!' or 'Go to the Devil!' less frequently than their grandparents and great-grandparents did. Rather, 'Piss off', 'Sling your hook' and 'Get stuffed' resound in pubs and clubs and on high streets. And instead of Hell as a deterrent, we've set up top-security prisons, detention centres, probation orders and ASBOs to deal with evil and criminality. Still, in Dante's Hell I can feel the full blast of these old-fashioned imperatives and what lies behind them.

From page one, I feel the writer grabbing my hand and guiding me through the underworld, where his awesome vision leaves me reeling. In front of the gates of Hell, I come across the Neutrals, who Gabriele has told me always sit on the fence, never making up their minds. At work, even if they disagree with some new management ruling, they'll never have the guts to hand in their resignation, but instead hang on, murmuring that things aren't too bad. I watch them, naked on the misty shores of the River Acheron, chased by swarms of cruel hornets and wasps. After that, Dante invites me to meet all his sinners, each variety accommodated in a specific zone of Hell where they are subjected to a *contrappasso*, or infernal comeuppance, as we would say today. With a shudder, I clock the absolute order the writer has imposed upon each sphere. There isn't a person, or a wisp of hair, out of place.

I feel sure Peter must have revelled in this order, and I long to be able to discuss the work with him. I suddenly feel cheated that we met just once when I was too young to remember. I wonder whether he has been plunged into Dante's Hell, and if so, in which circle he is, and what was his sin? In Canto 6, Dante punishes the gluttons, who are cut up piecemeal and buried in mud. For a moment I think I may have uncovered the motive behind Peter's murder. His overeating and weight problem, his gourmet kitchen stocked with so many delicacies, and his mania for stockpiling supplies in his freezers would seem to assign him to this place in Hell. Then I recall Singh's description of his corpse lying in the chest freezer. Peter's murderer did not sling him into mud or cut him up piecemeal, suggesting that in the killer's mind he was guilty of something else.

By late afternoon I've reached Canto 28, the section Caterina linked to Giovanelli's murder.

You can be certain no barrel, with its staves ripped asunder,
Was cut wider than this sinner torn from chin to fart-hole.
Between his legs, his guts were hanging down,
His innards and heart in full view, like that terrible bag
That turns everything we swallow into shit.

I gasp at these graphic images comparing the sinner's body to a gaping barrel. And the terrible butchery of Giovanelli's body prompts me to ask again who, out of the people I have met so far, could have the know-how to have committed that murder.

If the tomb thieves are involved, it could be Angelo. He displayed notable dexterity with a knife when cleaning and scaling the fish that afternoon on the lake. Or it could be the person who took a potshot at Doris; or, as Doris herself suggested, any number of people keen to gain control of the lion's share of the tomb thieves business. Alternatively, if Dante and his *Inferno* have anything to do with the motive for these crimes, Caterina might be guilty. Not personally – I don't imagine she would be capable of inflicting butchery such as that meted out on Giovanelli – but she might be masterminding the operation and have engaged people to act on her behalf. Her unwavering support of Dante's plan to reform society might have persuaded her to concoct a truly astounding plan to clean up Italy.

26

According to the chief prosecutor heading the two murder investigations, Romagnoli and Celentano were conducting the inquiry "with their usual efficiency". The two detectives had put phone taps on key suspects, carried out bank checks and been through Peter Farrell's address book with a fine-tooth comb, contacting as many of his colleagues, acquaintances, business contacts and friends as possible, many of whom they had called to the station for interviews. They often met with the same person on different occasions in the space of a few days, in the hope that they would catch them out by finding contradictions in their statements. At the end of each day they filed a painstakingly detailed report which they placed on the prosecutor's desk.

Following Mario Giovanelli's murder, they employed an identical procedure to the one adopted for Farrell. In the meanwhile, Celentano continued to visit Maria Farrell, following Romagnoli's instructions. Considering the international nature of many crime rings, the inspector argued, Maria might have made contact with the murderer or murderers from her home in the UK. He also reminded Celentano that Peter had left his niece a considerable fortune. Of the three principal beneficiaries of the will, she stood to gain most.

Although the two detectives had been working together for nearly a decade, they differed in their investigative approaches. Romagnoli tended to be more sceptical regarding human nature, and never let suspects off the hook until the case had been solved. Conversely, once Celentano was convinced a suspect was innocent, he preferred to write them off and focus his attention on the remaining suspects. In this case, however, even though he was convinced that Maria Farrell had nothing to do with the murders – she had come through her interviews with flying colours – he didn't argue with Romagnoli since ongoing investigation meant he was authorised – indeed, encouraged – to continue calling on her. And while he didn't tell his colleague or anybody else, he quite fancied the woman.

27

.

A loud ringing, and I pull the covers over my head in an attempt to shut it out. What on earth is going on? The din persists, telling me that whoever it is is determined to wake me up. Opening my eyes, I see the culprit: the phone on my bedside table. My gaze jumps to the clock. It's 9am, and Dante's *Inferno* is still lying on the bedcover from last night. It's open at the final canto, which tells me that I must have dozed off while reading it.

The ringing shows no sign of letting up, and I pull my arm from under the covers and grab the handset. It's Joanne, her shrill voice betraying her irritation. She's been trying to call me. "Maria, don't tell me you forgot our opening night? You know, your *Hamlet*; our *Hamlet*."

"Well, tell me the score," I mutter, snuggling back down in bed "I'm all ears."

"All ears? Who are you trying to kid? You didn't even ring me last night and you didn't answer the phone either."

I suddenly realise how estranged I feel from everything going on in Manchester. Yesterday was the first night in my theatre of my favourite Shakespearean tragedy, and I didn't even call Joanne to ask how it went. I tell myself that if *Hamlet* means anything to me in my present circumstances, it has got to be related to Prince Hamlet's attempt to avenge his father's murder. Today I can fully identify with his search for the truth, since I am doing my utmost to do something similar for Peter. While I wouldn't contemplate murdering the person or people who killed my uncle, I would be very happy if they found themselves behind bars. But I can't find the words to explain all this to Joanne, so I just say, "Apologies, my dear, I'm just so stressed out with all that's happening here. I really am very sorry not to have been in touch; just tell me how it went. The acting? The crits? The audience's reaction?"

"Well, we didn't get a standing ovation, but the audience seemed to like it. The actors did a good job, and even Jane, who until the dress rehearsal had some problems with her last scene, found a way of making Ophelia's final speech and song very moving. It's been a lot of work, Maria, but I'm satisfied, given the circumstances. There should be quite a few reviews out soon. What's new with you?"

So many things have happened since I got to Florence that once again I'm lost for words. It's impossible to explain over the phone, so I just tell Joanne about Dante. "I've been reading Dante's *Inferno*. It's indescribably dark. Last night I got totally absorbed in one particular passage, so I mustn't have heard the phone ringing. Forgive me."

"I didn't know you were into Dante. That's a surpise." Joanne sounds miffed.

"It's a long story. I'll tell you when I see you." For a second I stare at the *Inferno* again, before shoving it under the covers. I need to forget it, at least for now, and pretend that Dante and his dreadful vision of Hell never existed.

"I mean, why aren't you reading *my* play?" Joanne asks, piqued. "I hope you haven't forgotten that our first reading with the cast is scheduled for next week."

There's a long pause as she waits for my reply. I still haven't told her that I won't be able to make it back to Manchester just yet. I've been putting it off, but now I blurt out, "Joanne, I don't think I'll be back home in the next few days. In fact, I'm certain I can't leave things here for a while yet. I'm in the thick of so many things. Does that make any sense?"

"I suppose it's got to," she says drily. "But you know it's not ideal if I have to direct my own first play."

"Let me have the *Hamlet* reviews as soon as they're out," I say, changing the subject. Then in the next breath I murmur something about an urgent engagement. It's a white lie, but I simply have nothing else I can tell her.

28

Turning the shower on full blast, I stand under the jet of piping hot water, letting the citrus gel pamper my skin. Hot and cold water. Cold and hot. A voice in my head is bawling out instructions: *Enjoy yourself this weekend, come what may!* Caterina has invited Gabriele and me to spend the weekend at her place in the country. The voice warns me that it really won't be a quiet weekend: *Once you're there, try to find out more about Caterina's obsession with Dante, and her gardener Alfonso Guidi. You never know, there might be something significant there.*

I dry myself, vigorously massaging my body with the towel. A quick spray of perfume, a touch of make-up, and I dart to a chest of drawers and pull out some underwear, followed by an orange dress and a matching scarf from the wardrobe. From a box I retrieve a beige bag and shoes; my spoils from a second trip to Anita's boutique. Taking a peep in the mirror, I ask myself what today's score is. Eight out of ten; nearer to nine? What will Gabriele say?

I pelt downstairs and through to reception. Perched on the edge of his seat, my friend is reading a magazine, an unlit cigarette between his fingers. On seeing me, he jumps up, complaining that we're late, and makes a move towards the exit and my waiting car. To my disappointment, he does not even notice my new outfit.

After a shortish drive we are climbing into the hills above Florence, where cottages and villas are dotted here and there, and an occasional farmer works in the fields. We are nearing the village of Fiesole when my companion points to a large detached house. In the garden, a figure is moving about amongst trees laden with white-and-pink cherry blossom; a reminder that May is already here. "That's Mario's house and that's probably Ilde, his wife – I mean widow," Gabriele informs me.

As we draw nearer, I notice that the woman is lumbering around the garden, making the atmosphere feel heavy and sad. On impulse I suggest we pay her a call; a fortnight has elapsed since Giovanelli's murder, so it seems all right to meet her and ask her a few questions.

Just the same, Gabriele is doubtful about the reception we might get. He explains that it will depend on whether Mario mentioned his feud with Peter, or his more recent clash with Gabriele. If he did, she might well send us packing. To avoid upsetting her, it will be best not to tell her I am Peter's niece; rather, I should pose as a university colleague over from Oxford. "So yes, let's give it a go. But best tread carefully," he concludes.

As I park the car in front of the house, Ilde looks up as if rousing herself from a daydream. I watch her quickly fastening the top buttons of her crumpled blouse and pulling her skirt zip round to the side in a last-minute attempt to make herself look presentable. That done, she picks up a wicker basket and carries it to a nearby table, letting some lettuce spill out onto the tabletop. She must be in her late forties, her gaze too distant and grief-stricken to register surprise or anger at the sight of us. The way she shuffles slowly towards us suggests that her husband's murder has knocked her for six.

Once Gabriele has done the introductions and apologised for bursting in on her, he reveals that he has decided to find out all he can about the murder of his two colleagues. He speaks slowly, so I manage to get the gist of what he is saying. As he pronounces his own name and Peter's, describing Uncle as an old friend, Ilde does not react, but when he mentions the police investigation, complaining that they seem to be making little headway, she nods. Then abruptly, Gabriele's tone changes and I get the impression that he is commiserating with Ilde about her husband's death.

There's a silence before she turns to me, holding out her hand to clasp mine. It trembles slightly as she whispers, "I'm pleased to meet you. I hope you are enjoying Florence, Maria."

She is soon motioning us to a wooden bench, where she invites us to sit down. Her voice is barely audible as she explains that she still can't imagine why anyone would have wanted to murder her husband. Each time she says his name, she touches an emerald ring on her finger, twirling it round to hide the enormous gem, as if to remind herself, and perhaps signal to us, how drastically things have changed since Giovanelli's passing.

The chinking of china and the aroma of freshly ground coffee suddenly fill the air. A woman in a blue uniform and a white apron has emerged from the house and is arranging a tray of coffee and biscuits alongside the lettuce already on the table. While we sip our coffee and munch the biscuits, I do my best to engage Ilde in some small talk. "Your garden's really beautiful! And I see you grow your own veg," I say, pointing enthusiastically at the lettuce. "Is it organic?"

In her broken English, Ilde does her best to reply, until Gabriele cuts in, broaching the subject of Etruscan antiquities and the tomb thieves racket. Now she falls silent. Not to be put off, he tells her she can, and must, tell him all she knows if she wants Mario's murderer brought to justice. She needn't be afraid that he'll inform the police; there are loads of people in Italy – like her husband, perhaps – who have connections with the tomb thieves.

Ilde's eyes open wide. When she speaks again, her voice is louder and more assertive. "Yes, there were people who came and went, not to mention cash that dropped out of the blue. But I never asked questions. Ours was a traditional marriage: I took care of the house and the children, and he managed the rest."

Her matter-of-fact tone makes me suspect that she is telling the truth and probably has nothing important to tell us. Feeling deeply sorry for her, since she is looking increasingly distraught, I whisper to Gabriele that we should be going.

However, as we get up to leave, Ilde makes a surprising move. Getting down on her hands and knees, she begins scrabbling under the bench where we've been sitting. To my astonishment, she pulls out a key and goes over to a small garden shed. Having unlocked the door and gone inside, she returns, with a red metal box which she places on the table. Opening the creaky lid, she takes out something wrapped in bubble wrap, which she quickly removes, revealing a black object. About the size of a loaf, it looks remarkably like the thing I saw Gabriele and Angelo haggling over, that afternoon by the lake.

Gabriele takes hold of the object, stroking it. A slight tremor in his voice betrays his emotion and recognition as he asks, "Where did this come from?"

"I don't know exactly. Somebody dropped it off in the late afternoon of the day Mario was murdered. There was nobody at home at the time. The caller left it in the porch with a note saying Mario was expecting it. What do you think it is?"

She's barely finished when Gabriele intervenes, placing the object squarely back on the table and beckoning Ilde to sit down. "Come closer, Signora. And you too, Maria – have a look. This little hut is actually an Etruscan funerary urn. It's very beautiful, and look, it's in excellent condition. The early Etruscans made these replicas of their own houses to act as the final resting place for their ashes. Look, there's even a little door in the side, and these delicate swirls on the roof are meant to suggest smoke puffing from the chimney. At least, that's my theory. We're talking ninth century BC. It's a real treasure!"

Ilde listens carefully, without the slightest reaction. We say goodbye and have nearly reached the car when Gabriele unexpectedly turns back. I hear him telling Ilde she ought to find a safer place for the urn; it is very valuable. As a parting gesture, he pushes his card into her hand, saying that if she decides to sell it, she should get in touch.

Back in the car, he lights up, and I notice his hand is trembling. He's visibly shaken by what we've discovered, and tells me firmly to forget what I have witnessed. I suspect he is furious that Giovanelli did him out of a little gem of Etruscan antiquity. I don't let on that I heard him haggling with Angelo that afternoon at the lake, and instead remind him that we need to find out who delivered the urn to Giovanelli's house. This person might be crucial to our inquiry. Gabriele makes no attempt to answer.

29

Leaving Ilde and the mysterious urn behind, we resume our journey to Caterina's. The meeting with Giovanelli's widow has suggested an intricate web of connections I knew nothing about. Besieged by a scary catalogue of ideas, suppositions and hypotheses, I force myself to concentrate on the bends in the road ahead. It is dead easy to drive around Florence, where the streets are mostly straight and flat, but these country lanes and roads are a nightmare. The experience of meeting Ilde makes me want to forget our murder investigation, at least for the weekend. Her grief felt so excruciatingly tangible, it has got under my skin.

I need to lighten up, and start chatting to Gabriele about the work Singh and I are doing to clear out Peter's flat. "I've decided to stop reading Peter's diaries for the time being. The kitchen's finished and I've managed to sell a lot of stuff or give it away. I'm really pleased you accepted that tea service and the set of Venetian wine glasses. Instead Singh doesn't want anything on the premises; he has nowhere to store it. I'll be shipping some of the small items back to England. At the moment we are concentrating on Peter's bedroom and wardrobes. They're bulging, but, like the rest of the flat, everything's clean and tidy. Singh's turned out to be an angel. He's so practical. I really don't know how I would have managed without him. By the way, I'm looking for somebody who could use Peter's more recent clothes. They even bury Singh, who isn't exactly slim. And after Singh tried them on, I put them on myself and we were creased up laughing. They almost drowned me."

"Oh, did they?" Gabriele chuckles. "Do you enjoy dressing up in men's clothes?"

"In the theatre, we call it cross-dressing. Shakespeare and his company were into it because male actors played both the men's and the women's parts. The church authorities at the time refused to allow women onstage. And it's fascinating that in some plays, the women (who are actually young male actors in disguise) get it into their heads to dress up as men. Take Portia in *The Merchant of Venice*. In that play, as in other comedies, the plot gets quite complicated. The boy actor playing Portia dresses up as a lawyer and changes her name to Balthazar, in order to put Shylock on trial. She then cross-examines Shylock and manages to catch him out on the question of the pound of flesh."

"Is that your Shakespeare lecture finished, Maria? I knew almost all of that. I studied Shakespeare at school, remember," Gabriele remarks scathingly.

"Sorry!" I pull myself up, realising how schoolmarmish I must have sounded. "Still, cast your mind back a good few years. At one time, Peter must have looked like he'd been a prisoner in Auschwitz. There's a wardrobe with clothes that would fit a concentration camp survivor; I tried on a pair of trousers and couldn't for the life of me do up the fly – the waist was so tiny. How many years ago would that have been?"

Gabriele's expression saddens. "He was still very slim when we first met at the end of the 1970s. The weight thing was actually quite recent. He put on a lot about five years ago when high blood pressure forced him to give up smoking. He started overeating and drinking more than he should as a form of compensation, I suppose. The more weight he put on, the less he exercised. And Singh was no help – actually, he was a hindrance. The moment I was away on business, he cooked Peter all the wrong foods. What do you call it? Comfort food?"

"Or solidarity food, seeing that Singh is also overweight. So, no more academic research for Peter?" I quiz, remembering how Uncle graduated from Oxford with a first, then, after a few years in Italy, decided to quit his university job.

"Peter had done his bit for academia. At least, that's what he claimed," Gabriele continues. "He wrote two books on contemporary art, both published by a leading press. Then in his fifties he left his full-time job to devote more time to his research and our art business. However, he still went out to lunch occasionally with colleagues from the old days. A few remained good friends, but he steered clear of others. Giovanelli was in the latter category. Peter called him 'the upstart crow from the south' – referring to Shakespeare, I think."

"Right, except for the southern bit – that must have been Peter's invention. It was actually Robert Greene, a playwright and pamphleteer, who ridiculed Shakespeare. He was Greene by name and green with envy. He hated Will's guts, considering him a hard-nosed young actor from the provinces who had come to London on the make."

"I didn't know that! Peter was just the same. He couldn't stand Giovanelli's arrogance, and swore that he must have been given a leg up by somebody with influence. I remember his words distinctly: 'Otherwise, I'm sure he would never have been offered that post.'"

I've just glimpsed another side to Peter: his hatred of nepotism. Evidently, to his mind, the illegality surrounding the tomb thieves was one thing, but other forms of corruption were far more deplorable.

We've just reached a village with rows of picturesque cottages on either side of the road, each with a neat garden, vegetable patch and olive grove. "Every stick and stone," Gabriele remarks, "belongs to Caterina."

"The jammy sod! The entire village?" I exclaim, incredulous.

"Yes, Maria!"

I recall how Gabriele suggested visiting 'Caterina's little place in the country', and quip, "Isn't her palace in Florence enough for her?"

"No, darling. Look up there, on the hill. That castle's hers, too. Thirteenth century and national heritage. Remember the sketch of the castle on the wine bottle she showed you when we had lunch at her place? Well, what you see up there is the real thing."

Stopping the car, I get out to take a better look, my eyes trawling the battlements. The drawing wasn't a patch on the castle staring back at me. On top of the stark grey walls, two tiny figures are moving along a walkway, their silhouettes appearing and disappearing behind the crenels snaking against the sky.

Gabriele has whipped out some binoculars and is scanning the figures. "It's Caterina and Alfonso," he remarks sardonically, "warts and all."

"Jealous?" I ask, settling back behind the wheel and resuming the steep climb to the castle.

"Not at all!" he chuckles, refusing to be baited. "Just glad I brought these binoculars with me. They were a present from Peter."

Before we reach Caterina's, I think I'd better let Gabriele know about my suspicions. Weighing my words carefully, I confide, "It's Caterina's obsession with Dante that interests me; I mean Dante the political figure and reformer who wished to put society right. You see, I don't think we should rule out... I mean, she might have something to do with the mur—"

Before I can finish, Gabriele blows his top. "You're off your rocker, Maria, if you suspect Caterina. She's had a bee in her bonnet about Dante and the corruption in Italy ever since I met her. You heard me telling her she doesn't understand a thing about politics. She's a moaner and groaner, and that's about all. She's just typical of that lot!"

164

"That lot? You don't sound as if you like them very much."

"Of course not. I am an outsider. I've been adopted, you might say, by Caterina's circle, perhaps because I'm cultivated and fairly well off. As I told you, as a young woman she experienced her share of financial hardship. Then she managed to marry into money, and her late husband poured millions into her properties. Still, coming back to your suspicions, you forget, or are simply unaware, that loads of Italians are fed up with the corruption here."

Refusing to accept that Caterina is necessarily innocent, I outline my theory about why somebody might have decided to mete out Dante's punishments in the year 2000. I explain that it is seven hundred years since 1300, when Dante set his *Divine Comedy*, and that seven is an esoteric number in the Kabbalah.

Hearing this, Gabriele flips again, yelling that he has no time for such crap.

"I admit I've no proof, but what I'm saying is that not everybody goes round claiming Dante as their uncle of long ago and saying that, had he lived today, he would have cleaned up society. When we see her, just pay attention to what she says. And if she gets onto Dante, I'm going to encourage her to talk."

Still seething, Gabriele tells me to make a sharp right, and in no time we're bumping along a dirt track. In the distance, I catch sight of some tall iron gates where the track finishes. The moment I switch off the engine, Gabriele gets out and walks to the left of the gates, fumbling with something set in the wall. A second later he brandishes a loose brick, while pointing at a bell. He presses it jubilantly. The heavy gates are soon creaking open. "Drive in!" he calls.

30

Once through the gates, we find ourselves in extensive parkland. To our immediate left is a swimming pool, and beyond that, a garden. To the right, a car park, where I pull in. Close up, the castle is awesome, its massive walls rising a few metres from where we're standing. I feel an irresistible urge to touch one of the huge granite slabs still in place after hundreds of years. Moving close, I let my fingers run over the rough surface, potted with tiny dents and ancient cavities teeming with insects. Looking up, I catch sight of the dozens of arrow holes in the upper parts of the brickwork; reminders of the Guiccioli family's military past and the battles they fought to defend their terrain.

A tiny door in the castle wall opens, and Alfonso emerges dressed in bright green overalls and a cloth baseball cap. Ignoring me, he gives Gabriele a hug. As they were at Caterina's palace in Florence, the two men are soon in conversation, seemingly oblivious to my presence.

It is a relief when Caterina appears through the same door, wearing old pants and a shapeless top. She comes towards me, her face tense and drawn. In one hand she holds a pair of secateurs, and with the other she flicks a lock of damp hair off her forehead. After a frosty hello, she tells me what is bugging her. "Alfonso has just been trimming those bushes over there. I've been supervising the operation; hence all this sweat and anger." She scowls, mopping the perspiration off her face and neck and pointing to two bushes at the far end of the garden, separated by a marble statue of a naked woman. "Come and take a look for yourself, Maria."

I follow her down a path in the direction of the statue, wondering how she can get herself into such a lather over a couple of bushes.

"This is my Venus, the Goddess of Love," she says fondly, looking up at the enormous figure. "She's a beauty, don't you think? I need order and harmony for my peace of mind. I need them like the air we breathe. Today, though, I'm fuming because I've not quite achieved what I am after."

Glaring in Alfonso's direction, she hollers at him to join us, and he walks over, Gabriele traipsing behind. Without wasting a moment, Caterina shoves the secateurs into the gardener's hand. "Go on, trim this one a little more. I've already told you, Alfonso, I'll settle for nothing less than absolute symmetry."

There is a pause before the gardener firmly replies, "You've got it wrong, Contessa. These two bushes match perfectly."

"You'd try the patience of Job. Look, Maria, at this hodgepodge," Caterina sneers, pronouncing the last word emphatically. "Don't listen to him. He rarely does anything right first time. And even worse, he can't take criticism. Still, I don't give a hoot, do I, Alfonso? I'm always on your back."

By this time Alfonso has had enough. Seeing that his line of firm resistance has failed, he takes to pacing around the lawn, shouting, "*Non ci sto!* I won't stand it!"

Caterina turns back to me, adding scathingly, "Whatever you do, Maria, don't watch him. That's just what he wants. He's attention-seeking. He's just turned sixty, but sometimes he behaves like a six-year-old. To break the deadlock, we need the unbiased professional opinion of a theatre director who has been trained to recognise and create visual beauty. We need your opinion, Maria."

Before I can tell her I'd rather stay out of their argument, a second man walks through the tiny door. He is dressed in a bathrobe, with a towel slung over his shoulders. I realise I've seen him somewhere before. But where? Then it clicks. He's the man who came to my rescue by the Arno, when I was trying to clinch the deal with Deirdre.

If he recognises me, he hides it perfectly. He gives my hand a courteous shake and says teasingly, "If you knew Caterina like I do – I suppose you're Peter's niece? – you'd realise she's been saying the same thing for centuries. She manages to keep her gardens in order, or nearly, but not much else beyond these battlements. The real work is left to people like Alfonso and me. And, to make matters worse, she's got the most terrible temper."

Gabriele, who has been standing beside me all this time, whispers, "He's certainly right about her temper. She can be obnoxious. But take the rest of what they're saying with a pinch of salt. They revel in bad-mouthing each other."

I catch the newcomer looking daggers at Caterina, after which he throws me a sly wink. "Remember, Caterina, who gets the jobs done and keeps the world outside here ticking along."

A pinging interrupts him. It's a text message on his mobile, which sends his eyes darting to the display. "*Cristo!* Never a dull moment; not even on a weekend. There's another crisis festering in Rome. Still, it can wait."

On this note, he promptly turns back to me. "May I introduce myself?" Pointing to Caterina, he adds slyly, "Nobody else will. I'm Federico Nitti, her dogsbody."

At this, Caterina's face turns livid and she barks, "Dogsbody, my foot! The man's a third-rate politician who spends his life commuting between his home, down the road from here, and Rome, on what he euphemistically calls 'urgent matters of state'."

She sneers. "He's always got some political crisis or other to deal with, along with even more urgent and compelling affairs of the heart."

"There she goes again. She's getting her own back for what he just said about her." Gabriele sniggers.

I decide to put a stop to their bickering. Relying on my director's judgement, I weigh up the bushes like elements in a stage set and pronounce my verdict. Caterina is right, I conclude; the right-hand bush still needs some work.

"Good Lord, what have you done, Maria?" Federico exclaims. "She'll be on her high horse for the rest of the weekend."

And he is right. Caterina looks jubilant, raring for further combat. She pounces on Alfonso, instructing him to finish the job properly, otherwise he'll be fired. Without a word, he brandishes the secateurs in her face, before sloping off towards the bushes. She's won the round, and he sets about lopping off some more leaves and branches until he's achieved perfect symmetry. For the first time this afternoon, I catch a smile on Caterina's lovely face as she declares, almost sweetly, "Teatime, my friends. But please go and get your cases from the car, you two. And by the way, Maria, that orange outfit really suits you. It's a huge improvement on anything else I've seen you in." Fingering my dress, she adds, "Still, it's a shame the silk is not top-notch. You can't beat Como silk. I've been so busy, but I really must take you to Giuliana, my dressmaker."

This attempt to influence my wardrobe once again strikes me as controlling, especially on what should be a leisurely weekend in the country. I find it irritating to think that Caterina might be on a mission to change the way I look.

As if reading my thoughts, Federico chips in, "She never gives up, Maria. You'll see; she'll manage to drag you along to that dressmaker of hers before you leave Florence."

Caterina cocks her head at him, another smile touching her lips, as she motions us through the castle door into a quadrangle, where two turreted keeps are connected by an overhead bridge.

The castle, she explains, is built like an onion, in concentric rings designed to offer maximum protection against invaders. I realise excitedly that we've just been admitted into the second circle, where under a white canopy a table is laid for tea and a maid is arranging a teapot, cups, plates, a sponge cake and biscuits.

Once we've settled down and are enjoying the tea, our hostess starts grinding an even bigger axe. Federico comes under fire yet again. "I've been thinking that I'd really like to build some bungalows on that plot of land in the village by the church. And it's something I need to do pretty quickly. Starting date, builders on site – early autumn if possible; I mean, the moment I've sorted out the paperwork and got planning permission. Certainly no later than next October."

"It's out of the question. You know perfectly well that's a green area," comes Federico's unyielding reply.

"Nonsense," Caterina growls, kicking off her shoes and resting her feet on the edge of his chair.

Silence reigns, while she rolls a cigarette and I stir my tea, my eyes riveted on the golden liquid swirling in the cup. I am wondering what will happen next when an ear-piercing shriek cuts the silence. A wasp has settled on Caterina's foot, and, a split second later, she's racing off, the insect in hot pursuit. In a flash, Alfonso comes to her rescue. Grabbing a pole with a net on top of it, he lunges after her. While Caterina cowers behind the terrified maid, the gardener circles them both, manoeuvring the net. I have to stifle a giggle; the scene is turning rapidly into a slapstick farce, unfortunately with second-rate actors. A few seconds later, Alfonso has caught the offender and proudly carries off both the net and the wasp, like prize trophies. We are enjoying our tea again when the 'wasp-stalker' returns, with a warning that he's released the insect into the parkland outside the castle. I notice that both Caterina's and Gabriele's eyes are fixed on him, and it is not hard to understand why. Alfonso has taken off his overalls and is wearing just a vest and a pair of shorts, revealing an attractive body in perfect shape.

Once tea is over, Caterina issues further orders. First, she reminds Alfonso about an old peach tree that needs cutting down. Second, she reiterates her instructions to Gabriele and me to take ourselves and our cases off to our rooms. She'll see us at dinnertime. That settled, she promptly disappears into the nearby keep, with Federico in tow.

31

Left to our own devices, I quiz Gabriele as to whether he has noticed anything unusual so far.

"Drop it," is his gruff reply. "Enjoy the weekend, the fresh air, the quiet, and what's bound to be some excellent food and drink."

His forecast of peace and quiet, however, is soon shattered by another roar, this time coming from the quadrangle below. A few seconds later, Alfonso comes hobbling through the door, cursing, his face ashen with pain. A stone flowerpot has just fallen on his foot, and he collapses on a nearby chair, allowing Gabriele to help him pull off his boot and examine the damage.

Once the gardener is feeling better, I seize the opportunity to have a chat with him, and ask Gabriele if he wouldn't mind interpreting.

"Mind? Not in the least," he replies, a twinkle in his eye.

"I thought you'd say that." I smile back.

Gabriele is still looking anxiously at Alfonso's foot, when the latter admits, "After all these years gardening, it was a damned stupid thing to do."

"Those heavy boots probably saved you from breaking something," I reassure him. "Still, why don't we wait to see how you're feeling later and then decide if you need to go to A&E?"

By now he's looking more relaxed – the colour has returned to his cheeks – so I inquire, "But tell me, how long have you been working for Caterina?"

He replies affably, suggesting he is lapping up the attention. "It must be about forty years. When I left school at fifteen, I worked in our family business; a trattoria in the suburbs of Florence. That is, until I fell in with some no-goods, as my dad called them. I got in with a bunch of small-time crooks, who had me well and truly in their thrall. Then Dad met Caterina and her husband. If I remember correctly, they came to our trattoria for dinner one evening. They were such a handsome couple, like two film stars of the time."

"From which film, Alfonso?" Gabriele chips in playfully.

"Oh, that's irrelevant!" comes Alfonso's stern reply. "I'm just telling you that the countess was gorgeous – twenty-five or thereabouts; a couple of years older than me – and Dad, who was keen to get me out of the clutches of those delinquents, asked her if she needed any help. She didn't hesitate. She gave me a job, and I've been with her ever since."

"Did you train as a gardener?"

"I've had no formal training. You could say she trained me. She bought loads of gardening books in the early days, and we ploughed our way through them."

"Did she never want a career herself?"

"Of course not. There was no need. She would have liked children, though, but none came along." He breaks off abruptly. He's evidently touched on a subject he isn't supposed to discuss. His eyes hold mine, seeming to beg me not to repeat what he's just disclosed. Soon after, he picks up the thread of his story. "Truth is, she took me under her wing and protected me from that bad lot."

His voice has lost its spark and he has evidently lost interest in what he's been telling me. He makes a move to leave, but I touch his arm, asking him to stay. I want to know what he means by 'under her wing'.

Sitting back down, he explains, "The countess has kept me on the straight and narrow all these years. She even tried to stop me tearing round on my motorbike, but she didn't manage that one. I've always loved anything that moves fast – horses, racing dogs, sports cars – and there she was, badgering me to learn about gardening. And lo and behold, she succeeded!"

Alfonso's remarks make me understand that I am not the only one Caterina has set out to 'reform'. And he has apparently come in for some harassment, too. He goes on: "She's a perfectionist, demanding perfection from each and every one of her employees. I managed to work my way up, and for the past ten years I've been her head gardener. There's this garden – the Italian Garden, we call it – then there's the garden in Florence, and a third one at her London home. The one in Chelsea has a Victorian herb garden and a rockery. She calls it the Victoria and Albert Garden. It's very grand, and sometimes features in those home and garden magazines; you know, the glossy ones. It has won a few prizes. Mind you, I still find the weather in England depressing; I panic the moment we get there. You never know what it's going to do from one second to the next. I got so depressed the year the hurricane tore up Kew Gardens. When was that? We lost so many trees, I felt like crawling under a bush and hibernating. But now you must see the lavender bed, Signora Farrell."

He leads me through the tiny door into the garden. Covering a huge rectangle, the lavender is in full bloom, its fragrance overpowering. Breaking off a sprig, Alfonso rubs the mauve flowers between his fingertips, brushing the scented powder under my nose. I draw back. It smells nauseatingly sweet, and makes my nose itch. Seeing my reaction, he explains, "Lavender perfume actually has a very different fragrance. To make it, the lavender is mixed with a complex bouquet of spices and herbs. At the moment, the countess is having a go at making her own. If it works out, we will make both lavender perfume and soap. A top perfumer came from London only last week to discuss a very special blend for an exclusive new brand. In England, in my opinion, you make some of the best lavender perfumes; even better than France's. Still, I don't know how long this idea will last. She's always got some fad or other on the boil. She had the conservatory filled with orchids last year. She was going to start selling them, and managed to co-opt the professor. He even bought a hammock and a couple of recliners to put in the conservatory, and they spent hours in there chatting about art, the horrors of today's society, and a marketing campaign for the orchids. Don't ask me what put the kibosh on the orchid lark."

He glances at his watch. "I've talked too much, and you two had better go to your rooms and get dressed for dinner. It's in half an hour. Don't be late; Her Ladyship is the only one who can be late. She does not suffer latecomers lightly."

Gabriele rushes off to retrieve our luggage from the car, and I notice Alfonso hanging behind. With his friend out of the way, he says, in broken English. "In your room, Signora Farrell, you find a bar of lavender soap and some perfume. You can try them now, or when you back in Florence. There is also a questionnaire. Very soon the countess decide whether it's worth to go ahead. I be grateful if you could fill it in. Here's my card; call me if you have any questions."

As Gabriele returns, Alfonso throws me a smile before limping off, cursing his aching foot at the top of his voice. On that cue, we make for our rooms, lugging our bags up the spiral staircase of the left-hand keep. Upstairs, I glance around my spacious room, which has a raftered ceiling and a comfortable double bed. The floral bedspread and matching curtains give the place a light, airy feel.

Once Gabriele has left his bag in his room, he joins me, and we settle down on two wicker chairs by the window. I want to go over what has happened since we arrived. "She's a control freak, bossy and a manic perfectionist," I kick off. Then, knowing full well I might be treading on sensitive ground, I ask, "Do you think there's still something going on between Caterina and Alfonso?"

"It was a brief fling, Maria, years ago," Gabriele replies, irritated.

"He certainly seems to have a close relationship with her," I insist, scrutinising my friend's face, trying to work out what he is thinking. Is he, I wonder, resentful of Caterina's relationship with Alfonso?

He pauses, before saying bitterly, "The poor man's securely squashed under Caterina's aristocratic green thumb. You saw how she treats him: like a fool who doesn't know how to do his job properly."

"Still, Alfonso strikes me as harmless enough. He even chose not to kill that wasp, and went to a lot of trouble to catch it. Her friend Federico struck me as far more interesting for our investigation. He's a doer, isn't he? She said he was a third-rate politician. Is that correct?"

"That's just their usual banter. In reality he's a highly influential figure in—"

Gabriele's answer is interrupted by a gong summoning us to dinner.

I chew slowly, savouring the food – a delicious wild asparagus risotto followed by an assortment of roast meats and vegetables. But the evening is spoilt by another row. Caterina never stops badgering Federico about implementing new legislation regarding green zones, while he insists that she has just got to be patient. He'll get round to it, but in his own good time. Refusing to see reason, she fumes, "I don't want to hear that you're *going* to do something, darling. Just tell me when you've done it. Then I'll be happy. What I'm asking is easy-peasy for the likes of you." Blowing him a kiss, she pushes his mobile into his hand, prompting him to make a call.

I notice Gabriele throwing me a weary look, as if to say, *They're at it again.* Then he confronts Caterina, warning her not to be so tiresome. Federico, he reminds her, never fails to give her a hand whenever he can.

The politician nods gratefully, before facing his adversary again. "You've got to understand, Caterina, that even though I am on the urban planning committee, I have to go through the usual channels. Especially since my party is in opposition, procedures have to be regular and above board. There can be no visible shortcuts. I can, though, if we're lucky, find a loophole or two and then proceed. But with extreme caution."

Caterina scowls, standing her ground as firmly as the marble Venus in her garden. And by the dessert course, it is obvious that she's winning. Spooning a dollop of chocolate mousse into his mouth, with his other hand, Federico makes a call on his mobile.

A few seconds later, he waves the phone under Caterina's nose. "*Soddisfatta, mia cara?*" 'Satisfied, my dear?' "Even though it's Saturday evening, I've just managed to put the proposal on next week's agenda. We'll be discussing possible new regulations concerning green zones in various regions, Tuscany included."

Without so much as a thank-you, Caterina throws him a haughty glare and sends for some coffee. "It's about time, that's all I can say. Sorry, Maria; sorry, Gabriele. Coffee, dears? Black or white? Sugar? I always have to fight tooth and nail to get anything done round here. You see, there's no Pied Piper in this village to get rid of the rats. Everything depends on me. If I can manage to build those bungalows, I can make headway on a little project I've got in mind. I knew he could do it if he wanted to. And hey presto, he's just set the wheels in motion."

She is speaking as if Federico were no longer sitting opposite her. Not that he seems to care. He is contentedly polishing off a second helping of mousse, licking the chocolate off his lips.

"A man in his position, on the steering committee," Caterina rattles on, going over to him and giving him a peck on the cheek, "can always find a loophole, providing he puts his mind to it. Can't you, darling?"

He scowls at her, then pours himself another glass of wine. Throwing me a doleful glance, followed by a sly wink, he bows his head, eyes glued to the floor, shoulders bent. It strikes me that he is very convincingly performing the part of a long-suffering victim. He's undoubtedly a fairly talented actor as well as a top politician.

Later, snuggling down in my comfortable bed, I reflect on the conversation at dinner. Caterina strikes me as a bundle of contradictions. Sometimes she bangs on about cleaning up the country, and she never tires of expressing her disgust at how badly people behave. But this evening she had no qualms about goading Federico into bending planning regulations to her advantage. I realise again, as I did regarding Gabriele's involvement in the tomb thieves racket, that Italians can be very inconsistent. This of course makes it a nightmare to understand what they are really up to.

The following morning, I wake up at six and, try as I may, I can't get back to sleep. I'm dying for a coffee and decide I'll try to find the kitchen and make some. Pulling on a dressing gown and slippers, I tiptoe down the spiral staircase and out through the door into the quadrangle, heading for the second keep, where I seem to recall I saw a door marked 'kitchen'. A compelling refrain of *Coffee, coffee, coffee* propels me along, and once inside the keep I soon find the kitchen on the ground floor.

The kitchen is small compared to the other rooms in the castle. Cream-coloured cupboards, 1930s style, line the walls. In one corner there's a hob; in another, a simple marble table where a blue-and-yellow majolica vase stands, full of magnificent white roses. After a quick sniff at the flowers, I set about searching for the coffee and a pot. As it percolates, I relax, enjoying the tantalising aroma. A few sips of the strong liquid and I can feel my head clearing, and I decide to take a stroll.

In the quadrangle outside, the door leading to the park is ajar. I hear voices, and tiptoe towards them. A few tentative steps further and I'm through the door. Taking care not to be seen, I position myself under a tree by the conservatory.

From here I can peer through the glass panes to where, against a backdrop of brightly coloured flowers, Caterina and Federico are lying naked, side by side, on one of the recliners. Their lively banter is punctuated by gales of laughter and an occasional hug and kiss. As I creep back to my room, it occurs to me that, if Caterina is the mastermind behind the murders, she may have enlisted Federico's help.

32

On this occasion, Kim was alone and itching to kill. It was nine in the evening and he collected his gear, throwing some plastic gloves, a hood, a hammer, rubber boots and a plastic sheet into a suitcase. Choosing a stylish suit from his wardrobe, he put it on, admiring his appearance in the wardrobe mirror. Then he left the house and made for his car.

After a long drive, he checked in at the hotel where Doris Gainsborough was staying, and went to his room.

The lady in question was getting ready for bed. She took off her clothes, pulled on a nightdress, removed her make-up and contact lenses, and brushed her teeth. She yanked the floss upwards, making her gums bleed and thinking about how much she would have liked to make love with the man she'd spent the evening with the night before.

After a dinner date, they'd come back to her room, where they'd indulged in some heavy petting. She was just getting aroused when he cooled off. Doris wasn't a woman to take such a snub lightly. She'd sworn like a Trojan, slapping his face and sending him packing.

Still simmering with anger, she massaged some night cream into her wrinkled skin, regretting that she hadn't hit him harder. She began to go over her schedule for the following day, hoping that the exercise would help calm her nerves. Her spirits lifted as she remembered that she'd be lunching with Gabriele at her favourite restaurant near the Ponte Vecchio. She would order some vintage Brunello wine, a starter of liver pâté, and a T-bone steak; the local specialities she relished whenever she visited Florence. While Gabriele always did his best to make her feel fabulous, she didn't kid herself that his flattery was genuine. She knew perfectly well that he was keen not to lose the lucrative business she brought with her from America.

She revelled in the power she had over him, and felt elated when she remembered what he'd told her on the phone. He'd found a valuable piece for the client she had lined up in New York: an Etruscan vase; a little beauty. Flushed with excitement, she focused on their usual rigmarole whenever they negotiated a deal. She would do her best to knock the price down, and initially Gabriele would turn down her offer. But in the end, after some haggling, they would agree on a figure – always in dollars, because Gabriele wanted the money paid into an American bank account. Afterwards she would have time to relax and enjoy the exquisite food and wine as they ran over minor matters like transport costs and a delivery date.

She returned to the bedroom, feeling much better. Once in bed, she listened to her favourite love song that unfailingly worked better than any sleeping pill.

She was just drifting off to sleep when she heard a knock on the door. Hearing the voice of the man she'd sent packing the night before, she dragged herself out of bed, still heavy with sleep. She opened the door, half-presuming he'd come to apologise, but the moment their eyes met, he grabbed her, stuffing a cloth in her mouth to stop her screaming. Propelling her into the bedroom, he pushed her down onto the bed. His hands searched for her throat, then his grip tightened until she lost consciousness, after which he hit her head, with a hammer. A single blow and he had cracked Doris's skull.

The action was quick and brutal. After switching on the light, for a moment he stared at the lifeless body, seemingly uncertain whether to continue. Then he proceeded to pummel her flesh, watching it turn from yellowy-white to black and blue. He moved like a robot, following the carefully planned instructions from a voice in his head: Open suitcase, pull out sheet, wrap up body, double body up and bundle it into case, shut lid, turn key in lock. The first step over, he breathed a sigh of relief that Doris's body had fitted neatly into the case. Second step: Clean room very thoroughly, using the cleaning materials you have brought with you.

Deciding it was safer not to return to his room, Kim sat in an armchair, his eyes fixed on the ceiling. He would wait here a few hours before leaving the hotel.

At five o'clock, he got up and, pulling his case behind him, went down to reception to check out. He was relieved to find the place swarming with holidaymakers who, like him, were leaving at the crack of dawn. He joked with the woman at the desk that he was glad he wasn't the only one with an early flight.

In the cool morning air, he headed for the car park. Opening the boot of his car, he heaved the case inside. Switching on the engine, he put the car into gear and was soon making for the outskirts of the city. In his mind's eye he could see the pond in the marshy landscape where he planned to dispose of the body. The muddy water was already sucking his victim into its dark abyss.

The following morning, a chambermaid was making Doris's bed when she noticed bloodstains on the sheets and carpet. She promptly alerted the manager, who in his turn called the police.

Shortly afterwards the crime squad were on the scene. Seeing that the room's occupant was nowhere to be found, and that her key was still in the room, Romagnoli decided to treat the case as a murder inquiry.

A couple of days later there was another emergency call from the Maremma area in Southern Tuscany. A writer had been out walking his dog. He'd taken his usual route, skirting a pond in a thicket in the middle of a marsh not far from the sea. On reaching the pond, he had come across a mangled body, half visible in the muddy water.

The moment the report came in, Romagnoli and Celentano set off to the crime scene. Seeing a police van and an ambulance already parked beside the road, the detectives left their car and continued on foot. Then, in the nearby thicket, the sound of voices told them they had nearly arrived. Catching his leg on some brambles, Romagnoli cursed, pulling out a handkerchief and wiping the blood trickling down his leg. Why, he moaned, hadn't he put some plasters in his pocket.

A moment later, they emerged from the thicket to see three uniformed men lifting something out of the water. Celentano's stomach tensed as, drawing closer, he realised how tiny the corpse was. Even after all his years in the force, the sight of this pathetic little bundle being lowered onto a plastic sheet made him feel sick.

The two detectives approached the corpse and weighed it up. For once they were in agreement. The body was most probably that of Doris Gainsborough, who had recently gone missing. What's more, Maria Farrell had informed Celentano that she had met the American woman, who had been a good friend of her uncle's and many of the people close to him. Corroborating that statement, in Doris's address book Celentano had found the phone numbers of Maria Farrell, Peter Farrell, Countess Guiccioli, Alfonso Guidi and Gabriele Foschi.

Even though he had no hard evidence to support his hypothesis, Romagnoli suspected that Doris's murder was almost certainly related to the previous two. Right now, though, the body had to be identified, and he wondered whom they should call – Doris had been visiting from abroad, after all. He was of the firm conviction that men were generally more capable of handling the procedure than women. They therefore contacted Gabriele Foschi.

A few hours later Celentano was standing next to Foschi at the morgue. The latter's face turned pale as the pathologist uncovered the body. His gaze roamed over the battered shell on the stainless-steel table, and he felt numb. The corpse looked so alien, so different from everything he'd ever associated with a human being. He'd chosen not to identify Peter's body, but in this case he'd agreed. The shape of the head looked like Doris's, as did the distinctly angular chin, even if the features of the battered face were beyond recognition. What made him certain, though, was a large, ugly mole on the victim's neck. Last time he'd met Doris she had told him it was bothering her and, once back in New York, she had an appointment to see a dermatologist.

Foschi nodded to the detective to indicate that he had seen enough. Outside in the morgue's tiny garden, he confirmed that, to the best of his knowledge, the corpse was that of Doris Gainsborough. Though distressed, he was eager to talk about the woman he'd seen only days before. He carefully tailored his version of the meeting at her hotel, making no mention of her trouble with the tomb thieves, or the discussion they had had about Giovanelli's murder. Nor did he reveal that, a few days after, he'd arranged to have lunch with Doris at a trattoria near Ponte Vecchio, but she had failed to turn up. All he said was that, accompanied by Maria Farrell, he'd gone for drinks with Doris at her hotel, and Countess Guiccioli had shown up later. He added that Doris had been in high spirits; still enjoying her work in the art world. And, of course, they'd talked a lot about Peter Farrell, reminiscing about Doris's friendship with him.

Celentano listened carefully, suspecting that Foschi wasn't telling the whole truth. The police had received a tip-off concerning the dealings of both Peter Farrell and Mario Giovanelli with a group of local tomb thieves. So, Celentano mused, couldn't Doris have likewise been in on the racket?

The following day the headline in a regional newspaper said, 'Body of American Millionaire Discovered in Maremma.'

33

After the weekend at Caterina's I decide to have a couple of days off from the clear-out. I need time to think about what I've learnt and the people I have met so far.

I go roaming around Florence, finally managing to visit the Boboli Gardens and the Palazzo Pitti, which leave me exhausted, but overwhelmed by their beauty. Nonetheless, in contrast to the amazing gardens and artworks all around me, every so often my mind returns to the gruesome murders that have happened in such quick succession.

That evening, as I have on many others, I return to my hotel and have a chat and drinks with Franca and Carlo, enjoying the chance to try out my rudimentary Italian. For the first time I tell them why I came to Florence, and they look flabbergasted. I can only suppose that it's one thing to read crime stories in the paper or see reports on television; another to meet a relative of a victim. Lost for words, which isn't at all like her, Franca does her best to console me, reassuring me that the murderer is bound to slip up soon. Carlo retorts cynically that, decades later, the notorious

Monster of Florence is still on the loose. Feeling tired, I head off to bed, with the frightening thought that the killer or killers might well manage more murders before they are caught.

Following my short break, I'm keen to make up for lost time and arrive at Singh's lodge at eight o'clock instead of my usual ten. Looking through the window, the table is laid for breakfast: a large plate with a generous helping of bacon, scrambled egg, sausage, mushrooms, tomato and fried bread. The fry-up, which I've only smelt the remains of on other mornings, is there in all its glory.

Singh is carrying a coffee pot to the table when he notices me, but makes no move to ask me in. Instead, with his finger, he points to his food and his watch, making a circular movement, following the hand round twice, after which he points to the ceiling. His mime appears to be telling me, *I need to finish my breakfast; I'll join you in a couple of hours.*

This morning, although I know perfectly well that he's got his caretaker's job to do, his lack of flexibility really gets up my nose. Sticking my head round the door, I jibe, "Should you really be eating all that fat, Singh? It won't do your gout any good. You'll make yourself ill."

"It's only once a week," he replies sheepishly. "A little reward for my hard work. The rest of the time it's half a grapefruit, fifty-five grams of cornflakes, skimmed milk, and black coffee or tea without sugar. Oh, and a piece of toast; twenty-five grams."

The way he trots out his usual breakfast makes me suspect that he is reeling off the details of a diet he's never actually tried.

Getting to his feet, he moves to the fridge, taking out a bottle and unscrewing the top. Holding it high above his plate, he allows a liberal blob of some yellowy liquid to engulf his sausages. "My own special curry sauce – extra hot. Only today, though. I'd let you taste it, but by the look on your face, Maria, I don't think you'd want to at this time of the morning. It's my little treat."

He sits back down, beaming and pushing another forkful of sausage and curry sauce into his mouth. I take his noisy chewing as a none-too-gentle hint that I'd better mind my own business and leave him to it.

Later that morning, as Singh and I are emptying the drawers and cupboards in the sitting room, I apologise for being so tactless earlier. He tells me to forget it and quickly changes the subject, beginning another short Italian lesson – "*Questa è la collezione di dischi del professore*. 'This is the professor's record collection.' Please repeat" – when the doorbell rings.

It is Gianni Celentano, whose doleful expression tells me that he is the bringer of more bad tidings.

"*Buongiorno*. You look very down, Inspector," I venture, keeping up the formality for Singh's benefit. I notice he has taken the detective's arrival as a cue to stop work, and is sitting on the carpet, his back against the divan, hugging a cushion to his stomach as if to shield himself from what Celentano is about to say.

"Another murder, Inspector?" Singh asks bluntly.

"I'm afraid it's Doris Gainsborough." Holding out a newspaper, Gianni throws me a long look. "Here, read this. I know you met her. She invited you for drinks one evening at her hotel, didn't she?"

Feeling like I've been punched in the stomach, I flop into an armchair and read the headline: 'Body of American Millionaire Discovered in Maremma.' I can see Doris's angry face again, the ashtray bulging under her jacket, and hear her vehemently complaining about the dearth of ashtrays at her hotel. Suddenly I feel a laugh coming on, but think better of it, seeing the grim look on Gianni's face. "How was she murdered?"

"I'm afraid I can't tell you that. What I can say is that her body was found in a muddy pond in the open countryside."

I just sit there without moving, imagining what might have happened to Doris. Then I hear a whisper behind me, interrupting my train of thought. It is Singh bringing us a tray of tea.

"It's hot and sweet. Here, have some. It'll calm your nerves. How about you, Inspector?"

I force the sugary liquid down my throat, as Gianni proffers some more details. "This, as you know, is the third murder in two months and the crimes are very likely connected. All three victims were part of the same circle of friends, colleagues and acquaintances. You can—"

I butt in, "While I didn't know Peter or Mario Giovanelli, I did meet Doris, and this makes her murder that much scarier for me. Can you understand?"

He clocks my words and adds, "Of course I can, Ms Farrell. I've already advised you to take precautions. Now, however, I insist you do exactly as I say. I presume you got yourself a mobile."

"Of course I did," I nod.

"Good. Keep it switched on at all times and remember our emergency line is open 24/7. Let us know exactly where you are in the course of each day. It's very likely that the murderer will strike again."

34

The warm glow of the five lamps above the crucifix of the tabernacle in Via Ricasoli soothes my racing thoughts, and I allow myself to float in the quiet stillness of Florence in the early morning.

After Celentano's news about Doris's murder, I spent the night tossing and turning, without a wink of sleep. Doris's dead body in the marshy pond just refused to go away. At five o'clock I got up, thinking I'd go for a stroll.

As I peer into the lamplight of the tabernacle, a voice in my head starts to pray: *Please, whoever you are, give yourself up. You need help; you must be very sick.*

First Peter, then Giovanelli, now Doris. I pull out my notebook and make a new entry for Doris, noting in capital letters that I need to check her exact date of birth:

Doris Gainsborough, born New York... (CHECK); died Florence, 10th June 2000.

Doris was doubtless one of the 'big fish' mentioned in the letter she showed us. Was she right in saying that there was a dealer or gallery owner whose aim was to take control of the entire market in Etruscan antiquities? If so, did he or she threaten Doris, then strike when the poor woman refused to stop trading?

My thoughts switch to the Dante connection. While I can understand that Caterina may have plotted to punish Giovanelli, she would have to be an utter lunatic to murder Peter and Doris, two of her closest friends. Once again I ask myself what the motive behind Doris's murder might be, and whether it is related to one of the punishments in Dante's *Inferno*. From the little I know about Doris, she spent her life perpetually angry.

I pull out my modern English translation of the *Inferno* and search for the canto devoted to the Wrathful. Flicking through the pages, I come to Canto 8, where Dante and Virgil meet some sinners who in life were forever angry. I read the passage quietly to myself.

> *"So many in the world above pretend they're kings*
> *But down here wallow like pigs in muck,*
> *Leaving behind them dreadful contempt!"*
> *And I answer: "Master, how I'd like*
> *To see this man thrown in the slop*
> *before we leave this lake behind us."*
> *   And he replies: "Before you see the shore,*
> *It is only fair your request be granted."*
> *Then soon after, under my very eyes,*
> *The mud-spattered crowd set about ripping him to shreds.*
> *I still thank and praise God for that.*
> *"Get Filippo Argenti!" they all roared.*
> *And that crazy man from Florence*
> *Dug his teeth into his own flesh.*

In this case the sinners have been slung into a marsh, doomed to bash each other around for all eternity. With mounting trepidation, I realise Doris's punishment resembles theirs. Her murderer actually threw her body into a muddy pool.

My gaze hooks on the lamps again, my thoughts returning to the person whose murder interests me most. The black-and-white photos of Peter and Dad as youngsters come to mind. *Click, click, click.* The images flit by, accompanied by the clicking of an old-fashioned slide projector. The photos of the twins in their teens seem to be telling me that I should focus on Peter's adolescence again and put to Gabriele the question I've repeatedly asked myself.

When I first met Peter's partner, I asked him if he knew why Uncle had been cut off from his family in England. When he swore he had no idea, I let the matter drop. However, the more I think about it, the more it seems likely that Uncle would have confided in Gabriele about the rift between my dad and him. This time I'm going to do my level best to make sure Gabriele spills the beans.

35

The next day I go for a stroll round the market in Piazza Sant'Ambrogio, where I'm meeting Gabriele. Inside the rambling covered market, trading is in full swing. The cacophony of voices and sounds, the rhythms and pitch of a myriad of voices buying and selling, fill the air. I marvel at the enormous variety of produce: fruit and vegetables, hams and salamis galore, a lot of which are seasonal and local. I buy myself some juicy peaches – "*Quattro pesche mature, per favore*." 'Four ripe peaches, please.' This simple sentence satisfies me that I can now speak Italian well enough to handle everyday things.

When Gabriele turns up, we leave the market and head down a nearby street. He wants to show me another of Peter's old haunts. As we enter the tea room, I notice that its walls are lined with dark wooden shelves displaying dozens of carefully labelled tea caddies in different colours. A sales assistant stands behind a counter, weighing out tea leaves on a pair of old-fashioned scales. There are only about ten small tables in the place, making it feel welcoming and intimate. People, who look like locals, are chatting and enjoying their tea and cake.

"You can take your pick – Indian, African, Sri Lankan," says Gabriele cheerily, once we are seated. "If you're into tea, you'll be spoilt for choice. The owner of this place has been travelling the world for decades to sample teas and bring them back to Florence. I'm sorry he's not in today, otherwise I'd introduce you. I'm having my usual: iced green tea with mint, and a Cornish cream tea." He points to a selection of scones and a dish in the display cabinet, labelled '*Panna montata dalla Cornavaglia*' 'Clotted cream from Cornwall'.

"Does it really come from Cornwall?" I ask in disbelief. "Is it really worth their while to import real Cornish cream?"

"It might simply be an excellent forgery." Gabriele laughs. "Still, there's much to be said for a good forgery of a masterpiece rather than a poor original painting. Quite honestly, I don't care; the cream here is delicious."

"You've convinced me. I'll have the same," I reply, tempted by the dense yellowy liquid.

A few minutes later, Gabriele slits his scone in half, smearing it with lashings of thick cream and strawberry jam, and I follow suit. I have to admit it's first-rate, Cornish or not.

Our merriment is soon cut short when Gabriele brings up his visit to the morgue, which has left him feeling shocked. I push a large piece of scone, jam and cream into my mouth, savouring the sweetness. I don't tell him that I already knew they had found Doris's body, and simply remark that I count myself lucky I wasn't the one called to identify it. Sipping my tea, I pose the question I need to ask him. "It's Peter. I know I've asked you before, but did he really never tell you why he cut himself off from his family?"

Gabriele pulls a cigarette out of a packet and taps it on the table. He looks troubled, making it obvious I've struck a nerve, so I try my best to reassure him.

"I realise it's something that's probably best left buried along with Peter. My dad never wanted to discuss the matter either. Only once he said something to the effect of 'Peter's like water that flowed away a long time ago. And you know perfectly well that water can't be made to flow back – naturally, I mean.' But today I feel it's my duty to unearth the truth. Not only have there been three murders, but the murderer has attacked people in Peter's circle of friends and acquaintances. The situation is becoming really dangerous. For you and me, Gabriele, as much as for anyone else."

He straightens his back, sitting upright, with fear in his eyes.

Just the same, I don't let up. "Listen, last night I had a nightmare. A voice was goading me into action. Peter was on the battlements of Elsinore Castle, dressed in a long overcoat, with icicles in his hair and beard. Like the ghost of Hamlet's father, he was telling me to avenge his murder and find the culprit. He was shivering and beating his hands together, trying to keep himself warm. Before he melted into thin air, he called out to me – 'Revenge, Maria, a foul and most unnatural murder.'"

"Not your *Hamlet* again! Forget it, Maria!" Gabriele replies scathingly. "You know as well as I do: with or without Shakespeare, our investigation is going nowhere. We're pretty hopeless detectives."

Then, a second later, his eyes roam my face. Pushing the cigarette back into the packet, he orders a second cream tea, maintaining the silence until the waiter returns with the order. When he speaks, the words come pell-mell. "Peter once told me that being an identical twin was the most difficult thing in his life. His relationship with Edward made him feel like a dog on a very short lead. 'I was chained to Edward', that's how he put it. To keep Edward happy, they had to do everything together. Your dad would settle for nothing less than an exclusive twosome. He wanted nobody to come between them. In their teens, this 'clinginess' – again, Peter's word – became unbearable. Peter was beginning to realise that he was gay, and had fallen in love with a boy they knew. Edward was fuming. He sensed that Peter was drifting away from him. They were eighteen, and had just taken their A Level exams and come through with flying colours. They'd studied the same subjects: English, Latin, French and History. Despite their success, however, they were as bored as badgers, longing to get out of Manchester. Their sights were set on Oxford or Cambridge, so they decided to sit the Oxbridge entrance exam. By then Peter was praying that he would get into Oxford and your dad into Cambridge, or vice versa. That way they'd automatically go their separate ways. But, as you know, Peter went up to Oxford, while your father just about scraped into Hull."

"I already knew a lot of that," I remark, disappointed. "What I need to know is *why* only one twin won a place at Oxford."

"A few months before he died, Peter wrote you a letter."

"A letter?" I exclaim, astounded. "Why didn't you mention it before?"

Gabriele has put his bag on the table and opens it, cocking his head apologetically. He takes out an envelope, and my heart leaps as I catch sight of my name on it. "When Peter gave it to me, he was adamant that he didn't want you to read it until after his death. With all that's been going on, you can understand, I hope, why I didn't give it to you sooner."

"You've kept it in your bag all this time?" I ask, incredulous, opening the letter.

"Sorry, I should have given it to you before."

Remembering Caterina's description of Peter, at our first meeting, as her 'unpredictable Albion', I ask, "Do you think this is another of Peter's little surprises that he's pulled out of a hat?"

"I honestly don't know. Go on, read the letter," Gabriele replies firmly.

I rip open the envelope. There is a single sheet of notepaper inside, with Peter's neat handwriting on it. He begins by instructing me to find a safe containing a letter, after which the rest of the text sounds like a riddle:

Dial 999, that's my advice.
Add one, and in a trice
I'll take you where
You're bound to share
Fine food and wine;
The pleasure's mine.
They'll solve the mystery
of your uncle's history.

Without breathing a word to Gabriele about the contents of the letter, I thank him for the tea and say goodbye. I need to be alone, and on my way to the flat, I keep running over the riddle Peter wrote. I feel deeply frustrated that I can't make head nor tail of it. How can somebody who is dead and buried annoy me so much? In a loud voice, I hear myself taunting Peter – "I won't let you thwart me, Uncle! I'm going to search your flat from top to bottom. You'll see; I'll find the safe and the letter!"

Once there, I make a beeline for his office, where I mooch round, looking behind books, inside cupboards and under carpets. I find nothing, and go through to the sitting room, taking down each painting in turn in case the safe is concealed behind one of them. Having searched all over the walls, I hunt for a loose floorboard. Nothing again. Flopping down into a chair, I tell myself that Peter would never have chosen such an obvious hiding place as behind a painting or under a floorboard. He was a veteran practical joker and far too clever to make the search so easy.

Remembering Gianni's instructions to let him or one of his colleagues know my every move, I ring him at the station to tell him I am about to call a taxi and go back to my hotel. To my surprise he says that he has just finished work, and we could have a drink together in the hotel bar.

36

"*Cin cin!*" Gianni moves his glass to meet mine. "That's a colloquial way of saying 'cheers' in Italian, Maria."

"I know. Carlo and Franca are always saying it," I reply, reciprocating and chinking my glass against his. "Then there's '*salute*'! Isn't that the equivalent of the English 'to your health'?"

"You're learning – very slowly, but surely," he teases, making a second toast. "But tell me, have you had time to see something of Florence? I know you've got plenty to do, but…"

"You're right – there's never really much time to switch off; except for the walks I sometimes take in an evening, and a recent visit to the Palazzo Pitti and the Boboli Gardens. But I must say I find it a bit awkward, having a drink here with you."

"I know, regulations and red tape. A detective should not socialise with somebody involved in a case he is working on. Is that what you're thinking?"

I nod; that is exactly what's on my mind. "Don't think I don't enjoy your company, but meeting you here doesn't seem right in the circumstances."

He shrugs and whispers, "I enjoy talking to you. And we're not in a public bar or café. We're in your hotel lounge, and the only two people here.

"Tell me about your job in Manchester. When I was at college, I went to the theatre a lot. Even though I studied law, I loved Rome's theatres and saw loads of plays starring some of the finest actors in Italy. But that was a long time ago. Now, at the end of a long day's work, all I want to do is enjoy a meal out, spend some time with my son, or have a blether with a relation or friend, as they say in Scotland."

"You certainly picked up some of the lingo, while you were in Glasgow!" I laugh. "I suppose theatre is my life. Derek, my ex-boyfriend, worked as my lighting designer, so we were always talking about our current production, the next one, or somebody else's show."

"Did you leave him?"

"He left me six months ago, but I'd rather not talk about it."

"Want me to tell you about my procession of Scottish girlfriends instead?"

"Did you say 'procession'? If you did, don't bother."

His eyes are dancing as he ignores what I said and pours some more wine into his glass. "When I was living in Glasgow, the women I met there, most of them Scottish, were generally friendly and... well, the usual thing for an Italian man, I suppose."

"The Latin lover type, you mean? And in your case, pretty good-looking, intelligent, and with a job that many people find intriguing."

"Do you think so?" He smiles and peers hard into his glass. "You see, after a passionate first date, the relationships – if you can call them that – usually fizzled out. I'm not saying it was the women's fault; it was probably me. They just didn't interest me any more, even as friends. Most of my real friends go back to my primary-school days in the Maremma."

"So what was missing from your Scottish relationships?"

"The fun side. Going out, having a drink, a good meal and a chat, without necessarily going to bed afterwards. I like a woman who appreciates good food and wine. Somebody who's a creative cook and into local food."

"That sounds like a tall order. You mean somebody born and brought up on a farm, who's vegetarian, maybe."

"Definitely not," he replies, laughing. "I'd like to fall madly in love with a gorgeous meat-eater, who's into art, music... and what else? You tell me. Is that too much to ask?"

"An all-rounder. Dare I say a Renaissance woman, with many strings to her bow?"

"That's an interesting way of putting it," he replies, mulling over my definition.

"It won't be easy to find her today."

Then he says, in a low voice, "I've written a sort of memoir about my time in Scotland. I try to capture what it felt like at the time. I hope to publish it when I retire."

"Can't you publish it now?"

"No, not in my present position."

"And no crime fiction, like some of your colleagues? I recently read a novel by a former Italian chief inspector. His books sell like hot cakes."

"I'd rather keep murder to my daytime job. In my writing I want to get to the core of those personal relationships where I get entangled. Is that the right word?"

"It all depends," I say, smiling and changing the subject. "When you came back to Italy from Glasgow, am I right in thinking you wasted no time in marrying an Italian girl?"

"Wrong again! Like so many Italians, I'm lucky to have an extended family. Parents, a brother and three sisters, five nephews and nieces, and more cousins than I can keep track of. In 1992 when I returned from Glasgow, they took me back into the fold."

"And your wife?"

"She was a doctor. I'd been back a couple of years when I met her at the hospital in Grosseto. I was there on a murder case to talk to one of her patients. She turned out to be my Renaissance woman, Maria!" He chuckles at the idea.

Then he glances at his watch, exclaiming, "It is ten to eight and my sister and son are expecting me for supper. I daren't be late. She'll have the pasta on the table. Be seeing you."

37

Shaking my hand, the woman standing at the entrance of Peter's flat introduces herself as Anna Biondi. Or, as she insists, "Just plain Anna; that's the way I like it. Italian art is very big in the States, and I am often over there on business. While there are some things I'm not too keen on – I mean, the food and the lack of history – I love the Americans' easy-going informality. Anyway, Countess Guiccioli told me you'd be waiting for me here. You should know I've already done my homework on the paintings and today I just have to finish my appraisal."

Anna is in her early forties; curly fair hair, her face skilfully made up, a stylishly tailored mustard suit setting off her slim figure. By her side is a large trolley-case. Once in the sitting room, she opens it and it is soon abundantly clear why she needs such a big one. She pulls out a notebook, a dozen or so hefty books, two catalogues, a sales manual and a medium-sized paper bag, all of which she arranges on the table. She's soon strolling round the room, taking a look at each painting. I marvel at her cool – not a single 'wow', 'oh' or 'ah' passes her lips. She is evidently used to rubbing shoulders with modern art's giants. Toing and froing between the table and the paintings, each time she returns to her seat she leafs through a book or two and jots down some notes. After about an hour, I make her some coffee and put it on the table in front of her. A faint smile flickers on her lips and she pushes the cup to the edge of the table, murmuring, "Not now, Maria; I'll have a break at four."

True to her word, at four sharp, I see her surreptitiously opening the paper bag and pulling out half a dozen grissini and a lump of cheese. She sits contentedly eating her snack, accompanied by an occasional sip of the now-cold coffee. Her face brightens as the food and caffeine kick in, and she enthuses, "You're in for a substantial sum, Maria. Gabriele Foschi's also a very lucky man! He already owns some prize nuggets – I saw them last year at a party he threw for his birthday – so the paintings he inherits will swell what's already an outstanding collection. But tell me, what are you going to do with yours?"

"Ah… I haven't quite decided," I say hesitantly, taken aback. Her query has made me realise that I haven't given any serious thought to the question of the paintings. "I have to confess I still haven't got any further than thinking about their division between Gabriele and me. I'll be selling them, I suppose."

By now Anna has finished eating, and I catch her glancing at her watch and muttering that she really ought to be getting back to work. On this cue, I decide to take myself off to the botanical gardens for an hour. I need a breath of air and time to think over what she has just asked me.

Soon after, I am strolling around the gardens with Singh. I asked him to come with me as a way of saying sorry for telling him off the other morning about his eating habits.

We are admiring the blooms in the orchid house when he recalls the flowers he used to see as a boy in India. While he adores the flowers here, he is disappointed that they have no scent. "I loved the scented jewel orchids my grandmother grew. *Bellissimi fiori!* Beautiful flowers!" he exclaims, his voice tinged with nostalgia.

It is coming up to closing time and, with very few visitors left in the gardens, I quietly consider my options. Am I really going to sell all the paintings and stash the proceeds away in the bank? And where will the paintings end up if I sell them? Most likely in the palatial homes of art collectors, who might be anywhere in the world. I don't like that idea one little bit, but nor do I want or need all the paintings. I could sell two to refurbish my house in Manchester and provide me with a nest egg for a rainy day. And why not? I might even buy myself a small studio flat in Florence with part of the money from the sale of Peter's flat. I could also give Singh a hand. He's turned out to be a guardian angel over the past few months, and deserves a reward.

"How about a trip to India?" I blurt out, making Singh jump. "How about that? I can arrange everything – your fare, hotel and so on. You could visit your relatives and your childhood haunts."

He looks bewildered, his gaze alighting on one particularly beautiful pink orchid. "That's very kind of you, Maria. But I have my job here. I really don't know if my boss will give me time off. Let me think it over."

Out of the corner of my eye, I can see one of the gardeners approaching. He is jangling a large bunch of keys, signalling that it is time we left. Grumbling about us being the last to go, he accompanies us to the exit. Out on the pavement, the gates clang shut behind us, and I watch the man giving the huge key a couple of sharp turns. At that moment I do something I've never done before. I look up to the top of the iron gates and read the words inscribed there: '*Giardino dei Semplici*'. I ask Singh to translate and he replies solemnly, "A Garden for Simples; in other words, medicinal herbs and plants."

The name seems to answer the question I've been wrestling with for some time. While the garden's founders believed medicinal herbs and plants could heal people, I strongly believe art to be therapeutic. At that moment I decide to give three of Peter's paintings to Manchester's City Art Gallery. It has a policy of free admittance, and I'll ask them to create a special section for Peter's paintings.

The sky is turning dark as Singh and I slowly wend our way back to the flat. I keep silent as I go over my plan. Maybe I could even introduce a special programme at the gallery's teaching centre, so that people with no specialist knowledge can learn about the nuts and bolts of Italian art history.

Back at the flat, Anna is looking elated, making me ask, "I suppose you're done, then?"

"One hundred per cent." Her voice rings triumphant. "I feel electrified. These painting are so very special. And just look at him. I call him the young *Mona Lisa*. He's androgynous, enigmatic and so sad, don't you think?" Pointing to Picasso's young man, her fingers stroke the simple wooden frame. "I can tell you a secret, now it's all written down and the valuation's complete. Out of the whole collection, this boy's my favourite. Now, as soon as you like, you and Gabriele can divide up the paintings. But what a shame! They sit, or rather hang, so nicely together. You need to fix a date and time for the formalities when you, Gabriele, the countess and Dr Manetti are available. Even if my job is done, I hope I can be present. And by the way, some of the paintings have exceeded my expectations financially speaking."

On that optimistic note, Anna repacks her case, pulls on her jacket and sets off home.

Pouring myself a drink, I sink down into an armchair, my eyes settling on Picasso's young man. Whenever I look at him, he seems to be teasing me. For the umpteenth time I challenge him to divulge his secret, but he refuses to be baited. I chuckle, suspecting that the enigma surrounding him is probably what makes him so attractive.

I decide I'd better be heading back to my hotel, and make my way downstairs. I'll say goodbye to Singh and get him to call me a taxi. In the hall there's an aroma of French fries drifting from his lodge. Even at this late hour he has no qualms about sharing the smell of his cooking with anyone who happens to be passing. A glance inside his room tells me he is watching a black-and-white Chaplin film while eating his supper. In his familiar sign language, he throws me a quick wave, pointing to his meal, then to the television. But this time he beckons me to join him. There's a bottle of Peter's red wine sitting next to the steak, and he pours me a glass. He's beaming now. "To your health, Maria!"

As I sip the delicious wine, my eyes fall on the drawing on the label: it's a sketch of an elderly man, with a paunch and a smile on his face. On his head, there's a straw hat; in his hand, a glass raised in a toast. The year on the label is 1999. "Is this a portrait of Peter?" I ask.

Singh nods, pointing at the label and saying, "The professor drew it, you know. It must be your uncle's last self-portrait."

As the cab speeds through the dark streets, I go over the events of the past few days. I've still not managed to fathom Peter's riddle, and I am no closer to finding the safe. Without Hamlet's mousetrap, or some similarly ingenious device, my investigation is going nowhere. Like Gabriele, I've got a feeling I am not really cut out to be a detective. Then I revert to a more positive matter, recalling my idea to send some of the paintings to the Manchester Gallery, and make a mental note to start talking to the people in charge. There is also my growing friendship with Gianni to consider. I am not sure what is happening, but it certainly feels good.

38

Nine o'clock, and another two armchairs have just disappeared through the door of Peter's flat, giving me an overriding sense of remorse. It was one thing to sort through his food and drink, shipping it home or giving it away, and to bag up his clothes and take them to an old people's home and a second-hand shop; it's quite another to sell off most of his furniture. The flat is looking steadily more uninhabited, making me feel terribly guilty to be dismantling the things Peter cherished for nearly fifty years. I slept badly last night, and my feet and ankles are swollen, with the heat. I sip some coffee, letting my eyes skim over the half-empty sitting room. I suddenly realise I just can't face another prospective buyer this morning, and ring the woman who's due here at ten to cancel her appointment. She can see the divans and the remaining armchairs tomorrow.

Outside, dark clouds are brewing and a steady drizzle has set in. It is the first really rotten weather since I arrived in Florence. I'm so down I feel like lounging around the flat, without lifting a finger. I decide the clear-out can wait, and read through my notebook, going over the details of the investigation so far. I have to admit that, after all these weeks doggedly searching for clues, nothing of great significance has come to light. There's the possible Dante connection and the *tombaroli* racket, but nothing that points definitively to a culprit. Despondent, my thoughts shift to Manchester, and I phone Joanne, who by now is well into the rehearsals for her play. "How are things?" I ask, doing my level best to sound bubbly and positive.

"Not bad. The usual," she replies, which I translate as *I'm really messed up, and not only am I having serious doubts about the worth of my play, but I haven't a clue how it will go down.*

I try encouraging her. "Come on, my dear tell me the truth. It's always a testing – at best exhilarating – roller coaster, directing your own play. I've been there, remember? But listen, I'm so sorry I've left you on your tod all this time. I might just be back, though, for the opening night."

Joanne's voice lifts a few notes at the prospect of my return, but then she quips, before abruptly hanging up, "Don't bother; we can manage without you, fat face!"

Suddenly my mobile pings. It's a message from Alfonso Guidi: *'Ha finito il questionario? Potrei passare dal professore per prenderlo.'* 'Have you finished the questionnaire? I could drop by the professor's and pick it up.'

This takes me aback, reminding me that Alfonso's questionnaire and the lavender soap are still in a brown paper bag in the kitchen. I go and fetch them, pulling the wrapper off the soap and smelling the scent. I read Alfonso's text again and feel a buzz of excitement as I recall the day at Caterina's. He looked so attractive and amazingly fit in his vest and shorts. I make a start on the questionnaire, and as I tick the boxes, I wonder whether it is a good idea to invite him round. Smiling to myself, I repeat Hamlet's line: "To be or not to be…" I quite fancy the man, but I don't know him from Adam. In the end, I decide to do a most un-Hamlet-like thing and throw caution to the wind. I make a spur-of-the-moment decision and text him: 'Finished questionnaire. Why don't you come by in an hour?'

A few seconds later my mobile pings again: '*Sì, certo. Ci vediamo alle undici.*' 'Yes, sure. I'll see you at eleven.'

The moment I receive his reply, I am overcome by doubts. I remember Gianni's instructions to keep the police informed about my every move, and stare hard at the phone on the table. Should I call Gianni to let him know that Alfonso is coming round? I pick up the handset, then put it down. I'll compose a text to Gianni and leave it ready on my mobile, just in case. I laugh out loud at the high drama this prospective meeting is turning into. Telling myself not to be ridiculous, I wash my face and hands using the lavender soap; it leaves my skin tingling and fresh. Thinking that I might just get Alfonso to divulge the secret recipe, I sit, gazing through the window at the beating rain.

The bell rings and I open the door to find Alfonso clutching a bunch of damask roses, which he pushes into my hand. Once I've thanked him for this unexpected gift, I hide my awkwardness by running into the kitchen to find a vase. He's sporting a beautifully tailored linen suit, designer sandals and a matching leather bag; a far cry from his gardening attire. He looks even more attractive than he did the day I saw him in Caterina's garden.

Without more ado, he flops down on one of the divans, complaining that his foot is still plaguing him after the flowerpot accident. I notice him casting his eyes around the nearly empty room, a worried look on his suntanned face. If I understand him correctly, he asks, "And where to God has all the professor's furniture gone?"

In my broken Italian I try to explain that Singh and I have nearly finished the clear-out and I will soon be putting the flat on the market. Alfonso makes no reply, but limps out onto the balcony, loudly cursing that his foot is still plaguing him. In the next breath, he calls out that the state of the window boxes will set my uncle rolling in his grave. How could I possibly have neglected them in this way?!

Seeing how upset he is, I decide to divert his attention. Handing him the questionnaire, I say playfully, half in English, half in Italian, "All the questions answered, my friend. I hope it's useful for your marketing research."

"*Brava!* Good work! Now we see."

I breathe a sigh of relief that Alfonso's voice sounds friendlier and more relaxed.

In heavily accented English, he suggests, "We go through it together if you don't mind, and control answers."

With his glasses perched on the bridge of his nose, he invites me to sit down beside him and begins skimming through my answers, commenting, in a string of monosyllables, "Fine... good... poor..." Then suddenly he stops reading and looks at me, a steely glint in his eyes that makes me stiffen. I realise the potential danger of finding myself on my own with this man and touch my mobile, ready to send the message to Gianni. Alfonso nuzzles up to me, murmuring that the lavender fragrance makes me smell sexy. I try my best to stifle a laugh. It has suddenly dawned on me how stupid I was to invite him round. It was one thing to fancy his good looks in the company of others; another to find myself alone with him and realise we have nothing in common.

I make a move to get up, but he pulls me down beside him. Holding me close, he starts humming the Mozart aria *Non più andrai* that he sang the day I met him. Immediately after, he attempts to translate the words into English – "*You will not be going anywhere, lovely butterfly*" – and my heart sinks as I clock the threat. Immediately, he changes tack, remarking coldly in his broken English, "You give questionnaire nine a ten. You are right. Lavender relax the mind, stop any negative thought, and that's good for you."

Clutching my fists to try and keep a grip on myself, I watch him walking to the door, but this time I panic as he pockets the key from the lock. I approach quickly, yelling at him to give it me back, but in response he spins round, a furious look on his face. Holding out my hand for the key, my fingers touch his for a split second before he pulls back. "Relax, and give me the key," I repeat insistently, praying he will do as he's told.

"No, Maria, that's out of the question." And he seizes my arm, propelling me back towards the divan.

Suddenly his mobile rings, and I can't believe my ears. His voice has turned friendly again. It's Caterina inquiring about a job she asked him to do. He courteously tells her he is busy, and she will have to wait until tomorrow. As if nothing has happened between us, he unlocks the door, throws me the key and says goodbye. I am left speechless, and stare at him, incredulous, as he walks to the lift. A voice in my head is taunting him, *What did you hope to get out of this meeting, Alfonso? A cheap sexual thrill? You're most probably a pervert who despises women.* The lift door is opening, and I wonder what makes the man tick. Even though my body is spotlessly clean, it feels soiled; a man whom I now find repulsive has touched me. As the lift door starts to close, I finally manage to speak. My tone is as casual and controlled as his. "See you, Alfonso. *Arrivederci.*"

Half an hour later, I nip out to buy some bread. The rain has stopped and the air smells like heaven. There's a young couple laughing and talking, a Japanese tourist taking photos of the botanical gardens, and on a corner an old man is begging, a cap on the pavement in front of him with a couple of lire inside. The atmosphere is so very ordinary, and I worship everything about it.

Then the memory of Alfonso's threatening behaviour overwhelms me once more, like a mighty storm. His mix of gentleness and viciousness brings to mind Shakespeare's *Richard III*. King Richard can be a charmer who makes women fall under his spell, but he is also capable of committing the most terrible atrocities. Could Alfonso be such a villain?

39

Back at Peter's flat, I'm feeling terribly confused and desperately need to clear my head and forget about what's happened. I remember Caterina's invitation to use her swimming pool whenever I want, and decide to take her up on it. A swim, some sun and some fresh air will probably do me good. Having collected a towel, a swimsuit and sun cream from my hotel, I jump into my car and head for Caterina's castle.

When I arrive, she tells me she is just about to start a Dante lesson.

"You can't still be studying Dante!" I exclaim, incredulous. "What can you possibly learn about him that you don't already know?"

"He's like Shakespeare, Maria; his work has so many layers that I never get bored. And you see, I'm lucky. I have an exceptional teacher. He's an actor, who tells me that when Dante wrote the *Divine Comedy*, he imagined it being read aloud or even performed. Dante would never have wanted his work studied as an academic book on syllabuses in high schools and universities.

You'll get a chance to meet my teacher at supper. See you later and enjoy your swim."

Left to my own devices, I stretch out on a sunbed by the pool and smother myself in sun cream. After the ordeal with Alfonso, I need to relax and enjoy the sun. However, my mind refuses to shut off, and I begin going over what happened this morning, move by move, line by line. I visualise Alfonso in Peter's sitting room as his mood swung unpredictably back and to, viciousness and aggression alternating with friendly normality. Soon the heat makes me feel sticky, and I decide to take a dip, but after just two lengths, I have to stop. I haven't swum since my holidays last summer and I am out of practice. Feeling disgusted with my performance, I pull myself out of the water and start heading back to my sunbed.

But calamity strikes. I fail to notice the slippery surface and end up spreadeagled on the wet tiles. I am lying there, my nose pressed against the cold, hard surface, cursing and praying I haven't broken anything, when a voice calls out, "Are you hurt, Maria? Hang on, I'll get a doctor."

Forcing myself to sit upright, I see a man in sunglasses bending over me. It's Federico Nitti. My legs and right hip are still smarting from the fall. Cradling my knees, I draw them up to my chest, holding them tightly.

With a look of concern, Federico crouches beside me. "I saw that! That was a nastly fall. How are you?"

"Just a couple of broken legs and probably my neck," I quip, groaning and gingerly sitting up.

"I'll help you up. Nothing broken by the sound of you." He holds my arm, guiding me back to my sunbed. "Now you've proved you can still walk, how about a drink?"

"Depends."

"On the drink or the company?"

"Both!"

"Gin and tonic?"

"Sounds good." And I slowly lie back on my sunbed, rubbing my arms and legs very hard. I notice that Federico's already brought out a tray loaded with bottles of gin and tonic water, glasses, olives and crisps, and placed it strategically between my sunbed and the next. I smile to myself. Sure of his charms, the man took it for granted that I'd accept his invitation.

He sets about making the drinks, popping a couple of ice cubes into each glass, followed by a single measure of gin, two of tonic, and a lemon wedge. The final touch: a couple of coloured straws. Once the operation is complete, he beams at me. "You're a lucky girl, you know! First, you had a very narrow escape. You could have broken a leg or three! Second, and more important, you are in the company of one of the finest gin-and-tonic makers in Tuscany."

Sipping my drink, and thinking that Federico is such a show-off, I switch to my detective mode, seizing the opportunity to find out more about him. I feel myself groaning inside, since I am about to ask something I've said several times since I came to Florence. "Where did you learn your English? It's really very good."

So far, the Italians on whom I've tried out this patter have opened up like corks popping out of a bottle of bubbly. Federico's animated response tells me that it's working again. "As a boy I went to England in the summer vacation to learn English. Later, at university, I read economics, and many of the lectures were in English. Then I spent three years at Harvard writing my PhD. So, all in all, I suppose it's Harvard's fault," he says proudly.

In response, I put on a deadpan expression and perform my best American drawl. "I just *love* your American accent, Federico!"

"You're not doing badly yourself. It's pretty obvious you are a professional!" He laughs as he knocks back his gin and tonic.

By now he has stretched out on the sunbed next to mine and is smoothing cream all over his face, confiding that the rest of his body is so used to the sun it never gets burnt.

"And why a political career?" I venture, hoping I'm not treading on sensitive ground.

"Politics is a kind of addiction. Once you're in parliament, you know perfectly well that you are in one day and you've got all this power, but the next, you might be given the boot. At the moment my party is in opposition and working 24/7 to oust the left-wing majority. It's not easy."

"So what makes you stay?"

"I get a huge buzz from the power it gives me. In my job, if you have a good idea, you can turn it into reality, something concrete, if you really want to. The life of a politician can be immensely satisfying."

"But it's also a dangerous world, isn't it?"

"Right. You can't trust anyone. Your closest friend will cut your throat rather than go down himself."

"I couldn't live like that," I remark. "In the theatre, people work as a team. There's bitchiness and jealousy, certainly, but ultimately, for a show to work, the company's got to stick together. Otherwise, the play is a disaster and everybody suffers."

"You lefties haven't got the balls. Take the lot who won your last general election," Federico retorts.

His generalisations astound me. "What do you mean, 'you lefties'? What makes you say that? It's not a matter of left or right. In the theatre we pull together to achieve a common goal in order to entertain and hopefully educate our audiences."

Sneering, he knocks back another drink. "I was referring to New Labour, the party you just voted for, no doubt. What exactly do they stand for? In the past, even if you disagreed with their politics, as I did, you knew where you stood with them. I mean, the likes of Harold Wilson…"

"After twenty years of Conservative government, New Labour look like they'll be bringing a much-needed change. I'm sorry, but the old-style Labour Party no longer meets ordinary people's needs."

"In Italy people like you are usually communists."

This last remark makes me fume. "What do you mean? In a democracy, communists have every right to exist just as much as anybody else."

I'm feeling tempted to drown Federico in my gin and tonic when Caterina shows up and interrupts what is turning into a mighty row. Dressed in a bikini and flip-flops, a rifle tucked under her arm, she looks bizarre.

"Just what I need to deal with your friend here," I jibe, pointing at the gun.

Patting Federico's head with the rifle butt, she attempts to cool things down. "Well, he's off out hunting, aren't you, dear? What is it you are after today?" She offers me the gun, winking slyly. "If you want to shoot him, it's all yours; go ahead."

"Rabbits," Federico snarls taking hold of the gun. "But next week, who knows? See you later."

Muttering something about darned communists, he swaggers off in the direction of the car park. Waiting beside a classy four-by-four, a uniformed chauffeur opens the door for my sparring partner. Soon after, the vehicle goes off like the clappers, with Federico performing a little wave through the window. He looks as pleased as punch, making me suspect that he is gloating about managing to wind me up.

"I can't stand his political ideas." I tell Caterina as the car disappears from sight. "I'm sorry, I know he's your friend, but he really is a prat."

"Left or right, in Italy, they're all the same. I know you can't understand, Maria. Most Italians don't either. Our government is always changing. One day the left are at the helm; the next, some other party. And people like Federico have a deep-seated hatred of communism. I'm sorry he's offended you, but I really must get back to my Dante lesson."

40

With a couple of hours to go before dinner, I lie back on the sunbed and pull out my notebook. On the first empty page I jot down today's date followed by:

> *Federico Nitti, a politician in his late fifties. He's in the shadow government and a specialist in environmental issues. He can be pretty obnoxious when he's had a glass too many, and shows zero tolerance of political opinions that differ from his own. He has little grasp of British politics, conflating New Labour with communism.*

I feel instantly better. There's nothing like writing about something to help you get it off your chest. I relax and doze off, my thoughts returning to Alfonso and what happened at Peter's.

After a snooze, I wake up feeling parched and decide to get myself a drink from the kitchen. In front of the open window, I freeze in my tracks. Caterina is stirring something on the hob, while

Federico pulls some dead rabbits out of a bag. "Don't invite me again when Maria is here," he snaps. "She doesn't understand a thing about this country or how politics work here. What a moron!"

"Hold on!" Caterina shouts, offended. "I've every right to invite whomever I want here. And don't you dare criticise Maria. You should concentrate on what I've asked you to do and not waste your time arguing with her. I know you've used your connections and have managed to get planning permission, but there are still some crucial hurdles to clear."

Without waiting for her to finish, Federico stumbles towards a rack on the nearby wall and selects a large knife. Knocking back a drink, he returns to the table, brandishing the knife and muttering angrily under his breath. He pauses, hovering over the table, where a grey rabbit is stretched out. Holding the knife high in the air, he points the blade at the little, limp body. A second later he's plunged it into the creature's flesh and is stabbing it over and over.

At dinner Federico looks subdued and scarcely says a word. Luckily Caterina's actor friend, Giacomo Andriolo, turns out to be excellent company, and we are soon chatting about the theatre. Giacomo is curious to hear what I know about Italian theatre.

"Apart from the giants like Goldoni, Pirandello and Dario Fo, very little," I confess. "And, oh yes! Some years back, I saw Fo performing his *Mistero buffo* in London. He was amazing."

Giacomo turns to talking about his own work. "I tour my Dante recital a lot; a bit like Fo with his *Mistero buffo*. You see, I believe that, even though Dante wasn't a dramatist as such, he wrote the *Divine Comedy* to be read aloud for a live audience. It really works in performance."

"Caterina mentioned that. It's a brilliant idea. But tell me, how on earth can Dante still manage to capture people's imagination today?" I ask sceptically. "How can a poem written seven hundred years ago still speak so powerfully to the present?"

"It's probably because Dante managed to talk about all human passions. Aren't they the same now as they were when he was alive? There's no real gap between them and us in this respect. Remember, too, that Dante called his work *Commedia*; the comedy of life. He didn't use 'Divine'; that adjective was added later. Sadly, it puts some people off reading him."

Giacomo's enthusiasm makes me want to find out more about his audience. "Caterina's been telling me that you perform Dante for huge numbers in the open air."

"Whenever I get a chance, I perform my Dante. I'm a Florentine born and bred, so whenever I do the show here, it feels really special. As I stand there, looking out at the spectators, it feels like Dante's there beside me. A man more or less my age, clutching a copy of his *Commedia*, and egging me on to give it all I've got."

The first course over, Federico gets up to go. He drily announces that he's got an early start tomorrow and needs to get to bed. Mumbling a quick goodbye, he hurries off.

Tucking into the second course, a generous helping of carpaccio dressed in olive oil and lemon and garnished with rocket leaves and grated parmesan, I ask Giacomo how he first fell in love with Dante.

"He came looking for me," he replies, laughing. "You see, I was born in Via del Corso, just round the corner from the church where Beatrice Portinari, the love of Dante's life, was buried. I first visited the church with my grandmother when I was three. And, you see, it was Nonna (that's Italian for 'grandmother') who first read me some passages from the *Commedia*. At the time, I couldn't really understand the words, but Dante made his entrance into my life at that very early age. Nonna could hear the rhythm in the lines, and conveyed it to me. I'm from a musical family, you see. Nonna was a violinist and my grandfather an orchestra director. Dante's musicality lives on in the *Commedia*, and leaps out in performance. And, well—"

A phone rings, interrupting our conversation, and Caterina goes out of the dining room to answer it, leaving the door ajar.

"That's fine. And how are things in Delhi?" She sounds worried. "Thank goodness… Good, good, I'm pleased if you've managed to start work on the hospital and still have some funding left… Yes, I am. I'm delighted. Federico Nitti will be coming to India too; he's the environmental specialist I mentioned. The bungalows here will be finished and rented out by spring 2001; at that point I'll be able to transfer more money. And there's good news. There's a rather substantial windfall in the pipeline."

Here's a side to Caterina I was not aware of. Although I met the two Indian boys at her home in Florence, I hadn't realised the scale of her charity work. And judging by what I've just heard, Federico is giving her a hand. Even though I don't agree with his politics, Caterina's conversation suggests that there is a more positive side to the man. He's behaved offensively and drinks too much but, I conclude, that doesn't necessarily mean he has anything to do with the murders.

41

I run through the rooms in Peter's flat, flinging open the windows to give the place a good airing. Most of the furniture has been sold, and the flat looks even bigger than before.

At ten Dr Manetti shows up to supervise the division of the paintings. A minute late Anna Biondi comes in. At two minutes past, Gabriele, Phoebe and Caterina arrive. Then, Angelo walks through the door. Manetti catches me staring curiously at the newcomer and whispers that I'll understand very soon why Angelo has been allowed to join us.

Once we are settled round the table, Singh comes in armed with a tray of coffee, shuffling along without saying a word. He's looking dejected, his shoulders bent, his eyes on the floor. I wonder whether he is thinking the same as me: that this will almost certainly be the last gathering at Peter's flat before it goes up for sale. Huddled together, Caterina and Gabriele sip their coffee, exchanging the odd word. Gabriele's frequent glances at his watch make me realise just how keen he is to get the division over with. As for Manetti, he is engaged in some light-hearted banter with

Anna: "You took your time, my dear. And know what? A little bird told me you sniffed out a fake the other day during one of your costly appraisals. Nothing to do with our treasured specimens, I trust?"

He seems not to have noticed that we are all waiting to begin, so I say, "Dottor Manetti! Would you mind if we got down to business, please?"

In a flash he spins round to face us. Visibly irritated, he makes it clear that he is not used to being told what to do. Then, like lightning, he changes tack and gushes, "Quite right, quite right, Ms Farrell. You want to be heading back to Manchester, I guess. You must be feeling homesick; you've had a long stay in Florence, much longer than you expected."

"Not really. Still, there's something we need to attend to, don't you think?"

"Quite right. And that's what we're all here for, including Dr Biondi." He throws Anna a mischievous smile, before handing her appraisal to Caterina. "We have of course to adhere to the instructions in Peter Farrell's will. At our first meeting I mentioned that Countess Guiccioli will be first to select a painting of her choice. Your Ladyship, please take a look at the valuation. The paintings are arranged in descending order of value. What is it to be?"

Caterina takes hold of the paper, her hand trembling slightly as her eyes scroll through the list, stopping at each item. After a glance at Gabriele and me, she gets to her feet and walks towards the paintings. Pausing in front of each one, it feels like an eternity before she speaks. "It's got to be the Warhol; it's not really my cup of tea, but it is at the top of the list," she says shrilly, unable to disguise her emotion. Then she turns to me. "Remember, Maria, when Doris talked about Andy Warhol that evening at her hotel? Years ago, Peter was adamant that Warhol was going places, while Doris and I were sure he'd got it all wrong. Today I must say I'm extremely thankful he refused to listen to us!" Her eyes are dancing as she remembers the furious arguments she and Doris had with Peter; then she goes on, "But know what? I've not chosen the painting to remind me of Peter; I have my own way of remembering him. I chose it because, according to Dr Biondi's appraisal, it's worth a small fortune."

I can't wait to know what exactly she means by 'a small fortune'.

Then, as if reading my mind, she teases, "I bet you're all dying to know how much is written here." Her hand rests on the frame of the Warhol, as if to say, *This belongs to me now*. And, without more ado, she reads out the figure, first in lire, then in pounds, her voice trembling with elation.

I conclude that the sale of this painting is very probably the windfall Caterina mentioned the other day when she was talking on the phone to her charity in India.

A rasping voice suddenly makes itself heard. Gabriele instructs Manetti to get on with the proceedings. He's adamant that he won't be kept waiting. I whisper to him to keep his temper, telling him he is behaving like an idiot, with no consideration for the rest of us.

Struggling to stifle what sounds like the beginning of a wicked laugh, Manetti fumbles in his briefcase and pulls out an old trilby. "I'm afraid you'll have to be patient a little longer, Professor Foschi. Here's the hat my client instructed me to use. In it there are two folded papers; one with 'FIRST' written on it, the other with 'SECOND'. You and Ms Farrell should dip your hands into the hat at exactly the same time and draw out a paper. Go!"

Gabriele's face has turned crimson as we plunge our hands into Peter's old trilby. We unfold our papers, and I come up trumps.

"Congratulations, Ms Farrell," Manetti says quietly. "Here's the list. Go ahead and choose your first painting." Apparently, having forgotten that he is meant to be impartial, he is grinning from ear to ear as he says graciously, "However, you may have some questions for Dr Biondi first."

"No, I don't think so. I'm ready. Anna has assigned the Picasso second place on the list, so I'm going to choose that. It's tiny and one of the artist's minor works, but yes, Pablo—"

I haven't finished when Gabriele hits the roof, wagging his finger first at Caterina and then at me. "She gets the Warhol, then just because she's Peter's niece, she gets the Picasso and the rest of his possessions. What did she ever do for him? Nothing, *niente*, nada." Beside himself with rage, he hurls a vase off the table, and it slams onto the parquet floor.

I watch, horrified, as splinters of blue and yellow china spill out everywhere, thinking this will be one less item that I'll be taking back to Manchester. Of course he's got a point – I never did anything for Peter; nor could I, since I only met him once when I was three. I just happen to be his niece. Just the same, the scene unfolding before my eyes is hard to stomach. This man, who's been so kind to me, is shaking from head to toe, a torrent of abuse spewing from his lips.

"For Christ's sake! Peter was stupid enough to leave her his flat and everything else; then, as if that wasn't enough, the silly sod left her half our paintings. They should have all gone to me."

I butt in, trying to show him that I understand where he's coming from. "I'm as puzzled as you, Gabriele, that Peter left me these paintings. Still, you can hardly expect me to refuse them. He wanted me to have them."

Gabriele is in no mood to listen, and goes on, even angrier than before, "You do realise that over the years, Peter and I bought the paintings together? Or don't you? That's what's so unfair. Each time we purchased a painting, he'd say, 'This one's mine, the next one is yours.' So we built up two separate collections. Among his paintings, the Picasso is my absolute favourite, and you know it. And, damnation, it will soon be on its way to a city swarming with barbarians. Christ almighty! It's going to Manchester, the dreariest hole in England, if not the world."

Slinging his bag onto the table, Gabriele storms out, heading for the toilet, with Phoebe prancing and barking at his heels. An instant later, a door bangs to. Gabriele has not been gone for more than a few seconds when Manetti strides out after him, looking ready to scalp him. Soon all hell breaks loose. Manetti can be heard hammering on the toilet door and yelling frantically, "How dare you behave like this, Foschi? Come out of that toilet, you vandal! You're acting like a five-year-old."

Shortly after, the solicitor reappears with the culprit in tow. While the muscles in Gabriele's face are still twitching, he's managed to get a grip on himself. His head bowed, he cradles Phoebe in his arms, whispering into her fur that he'll take the Dalí.

Mine, yours, mine, yours. In a few minutes the paintings are shared out, and Manetti declares Gabriele and me to be the owners of five little nuggets apiece. He informs us that in the next few days we will receive the official papers, and at that point we can dispose of the paintings as we see fit. I've arranged for a lorry and an armed escort to travel through Switzerland and France as far as Calais, followed by a ferry over to Dover and on to Manchester. Three of the paintings are destined for the Manchester Gallery, while the other two will be kept in a deposit box awaiting auction.

The meeting concludes with a surprise. Angelo has given Manetti a letter from Peter, with instructions that his winemaking equipment is for Angelo. This is an irregular procedure, the lawyer admits, since the beneficiary should have been included in the will. However, if I am agreeable, Angelo will receive the equipment. I nod my assent. From what I understand, Angelo and Peter got on like a house on fire, and this also means that the cellar will be emptied free of charge.

The sound of a door shutting makes me jump. Gabriele has slunk out without saying goodbye to anybody. His outrage leaves me feeling drained. My legs are shaking, and I have to sit down. The anger, derision and spite he showered upon me have left me wondering if he has been deceiving me all along. Did he manage to pull the wool over my eyes? Did he help me with my investigation, while secretly hating me and perhaps even covering up his involvement in the murders?

Seeing me sitting with my head in my hands, Caterina comes over and apologises for Gabriele's behaviour, then adds, "Still, you should try to understand. He and Peter worked together for more than twenty years and built up a magnificent collection of paintings. It is very unfortunate that your uncle did not recognise what he owed his long-term partner when it came to writing his will."

I make a move to leave; I know Caterina's got a point, but I am in no mood to listen to her peacemaking efforts. I'm about to return to my hotel when Angelo intervenes. He grabs my arm, telling me that he's already phoned his mother and she's rustling us up a quick meal. I can sleep over at their place and return to Florence the following day. I certainly don't fancy the idea of spending an evening alone at my hotel, and gladly accept his invitation.

42

Angelo's village lies halfway between Lake Trasimeno and Florence, and his house is small but welcoming. His mother, Lina, is waiting for us in a whitewashed kitchen, chock-a-block with pots and pans of all sizes, hanging on the walls and covering the worktops. Piled in a corner, boxes and crates of fruit and veg are waiting to be cooked and frozen. This is a busy time of year, Lina says, pointing to a glut of produce from her allotment.

The impressive array of starters on the marble table tells me that this is not going to be the 'quick meal' Angelo mentioned. Apologetically, Lina asks in broken English if it is all right if we eat in the kitchen. There'll only be the three of us – Gerda's just left for Germany – so it's not worth laying the table in the dining room. I detect a touch of jubilance in Lina's voice as she mentions Gerda's departure, and remember what the young woman told me about the close bond between mother and son.

We are soon enjoying some delicious food, but as my hosts labour to ask me questions about England in their very basic English, I start to regret accepting Angelo's invitation. I'm still upset after the scene at Peter's flat, and in no mood to try and understand them, or to make an effort to speak in Italian. I drink a bit too much wine, and by the time dessert is served, I am slurring as I compliment Lina on her cooking. In her stilted English, she does her best to keep the conversation going. "You next visit, you cook English food for us. I curious."

With Lina in the kitchen washing up, Angelo takes me through to the sitting room, where he pulls out the family album. The photos show his journey through life: as a baby, a small boy, a teenager and finally a grown man. Nearly all the pictures are of Lina and him, making me curious to know what happened to his father. He took himself off to Australia, Angelo confides, and never came home. I think that this explains in part the bond between mother and son, and suspect that Gerda probably went home when she understood that there was no real place in Angelo's life for another woman.

Closing the album, my friend pushes a tiny object into my hand. It is a solid gold brooch in the shape of a snake. "Etruscan," he says with satisfaction; "a present for my mother."

I turn it over, fingering it and imagining the upper-class Etruscan lady who owned it all those centuries ago. Angelo's face clouds over as he adds that, sadly, there'll be no more brooches, nor any other Etruscan antiquities, come to that. Recently he's had problems with his clients, including Gabriele. There's been some infighting, and the police have had him down at the station for questioning. Even though they haven't prosecuted, he doesn't want to put his family in danger. From now on, his fishing business and Lina's pension will have to keep them going. They won't starve, he concludes, throwing me a defiant glance.

"And what about Giovanelli? What was the story there?" I ask. "I overheard you and Gabriele haggling over the funeral urn, that day on the lake. We also called on Giovanelli's widow, who showed us something that looked very like it."

Angelo looks flabbergasted and, after a pause, advises me in his broken English, 'Best forget the business, Maria; it is in everyone interest."

I can hear Lina calling my name from upstairs. She wants to show me where I am sleeping, and has made up a bed in a tiny room overlooking the garden. I tell them apologetically that I need an early night and am soon snuggled up in the small but comfortable bed, fast asleep.

43

While Maria was staying overnight at Angelo's, there was a fourth murder. It was 11pm when Singh arrived back home. He'd been out to a late-night film and was starving. He quickly poured himself a glass of wine, took a swig and started to cook a huge T-bone steak; a Fiorentina, as it's called in Tuscany. This always reminded him of Peter – it was what they had indulged in whenever it was just the two of them. If Gabriele was away at a conference or on business, Peter would arrange a dinner with a top-secret menu. On these occasions he could eat the things he knew he shouldn't, with Singh as a willing accomplice. The menu was invariably a medium-cooked steak that nearly covered the plate, a generous helping of crispy French fries, a good dollop of tiramisu and a bottle of the finest Brunello wine.

Singh liked some background noise as he cooked, and switched on the television. The programme didn't matter; it just made him feel less lonely. Once he'd grilled the steak to his liking, he cut it into small pieces, staring satisfied at the mountain of meat on his plate. He was on his second glass of wine and munching on a grissini while he waited for the chips to turn crisp and golden. Like Peter, he found solace in food, and helped himself to a chunk of pecorino cheese. He remembered the last dinner he'd enjoyed with the professor, during which the latter had done something he'd never done before. Having drunk more than usual, he had begun to tell Singh about his twin brother, Edward. They'd never stopped scrapping and skin and hair used to fly over the most trivial things: a dirty handkerchief or a broken shoelace could sometimes set them off. Still, with tears in his eyes, Peter had told Singh that, despite their differences, he and Edward had always managed to make it up, they were so close. A hug, an apologetic smile or a gentle look would put an end to their quarrel.

The entryphone rang, cutting into Singh's train of thought. It was nearly midnight and he hadn't the foggiest idea who could be calling at this late hour. He bit into the cheese again, promising himself he'd finish it when the caller had gone. He quickly slugged down the remaining wine in his glass, switched off the cooker, drained the chips and picked up the handset. A muffled voice said, "It's Detective Inspector Romagnoli. We want a word with you."

Singh didn't hesitate. He knew the detective, because over the past couple of months he'd been summoned to the station three times. He shoved the bottle of wine into a cupboard, pressed the button to open the main door and steeled himself for more questions.

Through the lodge window, he caught sight of two hooded men striding towards him, one holding an angry pit bull on a leash. Singh froze, then, as one of the men entered his room and lunged at him, he did his best to kick his assailant in the crotch. Sadly, the man's athletic frame put Singh at a distinct disadvantage, and he failed to hit the mark. Still, he did manage to whip off the attacker's hood, after which the latter pushed him to the floor. Staring at the man looming above him, Singh realised who he was and started to sob. Kim reacted immediately, grabbing a cushion and pressing it over Singh's face. For a few seconds he held it there until his victim had lost consciousness and stopped breathing.

Now Robin, who had been watching the attack, sprang into action. Once he had selected the keys to Peter's flat from the key rack, *he began to help Kim pull the corpse into the open lift. Inside the flat, the pair dragged the body through to the kitchen, where Robin unleashed the pit bull, which set about savaging the corpse. It had been left without food for two days and, with all its feral might, it tore at the body. After the dog had had its fill and was sprawled out, exhausted, on the tiles, Robin finished the job. Grabbing a hatchet and cleavers, he hacked at the body; he had evidently got over his earlier squeamishness. While he did so, Kim carried a sack of soil into the bathroom and emptied it into the tub. He turned on the taps, gloating as he watched the water turning the soil into mud.*

On returning to the sitting room, the sight of Robin ensconced on the divan having a fag, with the dog snoozing at his feet, and the job only half done, sent Kim ballistic. Shoving the empty sack into his accomplice's hand, he yelled at him to throw the body into the tub and clean the place very thoroughly at once. Robin complied, returning to the kitchen, gathering up the mangled body parts and shovelling them into the sack. Afterwards, he took the sack into the bathroom and emptied it into the muddy bathwater.

Before leaving the bathroom, Kim played a little game. Peter's magnificent collection of perfumes had caught his eye. Paris, Rome, London. Which should he choose? He hesitated. It had to be Rome. Smiling, he tried to spray Robin with a perfume labelled 'Il bel romano', but the latter dodged out of the way. He'd had quite enough and wanted to leave the premises. Calling his accomplice "a f... spoilsport", Kim shoved the bottle into his bag; another keepsake of the man he'd murdered a few months before.

44

It's 10.30 and I get to the flat half an hour later than my usual time. Following Gabriele's violent outburst at Manetti's, I took a day off from the clear-out to see a little more of Florence. I wonder again at how Gabriele had managed to appear so composed and friendly towards me for so long. I particularly wanted to visit the Uffizi Gallery and Botticelli's *Allegory of Spring* and *Birth of Venus* paintings, and spent over an hour in the Botticelli Room. The artwork made me remember how I had imagined Caterina as an elderly Venus, and wonder if she was indeed as beautiful in her youth as the young woman in the painting. *How*, I mused, *can there be so much beauty in Florence alongside the horror of these murders?* I also popped into a travel agency to make inquiries about a trip to India for Singh, my spirits soaring at the prospect of being able to give him a special treat.

Performing my usual wave in front of the lodge window, I can't wait to tell my friend that a holiday is on the cards for him, if his boss will give him the time off. Approaching the window, I peer inside, my eyes landing on his chair. It's empty, and Peter's keys aren't on their usual hook. I guess Singh has already gone upstairs to make a start on my uncle's books.

As the lift climbs to the third floor, I start to plan my morning's work: sorting through Peter's library, reading snippets here and there, and perhaps listening to Singh telling me a story or two about Peter. I ring the doorbell, but there's no answer, so I try the handle. I stiffen when the door swings open, immediately thinking that the flat has been burgled and the paintings stolen. In a panic, I walk inside, calling out Singh's name, but there's no answer. In the sitting room there's a tantalising scent of perfume, and to my relief, the paintings are still there in what is otherwise an almost empty room. A divan, a couple of chairs, a table and a telephone are still piled up in the corner where I left them.

Once in Peter's bedroom, I notice the bathroom door is open, and look inside. My eyes fall on the bathtub, filled to nearly overflowing with muddy water. Then, looking closer, I shudder at the sight of a hand with two of its fingers chopped off, just below the surface. Unable to process what I'm seeing, I sink down onto the tiles and throw up. I grab a towel and try to wipe the vomit off my face and T-shirt, but the more I rub, the more noticeable the stains are. Desperate, I rush downstairs, deliberately avoiding the lift, afraid of being attacked in there by a potential assailant. Halfway down, I remember my mobile, and for a split second I think I should phone the police. But I keep running; I've just got to reach the entrance hall.

Once there, I find a young woman, one of Peter's neighbours, who tells me she is looking for Singh, and I exclaim, "I'm sorry, but Singh's gone. I mean, he's dead." A second later the neighbour calls the police, and we sit huddled at the foot of the stairs, waiting for them to arrive.

Not long after, sirens can be heard outside, and the main door swings open. Romagnoli, Gianni and the forensic team are soon striding through the hallway. I get to my feet, watching as Romagnoli and the forensics rush upstairs. Then I hear Gianni's voice very firmly and calmly seeking to quieten the wild thoughts that have overtaken me, but another voice, the one in my head, refuses to leave me in peace – *What if the murderer returns while you are sitting here?* it keeps repeating. When Gianni learns it was me who found the body, he allows the young woman to return to her flat. Ushering me into Singh's lodge, he tells me I have no option but to go down to the station for questioning, but first he'll make us a cup of tea.

"You mean imperial gunpowder?" I ask, smiling bitterly, tears welling in my eyes as I remember Singh. "There, that's it in the caddy on the shelf; Singh's favourite tea. Why Singh? Why such a good man? Know what, Gianni, I'm beginning to feel totally drained. I mean, I can't go on dealing with murder on a daily basis. It's wormed its way into my everyday life, my tiniest actions and thoughts. I no longer see the world as I used to. And Singh's brutal murder is the last straw; it's made me feel even more threatened. As I look at you now, I'm wondering whether you'll be alive tomorrow. Will *I* be alive tomorrow, come to that? I don't think I can take any more. I just want to get home to Manchester as soon as I can."

Gianni shakes his head. "I'm sorry, but you found Singh's body and, as I said, we need a statement from you. There is no way I can allow you to leave Florence, or Italy come to that." He squeezes my hand, before ushering me out to a waiting police car.

45

Vivien Newman is standing just inside the entrance of the police station, a pen and notebook in her hand. Dressed in a pink blouse and pants, her long brown hair pulled back in a ponytail, she scribbles something down. After a quick "*Buongiorno*; sorry to see you here again", she guides me down the by-now-familiar corridor.

I can feel myself shrinking at the prospect of yet another interview. This time, though, face to face with Gianni and Romagnoli, I have several things I wish to tell them. Finding Singh's body has made me feel like the killer is breathing down my neck, ready to kill again. I kick off with a description of the last time I saw Singh alive, and how I found his body in Peter's bathroom. I conclude by saying that I have absolutely no idea who could have murdered such a lovely man. Romagnoli is in the habit of repeating the same questions time and again, making me feel confused and exhausted. On the point of tears, I stare at Gianni, who's looking concerned. Then a sharp cough interrupts the silence, and Romagnoli asks whether I have anything more to tell them. On impulse, I plunge into the deep end, telling them about my enquiry into Peter's murder and Gabriele Foschi's role in that investigation. On hearing this, Gianni looks nonplussed, while Romagnoli goes ballistic. He is furious that somebody – and I can't help thinking that his fury is partly due to my being a woman and a foreigner – should dare to attempt to do his job for him. I apologise but say I felt it was my moral duty. He shakes his head but I plough on regardless, keeping my eyes riveted on the desk as I explain Caterina's theory about a possible connection between the murders and Dante's *Inferno*.

Romagnoli lurches forward, putting his hands on the desk and making eye contact; his by-now-familiar way of signalling that he is absolutely focused on what I am saying. Encouraged, I suggest that somebody might be so obsessed with Dante and the punishments he describes in the *Inferno* that he or she is bent on accomplishing in real life what Dante only wrote about. Romagnoli looks increasingly sceptical, but keeps nodding at me to go on. I point out that the murders of Mario Giovanelli and Doris Gainsborough tally perfectly with two punishments in the *Inferno*. I admit, though, that I have still to uncover a definite link between Peter's murder and Dante.

"I see. So, as far as we know, your theory works for only two of the three murders. And what about Singh, the fourth victim?" Romagnoli asks, throwing me a scornful look. "What's Dante got to do with his death?"

When I fail to answer, he shakes his head impatiently and winks at Gianni. Then, surprising even myself, I exclaim, "The Gluttons, Canto 6!" I read this canto several times when I suspected that Peter's sin might have been gluttony. "They are splattered in mud and torn to pieces by Cerberus. And remember, the murderer or murderers left Singh's body in a bath filled with muddy water."

"Cer-ber-us." Gianni pronounces the name, deliberately splitting the syllables as if it might help him to fathom the meaning of what I've just said. "Cerberus, the monstrous hound of Hell who tears the Gluttons to shreds. I remember reading that passage at high school. I was sixteen, and revelled in the gory bits."

Romagnoli scowls at his colleague, perhaps for relating a personal experience, prompting Gianni to switch quickly back to his detective mode.

"You aren't to know, Ms Farrell, but once forensics pulled Singh's body out of the tub, it actually looked like it had been ripped apart."

On that cue I pull my translation of the *Inferno* out of my bag and read the lines describing Cerberus.

Cerberus is haughty, cruel and feral.
With his three throats, he barks and slobbers
Over the people drowned in the water below.
He's got red eyes, a greasy black beard,
A huge belly, and claw-like paws
Which he uses to maul and quarter these souls.

Romagnoli lights a cigarette, tilting his head back and blowing smoke rings in the air, before asking, very deliberately, "Can all this Dante stuff really have anything do with the murders? Come on, Signora Farrell, let's get back to the facts. Has anybody you have met during your 'investigation'," he pronounces the last word scathingly, "acted in any way suspiciously?"

I stare back at him and decide to put some more cards on the table. "For a while I suspected Countess Guiccioli, who first suggested the connection. Recently, though, I have come to see another side to her and believe I was wrong. Today, Gabriele Foschi is high on my list of suspects. During the meeting at my uncle's flat to share out the paintings, his temper got the better of him and he showed how deeply he resents me. You have to understand that Gabriele is furious that Peter left me so much in his will. Then there is Federico Nitti. The man has a drink problem that makes him very aggressive. At the countess's castle, I watched him skinning and cutting up some rabbits. He certainly knows how to handle a knife with great dexterity."

By now Romagnoli is tapping his fingernails on the desk; a sign that his patience is wearing thin. He takes a deep breath before giving his orders. "Signora Farrell, these are mere suppositions. You would be well advised to leave any further inquiries to the people who are qualified in such matters. Skinning and cutting up rabbits can hardly be defined as incriminating behaviour or a recipe for murder. What you've told us will be of no help, I believe, in getting a conviction."

I now decide not to mention Alfonso's strange behaviour, for fear that Romagnoli will completely lose his rag. Still, he has a final question about a group of tomb thieves operating in the area. He has reason to believe that some of the people I have met in Florence are involved in buying and selling Etruscan antiquities.

I quickly decide on an answer which I hope will satisfy him. "Yes, I've heard the word '*tombaroli*' a few times in conversations between Gabriele Foschi and Caterina Guiccioli. However, they were talking in Italian so I couldn't understand exactly what they were saying."

The whole business of the tomb thieves seems so shady and complicated that I don't dare start telling Romagnoli what I know. I am also well aware that Peter and Gabriele channelled some of their earnings from the sale of Etruscan relics into their art collection, and that I will benefit from some of those paintings. Deeply uneasy, I decide I had better keep quiet.

Then Romagnoli jolts me out of my silent meanderings, informing me that he will file my statement and I am free to go.

46

A couple of days after Singh's murder, the police lift the sequestration order, and I am allowed to return to the flat. I have an appointment with the carriers I've hired to take the paintings to Manchester. The official papers have come through and I can dispose of the artworks as I see fit.

When I reach Peter's, I get a surprise: there are a couple of vans on the pavement, together with a police car. Two officers in uniform approach and inform me that the carriers will have to wait. Accompanied by the policemen, I take the lift up to Peter's flat, wondering what on earth is going on.

Waiting for us on the landing are two men, who introduce themselves as bailiffs. They have orders to confiscate Peter's paintings until further notice. There are no chairs left in the sitting room so I sink down on the floor, my back against the wall, watching the pair take down the paintings, carefully wrap them and place them in crates. Before my eyes, my plans for the paintings evaporate into thin air. Caterina and Gabriele are also in for a rude awakening. I kick myself, thinking that, when Angelo confided in me about his recent brush with the police and his decision to stop trading in Etruscan relics, I should have suspected it might mean trouble not just for him, but for everyone else involved in the racket.

The bailiffs leave, and I stare glumly at the empty wall. Then the entryphone interrupts my thoughts. It is Deirdre, reminding me that I asked her to call round this morning to go through Peter's books. I decide not to tell her that the paintings have just been taken away, and instead keep our conversation focused on the books.

Deirdre looks very different from when I last saw her. She is positively glowing, her red hair freshly washed and shining, her eyes sparkling, a matching black top and pants showing off her shapely figure.

"What's new?" I ask, trying to put a smile in my voice. "Work going well?"

She grins. She's just found herself a new boyfriend, an Italian bookseller, and can't wait to tell me about him. "We fell for each other hook, line and Shelley," she laughs as she tells me about the animated discussion they had when they first met. "Can you believe it, Maria – our love story is all due to Percy Shelley? Paolo swore blind Shelley's poem *Ode to the West Wind* was inspired by a real storm, but that's a load of baloney. Give me a break! Shelley didn't need a real storm to put his inner turmoil into verse. In 1819 he found himself in terrible financial straits. On top of that, he was having an affair, and his marriage to Mary was on the rocks."

"Surely it was a bit of both?" I butt in. "The combination of a storm, a huge gale blowing the leaves everywhere, and Shelley's private worries."

"You could be right," she reflects, smiling, "but don't tell Paolo when you meet him."

Perked up by a double shot of caffeine, we go into Peter's office so Deirdre can sort through the books arranged in neat piles where Singh and I left them. While she is busy choosing which books she wants, I sit at Peter's desk and try to imagine it in the little flat I am hoping to buy in Florence – if, I tell myself, I am allowed to sell Peter's flat, since it too might be confiscated before too long.

My eyes fall on Peter's riddle again. It is still sitting on the desk where I left it earlier this month. I read it aloud, curious to hear what Deirdre makes of it.

Dial 999, that's my advice.
Add one, and in a trice
I'll take you where
You're bound to share
Fine food and wine;
The pleasure's mine.
They'll solve the mystery
of your uncle's history.

"'Food and wine,'" she murmurs thoughtfully. "I'd say seventy per cent of the books Peter bought from me were art books, and the other thirty per cent were cookbooks or books on the history of food and drink. He used to joke that even though he was a terrible cook, he was a mastermind on everything to do with eating and drinking. Anyway, coming back to the lines you've just read, Peter adored Lewis Carroll, and particularly the riddles in *Alice's Adventures in Wonderland*. The Mad Hatter's question 'Why is a raven like a writing desk?' was one of his favourites. It sounds as if he meant you to fathom this riddle."

Deirdre's remarks prompt me to re-examine the words 'food and wine'. When I first discovered the riddle, I'd been too busy searching for the safe to think about anything else. I recall now how Singh once read me some entries from Peter's notebooks about his trips to the countryside. I have put the notebooks in a pile on the kitchen floor ready for packing, and go to get the one I want. The second entry that Singh read was dated 1999. Finding the notebook, I flick through it, stopping at Peter's description of his trip to Pontremoli.

20th October 1999

The tagliatelle and porcini are not a patch on last year. The chef not only skimped on the parsley; he added it too late for it to give the dish its full flavour.

Salvatore's been given the boot. It's a real pity! He's a lovely man, while the new chef's as thick as two short planks, as Mam used to say. The waiter let it slip that the present chef can't tell a porcini from a toadstool. God help us! This trattoria used to be a safe haven when Salvatore (no pun intended) was around!

Just the same, we had a great time because in the evening Salvatore invited us to his home and cooked us a mouth-watering meal.

This time the expression 'safe haven' jumps out at me. It strikes me that 'safe' means 'rescued' or 'protected', but also 'a place to keep and store valuables under lock and key'. While Peter flags up the two possible meanings of 'Salvatore' (as a Christian name and a 'saviour'), I wonder if he could also be punning on the word 'safe'.

On impulse, I decide I have to visit Pontremoli to meet Salvatore and find out what he can tell me about Peter's 'safe haven'. I catch myself repeating the name 'Pontremoli', like a mantra that might help me solve the riddle. Deirdre joins in, splitting the word into syllables and pointing to different meanings: 'Ponte', 'pon', 'te', 'tre', 'mo', 'lo', 'tremolo'. "Ponte tremolo," she says, translating the words into English as 'trembling bridge'.

I suddenly realise I don't have the foggiest idea where Pontremoli is, and begin rummaging among Peter's maps for one of Italy. Once I have found one, I spread it out on the floor, and Deirdre points to Pontremoli in the north of Tuscany, 160 kilometres from Florence. Her face lights up, her voice animated as she fills me in on some local history. "Pontremoli is well known for its small bookshops and its celebrated tradition of itinerant booksellers. They used to leave Pontremoli every spring to visit the surrounding rural areas. These booksellers mostly flogged popular books to farmers and country people who couldn't easily access the towns and cities. Even today, every July there's an important literary prize in the town called the Premio Bancarella. It's well worth a visit, if you're still around then." Even if nothing useful comes of my visit, she reassures me, it'll be an enjoyable trip.

I ask her if she'll come with me to Pontremoli right now. I would welcome the company, and she can translate for me when needed. I haven't seen Gabriele since the terrible scene he made at Manetti's, and have no wish to see him again.

The drive to Pontremoli takes us over the Passo della Cisa, a mountain pass a thousand metres high, along a road that turns into a tortuous snake the higher we climb. I shiver at the sudden drop in temperature and pull on a cardigan, knotting a scarf round my neck to keep myself warm.

As we drive, my friend keeps me entertained with stories of various people who have patronised her stall over the years. Some really famous celebrities – film stars, writers, musicians – have turned up in search of an interesting read. We are travelling through an expanse of woodland when she whispers, as if unveiling a state secret, "You should know, this is porcini territory, and a very special place. Some years ago I visited a fabulous restaurant nearby and got into conversation with a local man. He told me all about the giant mushrooms he gathered here. He got me so excited, and then refused to divulge the exact spot where they grow. Truth is, the locals will never tell you about their secret places." She still sounds cheated, even though years have elapsed since the episode.

Soon after, we start our descent down a steep hill, and the town of Pontremoli comes into sight. Sprawling in the valley below, it is divided by a river. A few minutes later, we reach the bottom of the valley and cross a bridge. Once we've parked the car, we get a chance to enjoy a better view of the river and the villas on either bank. I catch my breath at the sight of the well-kept, colourful gardens and terraces stretching down to the water's edge.

But what now? It seems pointless to search for the Trattoria della Posta where Peter ate two years ago. If Salvatore was sacked from there, the owner will probably not want to talk about him. Instead I suggest we head for the main square and ask around in the bars as to whether anyone has heard of Salvatore.

In one bar we get chatting to a couple of farmers enjoying a late morning coffee, but the minute we mention Salvatore their faces go blank. Then I notice a girl in designer jeans and a short-sleeved blouse, absorbed in a magazine. She looks oddly out of place among the swarthy farmers. As she sees us, she throws us a curious glance, after which her eyes dart back to her reading. Smiling apologetically, I ask her in my broken Italian if I can have a word. She stares silently back, so I try another tactic; I offer to buy her a cappuccino and a chocolate. A couple of minutes later, carefully balancing the promised fare on a tray, I walk back to her table and plonk them down. I catch her smiling; my ploy seems to be working. "Fancy something nice?" I ask her, dangling the chocolate in its shiny wrapper under her nose.

Chuckling, she takes it, undoes the wrapper and pops it in her mouth. Grinning like a Cheshire cat, she tells me what I want to hear. "If it's Salvatore Rossi you're after," she mutters, wiping the chocolate from her lips, "he lives in a cottage just past the oil mill. Cross the square and take the road to your left. After about five minutes you'll find an alley on your right and see a sign – '*Il Mulino*'. That means 'mill' in Italian. Go down the alley until you come to the mill, and on the same side of the road you'll find Salvatore's cottage. It's about a ten-minute walk."

Deirdre and I hurry off, and sure enough, a few minutes later we find the sign, and then the mill, its door boarded up and the shutters at its tiny windows closed. A little further on, we come across a dilapidated cottage, where Deirdre knocks and the wrinkly face of an old woman appears at an upstairs window. She scowls, waving and shouting at us to go away, and I decide it's best to let Deirdre do the talking. When my new-found friend inquires after Salvatore, the woman grows quiet, then, coming downstairs and appearing at the front door, she asks who we are and the reason for our visit. Deirdre's explanation seems to satisfy her, and she is soon nodding and pointing farther down the alley. "Go to the river. Salvatore's out fishing; you can't miss him."

As we resume our walk, the path narrows and the brambles get thicker. I stumble over a warped tree stump and curse loudly, making my friend crease up laughing at my attempt at swearing in Italian. My "Madonna, the pity of pigs and cows" doesn't sound quite right.

Laughing, she suggests, "Why don't you keep it simpler? Something like '*Porco zio, mi sono fatta male.*'"

"What does that translate as? Isn't '*zio*' the Italian for 'uncle'?"

"It is, but a decent translation would be 'Holy hell, I've hurt myself.'"

Complimenting her on the translation, but warning that we should get a move on, I speed up. I am anxious to talk to Salvatore.

At the river, I scan around and catch sight of a man sitting on a rock. He is gazing into the water, cradling his head in his hands, his shoulders bent. Hearing us approach, he turns, staring hard, displaying his haggard face. Getting closer, I notice that his eyes are sunken and his clothes look in need of a wash. He's holding a half-smoked unlit cigarette between his fingers, as if he can't be bothered to relight it. On hearing that I am Peter's niece, he throws me a mournful look and introduces himself as Salvatore. Then Deirdre gets to work translating what he says.

"I read about Peter's murder in the paper, and soon after the police came down to Pontremoli to question me. Even now I can't see why anybody would want to murder such a decent man. Still, Maria, you took your time getting here!" Seeing my puzzled expression, he continues, "Peter first mentioned you last year, and said you'd probably turn up after he was dead." Salvatore pulls a face, as if to say he didn't like what Peter said one little bit. "Straight away when I heard that gloomy forecast, I told him I hoped your visit would be in forty years' time." Salvatore shrugs his shoulders, mischievously mimicking Peter. "But he was adamant that you would drop by much sooner. And before he left for Florence, he gave me strict instructions that when you did turn up I should take you to the oil mill and let you hunt around in there."

We set off for the mill, with Deirdre and me on either side of our guide. He is limping and keeps a tight grip on a stick to steady himself, but this doesn't prevent him talking ten to the dozen. "Your uncle rented the mill from me six years ago, I think. He wanted to make his own olive oil, and enlisted my help. He never came down here for more than a couple of days at a time, but he was eager to learn as much as he could about how we make the stuff."

As with everything, I think to myself, *Peter wanted the very best. In this case, top-quality olive oil, cold-pressed and made with organic olives.*

Salvatore's expression turns sad as he recalls, "You know, your uncle enjoyed some good meals with my family. He just loved his food. After his murder, I decided to board up the mill. It brought back too many fond memories of his visits here."

47

At the mill, Salvatore does his best to open the door, leaning his shoulder and all his weight against the warped wood, swearing like a Trojan, but it refuses to budge. In the end Deirdre comes to his aid, grabbing a heavy iron bar and managing to lever the door open. She mutters that years of carrying piles of books have given her the strength of an ox.

Inside, I stare into what looks like a dark pit and notice our guide throwing me an apologetic glance as he opens the shutters to let in some sunlight. The lights aren't working, he says, because recently the electric company cut off the power. Jokingly, he adds that Peter has done a moonlight flit and apparently overlooked the most recent bills in his rush to get out of here.

In the middle of the room are a huge vat and a millstone, the latter with a long wooden shaft, crenellated at the top end and almost touching the ceiling. I find myself shuddering; it looks for all the world like a medieval torture device. Lines of olive-oil containers complete the decor. Taking a small cup, Salvatore turns on the tap of one of the containers, and some yellowy-green liquid flows out. He holds it out to me so I can smell the delicious fragrance; then makes a beeline for the exit, saying that, before I return to Florence, there are a few bottles waiting for me at his place.

Left to our own devices, my friend and I begin to search for the safe. Circling the vat, I peer inside, gingerly fingering a thin layer of dust on the surface. Then I look under and inside the containers, but find nothing. Meanwhile, Deirdre sets about inspecting some shelves, on which piles of dusters, a pitchfork, and piles of old clothes are arranged. In front of a dirty washbasin, I notice a mat on the floor and pick it up, releasing thousands of tiny insects. I've just uncovered a great deal of frantic activity, but no trapdoor.

Deirdre climbs a ladder propped in a corner and disappears through a hatch in the ceiling. On impulse I follow her and find myself in a tiny room lit by a skylight. It is sparsely furnished, with a single bed, a simple table, and a wooden chair with a towel draped over the back. It could almost, Deirdre suggests, be a monastic cell, discounting the colourful posters on the walls advertising Tuscan food and wine. I suppose it was here that Peter spent the occasional night.

Deirdre is still hard at work, quickly sliding the mattress off the bed to find more layers of dust underneath. By now she's fed up and suggests taking a break, but I refuse. Pointing to the posters on the wall, I ask her to give me a hand to take them down. At last, behind one of them (advertising Brunello wine), we strike lucky. "I can't believe it. The safe! It's the safe!" I cry, overjoyed. "Something told me you'd bring me luck, Deirdre!"

In sharp contrast to everything else in the mill, the safe is small, black, shiny and new. Pulling the riddle out of my pocket, I tap in the number 999, but the safe door won't budge. I study the riddle again, lingering on 'add one'. I try 1999, and magically the door swings open, revealing a tiny box. Opening it, I carefully examine the contents: a pair of cufflinks, three gold rings, a locket containing a black-and-white photo of Peter and Edward at about five. Then, at the bottom of the box, concealed by a piece of blue silk, is the real surprise: a powder-blue envelope. Written on it in Peter's immaculate handwriting are the words 'For Maria Farrell, my niece. You made it, clever girl!'

Grabbing the chair, I move it under the skylight so I can see to read the envelope's contents. My hands are shaking as I open the envelope. A single sheet of blue paper, again in Peter's neat handwriting, says:

Dear Maria,

I only met you once when you were just three years old, and it grieves me to think that you were probably never told about that meeting. For all these years I've cherished those few days in Manchester. I could see myself in you, and that was really special since I never had children of my own.

You must wonder why I didn't come looking for you again. It was out of respect for Edward; he wouldn't have liked it. In fact, it would have made him very angry. Still, you should know that I always loved you, and from time to time I had news of you from my cousin, Edith. I'm so pleased you're doing something artistic. It would have been awful if you'd become a secretary, a bank clerk or something dreary like that.

I want you to know what happened between Edward and me. Our relationship, as I suppose Gabriele has told you, was difficult, to put it mildly. That's typical, though, of many identical twins. We loved each other to bits, but there was friction. My homosexuality – I can say it today; I couldn't when I was young – irked Edward. He couldn't understand what was happening to me, but could sense that I was attracted to other boys, and he began to understand that one day he would lose me to somebody else. To cut a long story short, when we came to sit our Oxbridge entrance exam, I was at the end of my tether. I was in love with a young man called Jim and wanted to go to college with him. Edward kept saying that he and I would either swim or sink together. He was adamant that he would never let me go.

The day of our exam was almost upon us. Edward was a crammer and had been studying day and night. Just the opposite of me! I'd been enjoying this passionate affair with Jim and had hardly opened a book. Then I had this brilliant idea: I dreamt up a kind of 'merry bond'. You know, like Shylock's pound of flesh in The Merchant of Venice. *Come to think of it, that too ended badly. I told Teddy that if he really loved me, he had to prove it: he'd write my exam paper for me, and I'd write his. If he did so, I'd never desert him. To my surprise, he agreed. A part of me wanted to slap him and tell him not to be so daft, but I kept quiet.*

On the morning of the exam, we walked into the great hall together and took our places at two neighbouring desks. He wrote my name on the top of his paper and I wrote his on mine. The upshot: I made it to Oxford and he ended up at Hull. Soon after he found out about Jim, who had managed to get into Oxford with me.

That was the last straw. After the most terrible row, Edward never spoke to me again, even at our mother's funeral. I know I betrayed his love but, as you can see, I had my motives. I didn't deceive him out of wickedness, but spurred on by a need to be myself, to live my own life.

I'm so sorry you never came to visit me in Florence and I never got the chance to introduce you to this truly magnificent city and my darling Gabriele.

All my love,
Peter

On the return journey to Florence I deliberately avoid the motorway, instead choosing the country roads. I need to clear my head, and hope that the rolling hills and vineyards will help slow down my racing thoughts. But the words 'deceit and treachery' keep niggling me. I picture Peter's frozen corpse, and finally the details of his murder make sense. The answer probably lies in Dante's Canto 32, which deals with those sinners who betray the people closest to them.

> *Then I saw a thousand doglike faces*
> *Embedded in the ice.*
> *Recalling them I shudder,*
> *And always will, whenever I see a frozen pool.*

In the letter Peter confesses to deceiving his twin brother. How, though, could the murderer have known about this? Gabriele was the person in whom Uncle would most likely have confided. Was he to blame for his death, and perhaps even the other three murders?

48

It was 2.30 and Romagnoli and Celentano were just finishing off a hearty lunch to celebrate Romagnoli's birthday. Over coffee and a cigarette, they got to talking about the latest developments in the Peter Farrell case.

They had had a busy few days. On the basis of information Angelo Verza had provided about the tomb thieves racket, they had sent the bailiffs to Farrell's flat to confiscate his collection of paintings. Romagnoli remarked darkly that the three recipients of the paintings, who had probably already decided how they would spend the money from their sale, must have had a terrible shock; their considerable windfall snatched away soon after it fell into their laps.

Returning to the four murders, the detectives were forced to admit that they had come up with no new evidence or leads. Romagnoli laughed as he recalled Maria Farrell's last statement, which had pointed a finger at Dante. Once again he scoffed at her attempts to try her hand at conducting a murder investigation; but Celentano revealed that, in light of the woman's claims, he had reread Dante's Inferno. Maria's theory might sound far-fetched but, in the absence *of anything else, he suggested, they should not totally disregard it. Indeed, he believed they should keep a close eye on Countess Guiccioli, who, if Ms Farrell was correct, was obsessed with the* Inferno *and the Florentine writer.*

49

Gianni and I are sitting in Peter's almost-empty flat, enjoying a coffee. "No paintings to look at any more. Shame, isn't it?" I say, staring at the empty wall. "What are Italy's legal procedures in these circumstances? I mean, is there a chance I'll get the paintings back?"

His eyes hold mine, before he replies, "For professional and ethical reasons, I can't go into detail, Maria. Our murder investigation will need to be finished before the prosecutor can decide what happens to the paintings. I'm sure you can appreciate that the matter is complicated. The murders, the tomb thieves, Dante – if indeed you are right – and the paintings might all be connected."

"So there's not much hope of me getting them back. Is that it?"

"I can't answer that," he says firmly. "I really don't know."

"Have Gabriele and Caterina been informed?"

"They have, and, like yours, their paintings have been confiscated."

"And what about the flat? Is that likely to go the same way?" I ask hesitantly, dreading his reply.

"As far as I am aware, Maria, the flat is yours. According to the deeds, your uncle inherited it from a friend in the late 1960s."

"That was some friend!" My spirits soar and I am tempted to ask Gianni if he knows anything more about Peter's benefactor, but I decide against it. If the flat still belongs to me, at the end of the day that's all I need to know.

Shortly after Gianni has left, the phone starts ringing and I reluctantly put down Dante's *Inferno*. Caterina's actor friend Giacomo was right when he said that Dante, like Shakespeare, deserves in-depth study. And I have a very practical motive for reading him again. I wish to link each murder as precisely as possible to one of Dante's punishments.

It's Caterina on the phone, asking me to go round to her place; she's decided to go ahead with marketing the lavender perfume and needs my help. She's written a letter in English to her perfumer in London, and, seeing as it's about the contract and brand, she wants to be sure that her English is absolutely spot on. She sounds tired and tense, and I ask her what's wrong.

"Nothing to worry about," she replies, her voice shaking slightly. "It's probably because I am leaving for India in a few days and I have so much to do before I go. The last-minute rush is getting to me."

"It's such awful luck about Peter's paintings, isn't it?"

When she shouts back that the situation is a real mess, I pull her up short.

"Stop shouting, Caterina. I'll be round in about half an hour and we can talk about it then."

I phone Gianni to let him know where I am going. After all that's happened, I've made it a hard-and-fast rule to keep the police informed about my movements. Seeing as it's only early afternoon, I decide to walk over to Caterina's.

The air outside is clammy, boding a storm, and a strong wind is already getting up. By now I know the route from Peter's flat to Caterina's palace blindfold, and I am soon in Piazza della Santissima Annunziata, where the sight of the Hospital of the Innocents reminds me that I still haven't managed a visit.

Ten minutes later, I'm battling terrifying squalls of wind but, undeterred, I stop for a moment to admire the grey-and-white facade of the Basilica di Santa Croce. I'm standing mesmerised by its elegant simplicity, when suddenly I have a hunch that somebody's watching me. Looking round, I see a youngish man in a white raincoat, an umbrella in one hand, a mobile phone in the other pressed to his ear. The minute he realises I've noticed him he looks away and keeps talking.

I quickly cross the square and head down the familiar alley leading to Caterina's palace. Another quick glance behind me, and the man is still tailing me. Panicking, I grab my phone to ring Gianni, then tell myself I'm growing paranoid. Doesn't this very ordinary-looking young man, talking on his phone, have every right to be strolling around Florence on a hot, stormy afternoon?

Just fifty metres ahead, Caterina's palace comes into view. Another glance behind me tells me that my suspected stalker has disappeared, and I ring the bell. A single buzz, and Alfonso opens the door, a strange smile on his face. Instantly I recall our recent meeting and feel a deep sense of apprehension. Jingling a bunch of keys, he inquires how I am, remarking that it is considerate of me to have braved the storm to come and give Caterina a hand. She's her usual impatient self, he murmurs, the smile swiftly disappearing from his face.

Climbing the stairs to Caterina's apartment, a jumble of thoughts flashes through my mind: my upcoming journey back to Manchester, rehearsals for my production of *The Tempest*, a return trip to Florence for the sale of Peter's flat and, later, another for the murder trial if they catch the killer or killers.

Unlocking the door of Caterina's apartment, Alfonso pushes it open, steps back and motions me into the vestibule. We walk through the unlit gallery of paintings before coming to the sitting room.

What I see there fills me with horror. Caterina is tied to a chair, gagged and sobbing her heart out. All the windows are flung open, making the noise of the storm deafening. I head for the door, but Alfonso's hands grip my shoulders and propel me to a chair next to Caterina's. He orders me to sit down and, seeing me dithering, flips. This time he pushes me down. The countess and I, he announces coldly, are his next two victims. Hearing his words, an icy bolt races through my body.

Ungagging Caterina and threatening her with a gun, he tells her to translate what he's about to say, and she complies. "This woman is a wealthy windbag," Alfonso begins, pointing straight at Caterina. Then, hearing her voice tremble, he slaps her face. She braces herself and bravely makes a tremendous effort to keep translating. "So far she has utterly failed to keep her promises. She's only capable of talking non-stop about Dante and his *Inferno*. And now instead of rabbiting on about cleaning up Italy, she's embarked on the present madcap mission: she intends to save the entire Asian subcontinent. When I heard she was off to India with Federico Nitti, it was the last straw. I decided to kill her. Dante spent years writing the *Divine Comedy*, in which he gives details of his suggested punishments for the sinners of his day. She has had every opportunity to follow his instructions and implement his punishments, and she didn't! I therefore felt it was my duty to do something for real."

"Did Caterina know what you were up to?" I ask. I need to keep him talking in the hope that the police, or somebody else, will arrive before he murders us.

"No, I am proud to say that everything has been done without her knowledge. As for you, Ms Farrell, you've been poking your nose into things that don't concern you. Gabriele told me what you've been up to, and I'm compelled to put a stop to your meddling. You've not committed a particular sin like my other victims; I simply have to get rid of you. However, before I do, I wish you to know why and how I chose my victims."

I clock Caterina's terrified eyes and the tiny muscles twitching all over her face.

"Mario Giovanelli." Alfonso sneers. "That man deliberately set out to divide his colleagues into two factions. He was one of Dante's Sowers of Discord; Canto 28."

"When did you first meet him?" I ask, wondering whether Alfonso's hatred of Giovanelli dates back to the days when Peter fell out with his colleague.

"We met at Peter's place. At the time Giovanelli was still young and desperate to secure tenure. As he got older, his ambition knew no bounds. When Peter decided to take early retirement, Giovanelli had it in for Gabriele, who never missed a chance to rally colleagues to vote against his proposals and stop him climbing up the academic ladder."

I wonder again about the relationship between Alfonso and Gabriele, and remember that first time I saw them together in the palace courtyard. They seemed so close. Then it occurs to me that I will probably never find out. I could soon be dead.

"Doris Gainsborough." Alfonso's words break into my thoughts. "She was a foul-tempered woman, one of Dante's Wrathful; Canto 8."

"But is that the only reason you murdered her? In this day and age it is no sin to be angry, Alfonso. There are so many people around who have foul tempers."

"According to Dante, extreme anger, or ire, *is* a sin. Still, there were other factors. Like Giovanelli, Peter and Gabriele were tired of Doris's way of doing business. She had started buying Etruscan relics from other dealers, rather than exclusively from them. My main reason, though, was more personal. Ms Gainsborough argued with me a couple of days before I killed her. We sometimes saw each other when she visited Florence. We'd have a meal, a drink, then, depending… she quite fancied me, I think, and was always very generous, if you see what I mean. That evening she'd had a bit too much to drink, and when we got back to her hotel, she started coming on to me, but I wasn't in the mood. When I went to leave, she went berserk, slapping my face and insulting me. She had the nerve to throw me out of her hotel room!"

I stifle a shudder. The thought strikes me that Alfonso could have murdered me that day at Peter's flat, if I hadn't managed to play him along.

"Then there was Singh. He never stopped eating. He lived for his food, with no thought for the millions starving around the world. He was one of Dante's Gluttons; Canto 6."

"It was me who found Singh in Peter's bath."

Alfonso's unfeeling eyes stare back at me, telling me that he simply could not care less.

Still praying that someobdy will turn up to rescue us, I do my best to draw out my story a while longer. "I'm so sorry I didn't manage to send him to India to visit his relatives. I'd organised a holiday for him; I'd even bought him a return air ticket. Once he got to know me, he put his heart and soul into helping me sort out the flat."

"That may be, but he was a pig, forever stuffing his fat belly when there are people in the world who are starving, including his own people in India. How dare he?!"

"And Peter? You've still not mentioned my uncle. He was the first person you murdered, wasn't he?"

Alfonso nods, before continuing his catalogue of crimes. "I was very fond of Peter. He sometimes gave me a hand in the castle gardens, and some years he turned up for the grape harvest."

"How long had you known him?"

"Nearly forty years. He was already that lady's friend when I started working for her." Alfonso grabs a lock of Caterina's hair and gives it a tug to underline what he is saying.

"So, you remember Peter as a young man?"

"Of course."

"But tell me, why did you murder him?"

Alfonso looks daggers at me, then his eyes dart and fix on the wall as he says, very deliberately, "Peter committed one of the worst possible sins. He betrayed somebody very close to him: his twin brother. A week before his last birthday he invited me to dinner at his place. I gave him a beautiful yellow silk tie as a present, which I took back the evening I murdered him. Anyway, he got drunk and told me about the disgraceful trick he'd played on his twin. Peter's deceit changed your father's life forever, and for the worse, Maria. He behaved despicably. I decided there and then that I'd kill him."

"Canto 32?" I murmur, without telling him that I already knew about my uncle's deceit. "Alfonso, tell me. Was your plan to murder Peter, somehow connected with the fact that seven hundred years have gone by since—"

"Shut up!" he shouts angrily.

"So far you've mentioned Caterina and Dante," I continue, quickly changing the subject and trying to quieten him. "But did anything else push you to do what you did?"

"Here in Florence, right in the city centre, you can find the most horrific devils propelling sinners towards their deaths. They haunt me."

"What do you mean?"

"The frescoes inside Brunelleschi's Dome. Since I was a schoolboy I've made regular visits to look at those violent scenes of the Last Judgement; graphic images of devils hurling sinners to their damnation. I sometimes feel that I am one of those devils; a modern-day Lucifer with an important job to do. I have been called to get rid of the sinners of my day. But now I must get on with the business at hand. It's time. I'm going to kill the boss; then it'll be your turn."

At first I am dumbstruck, but then I pull myself together. I've just got to keep the conversation going. "And Caterina's sin?" I murmur feebly.

"You should know that, Maria, if you've read the *Inferno*." Alfonso points to the raging storm outside.

"Of course," I mutter, listening to the blasts of wind. "You've planned this murder very carefully, like the others. Adultery; Canto 5."

Alfonso goes on, glaring threateningly at Caterina. "The woman was unfaithful to her husband for many years and has had several extramarital relationships, including… That's enough said; I must get on with the job, and when it's finished, I'll leave her to float in these hellish gales, along with Dante's other notorious Adulterers, forever!"

He points the gun at Caterina, and I close my eyes. Clutching her hand, I sit there waiting for him to shoot. Then there's a massive bang, and I think he must have shot her. But, opening my eyes, I see Caterina still sitting next to me, shaking uncontrollably. Three men race towards us: Gianni, Romagnoli, and a third man; the one who was tailing me this afternoon. I feel sick as I catch sight of Alfonso lying in a pool of blood on the floor.

I must have blacked out, since the next thing I'm aware of is Gianni asking me if I can tell him my name. Turning to face him, I see his flushed face.

"Why do you want to know? You know who I am, don't you?" I ask confused. I look round and realise I'm in a hospital bed. "What am I doing here?" I blurt out, feeling desperate.

"We called an ambulance. You lost consciousness. The doctor said that when you came round, you might be suffering from amnesia, so I was testing you," Gianni replies grimly. "We got him, Maria."

"Who? Who the heck are you talking about?" I ask, confused.

"Don't you remember?"

As Gianni pronounces these words, bits and bobs of what happened start coming back to me. Alfonso, a gun, a storm, a letter, lavender soap, Caterina having a sobbing fit... but none of it makes much sense.

"You were at Caterina's, Maria, and Alfonso was about to murder you both. You do remember, don't you?"

"It's coming back. I just need to rest a bit."

"We managed to save you in the nick of time. You see, my young colleague tailed you to the palace. He's been keeping tabs on you for some days now, and he let me know you had arrived. A little later I tried phoning you, but when you didn't answer, I was worried and decided we had better go looking for you."

"Now I remember. Alfonso wanted to kill Caterina and me, and I did my best to keep him talking. I was playing for time, and for our lives. I kept asking him question after question, and he started to fill me in on the murders he'd committed. Then there was a gunshot and I thought I was dead, but no. There was Alfonso lying in a pool of blood. Is he dead?"

Gianni shakes his head, "No, Maria, he survived, with minor injuries, and is being treated here in this hospital."

Suddenly, DI Romagnoli comes into the room, and I tell him, "I am ready to make a statement, Inspector. I'm so grateful to you and your colleagues. I wouldn't be here if not for you."

For the first time, Romagnoli throws me a smile. "All in the line of duty, Signora. We'll need a statement as soon as possible. Your evidence will be crucial for the prosecution. *Arrivederci*."

50

A few days after our near escape, Caterina finally manages to take me to her dressmaker's. "It's just along here," she says, leading me down a narrow street, without a shop or a tourist in sight. "It's about time you came here. You'll see; your friends in Manchester won't recognise you when you show up wearing an exclusive outfit made in Florence. After what Alfonso nearly did to us," She closes her eyes for a second and pauses, gripping my hand, "I'm determined to involve you in what you might say are the trivial things in life – clothes – but some new and very special ones are bound to cheer you up."

After a few metres she makes a sharp turn down another nondescript street, and we are standing in front of a wooden door. A sign on the wall says, '*Piano secondo. Sartoria antica. Signora Giuliana Nespi.*' 'Second Floor. Traditional dressmaker's Ms Giuliana Nespi.'

Once Caterina has opened the door leading to the dressmaker's atelier, we climb to the second floor, where Giuliana greets us and shows us inside. In her late forties, she is slim, her hair cropped short with a fringe. She is dressed simply in a navy-blue cotton tube dress; her only accessories a necklace of exquisite pearls, a small silver watch and a tape measure slung round her neck.

"Isn't she just the spitting image of Coco Chanel?" Caterina whispers. "Such exquisite taste!"

Once Caterina has said hello, she introduces me. "Signora Nespi, I've brought my friend Maria for a new outfit. She's returning to England next week and needs something fabulous. A linen two-piece, perhaps?"

Giuliana remarks how sorry she is that I'll miss the rest of what looks as if it'll be a fabulous summer, and asks if I really have to leave. Nodding – I just have to get back to work – I look around the room. Rolls of fabric are stacked on shelves on every wall, with a huge cutting table in the centre. To the left, another room, whose door is open, reveals a row of sewing machines, where some women are making garments.

"Maria's a stage director," Caterina continues, fingering a roll of material the dressmaker has just got down to show us, "so this new outfit should be something she can wear for first nights or business meetings. Right, Maria?"

I've no sooner agreed than Giuliana suggests, "How about a linen suit? Wide tailored pants and a shortish jacket? It would suit you, I'm sure. I'm thinking Coco Chanel, brought up to date, of course, for the new millennium. Her clothes are classics; she was an absolute genius." Pulling out some catalogues, she shows me various Chanel designs. "If you like this one, I've got one already made up that you can try on. It's a size too big, but it'll give you an idea of how it will look. I can have one ready for you in two days."

The minute I try on the outfit, it feels good. The cut is superb, the material light and soft. I twirl round, studying myself in the mirror from different angles. Seeing my approval, Giuliana says she'll measure me, and is soon moving her tape measure deftly over my body at great speed.

"This outfit is an excellent start." I notice that Caterina's voice is brimming with satisfaction. "But Maria also needs some shoes, a bag and a scarf." Seeing my worried expression, she adds, "These are all on me. You saved my life, remember."

"Don't be silly. Anyone would have done the same in the circumstances."

Once I have chosen the accessories to match my new outfit, Caterina leaves a deposit for the goods, and we say goodbye to Giuliana. As Caterina and I walk down the stairs and onto the street, Caterina looks near to tears. "I don't think that's true, Maria, I mean that anyone would have done the same. You could have attempted to save yourself; made a deal with that scoundrel and to hell with me. You know, I feel very guilty and responsible for what happened. My only defence? I honestly never realised that Alfonso took what I said about Dante so literally. He seemed rather an independent sort of man. You heard him when he shouted me down over those two bushes in my garden at the castle. I truly didn't understand that I had such power over him to influence his actions. I will never forgive myself, and will have to live with the knowledge that my obsession with Dante's *Inferno* prompted a man to murder so many people."

I try to console her, but in truth I know that she will have to deal with what has happened on her own. "It's also the power of Dante, Caterina. After all these centuries his *Inferno* still manages to grip the reader's imagination in an extraordinary way. I have to admit he had me in his thrall from that very first night I read it. I just couldn't put it down. For Alfonso the effect must have been like a roaring tidal wave that swept away all sense of good and evil." Squeezing her hand tightly, I add, "What's important now is that he's behind bars and will serve a very long sentence. He'll probably never get out."

"However, you know, despite the atrocities he's committed, I am ashamed to say I miss him. I often had to fight to get him to do things; it was a struggle, but in the end he did them, and very well. Look at my gardens." She breathes a weary sigh. "Still, I'm off to India next week, and I'm hoping a change of air, and being miles away from Florence, will help. The Picasso painting would have made a huge difference to the work I want to do there, but I've made quite a lot from the sale of the bungalows. The money will go into building a new hospital in Delhi. I'm sorry I won't be seeing you again, Maria."

"I think you will. I'll be back for the trial, and for the sale of Peter's flat."

"See you soon then, my dear," she says, hurrying off home.

Now that she's outlined her plans for the hospital and her other charity work, I am pleased to note that this 'wealthy windbag', as Alfonso called her, seems to have recovered some of her energy and determination.

51

"You're looking great," Gianni exclaims on seeing my new clothes. "But where are you off to? Somewhere special?"

"They're a present from Caterina I'm going home. In two days I'll be back in Manchester, and straight into rehearsals."

Gianni's face turns sad. "I didn't realise you were leaving so soon."

"I'll be back for the trial and the sale of the flat. But right now I need to get back to Manchester and touch base."

We are in the reception area of my hotel, and Gianni exchanges a few words with Signora Franca. "Your long-term guest is leaving. Can't you keep her here a while longer?"

"No way," replies Franca, laughing. "She's been a real nuisance; so demanding. We'll be glad to see the back of her."

Their banter shows no sign of stopping, so I cut in. "Hurry up, Franca, you'd better get my bill ready. I'll be glad to get out of here; the sooner the better."

For the first time Franca gives me a hug, before heading towards the kitchen and calling out, "We'll really miss you, Maria.

You've been exceptionally brave to cope with all you have. If you ever return to Florence, I hope you'll be able to enjoy the many beautiful things our city has to offer."

Once Gianni and I have settled down on a divan, I ask him if he has interviewed Alfonso about the murders. "Yes," he replies, looking awkward. "But I can't give you any precise details. You will have to wait for the trial, okay? Your evidence detailing all that he told you and Caterina while you were held hostage will be put together with the interviews we are carrying out at present. What I can tell you is that he's shown no emotion whatsoever for the people he murdered. As he describes what he did, it's almost as if he is at church on a Sunday, confessing some minor misdemeanour to the priest. He sees what he's done as his 'life's mission'."

"'There is nothing either good or bad, but thinking makes it so,'" I mutter.

"What do you mean?"

"It's a line from *Hamlet*; something Prince Hamlet says to his friend Horatio. It just sprang to mind in connection with what you were saying."

"I don't follow."

"You just said that Alfonso claims that the murders are his life's mission. To the rest of us, they're heinous crimes; to him, they're heroic deeds performed out of a sense of duty to the community."

Gianni shakes his head. "He's got a totally distorted view of the world."

"But what about Dante? Have you asked him about the *Inferno*?"

"I have, but I can't disclose what he has told us."

"Well, how do you explain why he did what he did?"

"That's not like you, Maria; asking the police for help." Gianni chuckles. "According to the first psychiatric report, he's deeply impressionable and very easily led. For forty years Caterina Guiccioli ruled him with a rod of iron. For all that time he took things she said in moments of anger or distress quite literally, and in the past few months he started to act on them. He remains absolutely convinced that he acted ethically and in accordance with her wishes."

I am feeling exhausted, but I have to ask Gianni something else. "Alfonso was ready to kill Caterina and me. He told me why he was killing her – he pointed to Canto 5; the Adulterers – but said I hadn't committed a sin. He was going to kill me because I meddled in things that don't concern me. Is that what he told you?"

"He refuses to talk about his plan to murder you." Gianni shakes his head. "What I can tell you is that he regrets that he didn't manage to kill another of Peter's friends."

"Federico Nitti?"

"Mm. I can't tell you."

"If he had killed another person, that would have been seven murders, and seven is an important number in the Kabbalah." Seeing Gianni's sceptical expression, I let this drop. "Still, there's a final question I need to ask you. Thinking about the murders and the skill with which the bodies were butchered, where did Alfonso get his training?"

"The accused," Gianni says, "refuses to talk about that. Still, you can be sure that my colleagues and I will not rest until he has spilt the beans."

52

With Gianni by my side, I walk briskly through the city centre to the cathedral. Before I leave Florence he wants to show me the harrowing scenes of Hell that Brunelleschi painted inside the dome. He recalls how he visited the church for the very first time years ago on a school trip, and says that he still gets the shivers whenever he remembers those scenes.

Heading for a side entrance, he shows his police badge to the attendant at the ticket office, and the man waves us through the turnstile. At the counter, Gianni introduces me to Sandro, a childhood friend, and in a flash, Sandro calls to a colleague to take his place. "It is a great honour," he enthuses, "to accompany you both on a guided tour of the dome."

Sandro is soon leading us through a small door on the right and up a steep spiral staircase. There are 463 steps to the top, he tells us cheerfully, smiling at my astonished reaction. The climb is not for the faint-hearted, but luckily, every so often our ascent is broken by a slit in the brick wall on either side of the stairs, where we pause to enjoy a glimpse of the city. The higher we go, the more I can see of the roofs, domes and chimney pots of historic Florence, stretching out as far as the eye can see. It is truly magnificent.

"Are we on our way to Heaven or Hell, Sandro?" Gianni quips.

"Either," his friend replies. "You choose."

I am totally out of breath when we reach a narrow gallery circling the dome's roof. But to my surprise, we aren't the only visitors who have made it up the steps. An American couple are reading from a guidebook, while a group of German tourists on the other side of the gallery are pointing to the paintings and taking photos. I catch my breath as I take in the massive frescoes decorating the dome, wondering how the painters managed such a feat so many centuries ago.

Sandro is pointing at them, and explains knowledgeably, "In the upper part is Heaven, representing order, harmony and peace. It's here that the artists, Federico Zuccari and Giorgio Vasari, have immortalised themselves in self-portraits. Can you see them, there and there? It was Cosimo I de' Medici who commissioned this *Last Judgement*. Vasari began the work in 1572, and Zuccari took over in 1574 following Vasari's death."

Our guide's finger is now indicating the lower part of Hell, with its garish colours and larger and more dynamic figures. His tone has grown animated, revealing his passion for this masterpiece of Italian art. "Zuccari's style is startlingly different from Vasari's subtler and more delicate techniques. The truth is, he managed to create some of the most theatrically stunning effects in the history of painting. And for these images, where all Hell has literally broken loose, he took inspiration from Dante's *Inferno*."

"See, Maria?" Gianni breaks in, excited. "Just look at the turmoil and despair on the faces of those figures hurtling into the pit. You can of course recognise the devils by their horns and tails. They're intent on wielding their giant pitchforks and forcing the damned into the abyss."

A shudder races down my spine. The damned are mostly

naked young men, their faces twisted in fear and spattered with blood as they plunge into the hellish pit.

Sandro advises us to resume our climb if we want an even better view. And after another flight of steps, we find ourselves at the summit of the dome, our noses almost touching the paintings. At this height, energy seems to be pulsating from the fresco, sending shock waves through my body.

"Alfonso," I whisper to Gianni, so Sandro can't hear me, "told me that he admires these devils, or Lucifer, as he calls them. He fancies himself as a modern-day Lucifer; in his case, an ordinary man doing a much-needed job for the benefit of the community."

"I agree, he's actually very matter-of-fact about everything he's done." Gianni wipes the sweat off his brow. "But let's get out of here. Ten minutes is about as much as I can take in the company of these evil creatures."

As we head down the spiralling steps, my legs feel so tired that I have to negotiate the climb very carefully. At times there's a short break in the handrail, making the descent tricky. But Gianni, in front of me, seems to be flying down effortlessly, while managing to keep the conversation going. "I really am sorry you're going back to Manchester so soon, Maria."

"You've already told me. I promise, as soon as the estate agent finds a buyer for the flat, I'll be back. I want to get myself a small place in Florence where I'll be able to leave Peter's diaries and some of his books and other possessions. I want to read every one of the diaries. It's as though I've got to know him over the past few months, but I need to get closer to him."

On hearing this, Gianni stops suddenly in his descent. He looks round at me, a baffled expression on his face, and I try to explain.

"It's weird, I know, because Peter's dead and I never knew him. And then of course there's Dante; a dark, silent figure, out there in the shadows, pulling me back to Florence like a magnet."

On our way back to my hotel, we stop off at the special tea room and I buy a custard flan. "Fancy coming back to my hotel for some of this and a cup of tea?"

A broad grin lights up Gianni's face. "You're on, providing it's imperial gunpowder tea!"

Once back at my hotel reception, we settle down to enjoy some tea and cake. "This flan is delicious. It even beats my sister's," Gianni enthuses, brushing some crumbs off his shirt. "When all this is well and truly over, you'll have to come to our place for a meal and meet Tommaso– I've been telling him about you."

Gianni's invitation takes me aback, but I feel relaxed about getting to know his family. "We could meet up for a walk in the woods and look for porcini, or even better, truffles. Your stories about foraging for wild mushrooms have worked their magic on me."

"A hard climb to the top of the mountain, more like; a long trek at dawn before we find the first tiny mushroom," Gianni laughs. "I wouldn't want you to regret taking a trip out with a crazy bunch from the Maremma."

"It'll make a change from sitting in a rehearsal room, imagining Shakespeare's magic wood in *A Midsummer Night's Dream*, or Caliban's island with its spring water, berries, crab apples and monkeys."

"You're on, then, provided you cook Sunday lunch."

"I thought there'd be a 'but' somewhere."

"I've heard that your curries are terrific." He smiles, throwing me a challenging look. "Now, if there's one thing I miss about Glasgow, it's a first-rate curry in the West End."

"Deal done."

53

I am packing my case, thinking that I'll be back in Manchester by midnight, when the phone rings. It's DI Romagnoli's secretary. They want me down at the station as soon as possible. I stuff a few more things into my case and get up wearily. Refusing to think about what might be in store, I shower, get dressed and head for the police station.

Gianni is sitting at Romagnoli's desk with the young colleague who trailed me on the afternoon Alfonso took Caterina and me hostage. Gianni introduces him as Inspector Marco Crivelli, and explains that Romagnoli is out on a call. He carefully keeps his way of addressing me formal. "I wanted to inform you, Ms Farrell, that we made another arrest yesterday. The man has confessed to being Alfonso Guidi's accomplice."

I stare at them, waiting nervously to hear his name. Gabriele flashes to mind, then Federico Nitti.

"It's Angelo Verza," Gianni says quickly.

"It can't be," I say. "How did you catch him?"

"He gave himself up this morning, once he knew that Guidi

274

was behind bars and couldn't kill him. He's full of remorse; just the opposite of Guidi. He came to the station clutching Peter's old school tie."

"But why?" I ask remembering his kind hospitality when Gabriele and I visited him on the lake, but also his skill at cleaning the fish he had caught for our lunch."

"It was fear; unadulterated terror, Ms Farrell," Gianni replies. "Guidi was blackmailing him. He threatened to let the police know about Verza's involvement in the tomb thieves racket. He told him he'd get him and his mother sent to jail, and Verza, who idolises his mother, was certain the scandal would kill her. At first he paid Guidi what he was asking, but when he hadn't a lira left in his account, Guidi forced him to help him with the murders. Apart from being capable of gutting and scaling fish, as a young man, Verza was a butcher's apprentice, so he was able to butcher the bodies according to Guidi's instructions."

I panic, thinking that Angelo may have informed the police about the *tombaroli* business and my knowledge of their illegal activities. If so, I could be in trouble with the law.

"I've asked you to report to the station," Gianni begins, and I wait, dreading what he might be about to say, "to see whether you have anything to add to your statement before you return to England. Anything specific regarding Angelo Verza?"

Relieved, I reply that Angelo treated me very kindly, even inviting me to his home after my unpleasant ordeal during the division of the paintings. However, I don't think I have anything further to tell him.

"Then you are free to go," Gianni says, smiling as he closes the file in front of him. "We'll be seeing you in a few months' time for the trial, Ms Farrell. *Arrivederci.*"

I walk through the main door of the police station and down the steps, revelling in the bustle of the busy street. I need to get back to my hotel and finish my packing. Then it'll be time to head for the airport. I feel sorry that I haven't said a proper goodbye to Gianni, but that, I think, must be the way he wants it.

I have reached the Hospital of the Innocents in Piazza della Santissima Annunziata when I have an inkling that somebody is following me. For a split second, I am thrown back to the day Alfonso prepared the trap for me, and half-expect to see the plain-clothes detective talking on his mobile. I brace myself and turn round.

It's Gianni, clutching a bunch of flowers and saying he'd like to give me a lift to the airport. He guessed I could do with some help, since my case probably weighs a ton.

ACKNOWLEDGEMENTS

SONG "Bewitched, Bothered and Bewildered", lyrics by Lorenz Hart for the musical "Pal Joey", opened on Broadway, 1940. I quote two words, "Bewitched, Bothered ...." from the title.

SONG "Fragile", 1987, lyrics by Sting from the Album "Nothing Like the Sun"(1987). I quote the title.

Matador

For exclusive discounts on Matador titles,
sign up to our occasional newsletter at
troubador.co.uk/bookshop